<u>DEDICATION</u>

For My Family

THE SECRET OF ATLANTIS

(Joe Hawke #7)

Rob Jones

ISBN-13:978-1541124127
ISBN-10:154112412X

Other Books by Rob Jones

The Joe Hawke Series

The Vault of Poseidon (Joe Hawke #1)
Thunder God (Joe Hawke #2)
The Tomb of Eternity (Joe Hawke #3)
The Curse of Medusa (Joe Hawke #4)
Valhalla Gold (Joe Hawke #5)
The Aztec Prophecy (Joe Hawke #6)
The Secret of Atlantis (Joe Hawke #7)
The Lost City (Joe Hawke #8)

This novel is an action-adventure thriller and includes archaeological, military and mystery themes. I welcome constructive comments and I'm always happy to get your feedback.

Website: www.robjonesnovels.com

Facebook: https://www.facebook.com/RobJonesNovels/

Email: robjonesnovels@gmail.com

Twitter: @AuthorRobJones

THE SECRET OF ATLANTIS

CHAPTER ONE

Silvio Mendoza felt the rush of power coursing through his veins as he pushed his way through the Vienna rain. It was only a matter of time now before he would lay his hands on the greatest treasure of them all.

With only Aurora Soto and his own deluded thoughts for company, the former Mexican drug cartel lord scuttled along the backstreets of the Austrian capital. He disliked the city. He held no place in his heart for Baroque gardens, Sachertorte and opera houses. Mendoza was an outlaw, a man from the jungle who knew only the harshest realities of life, not this ludicrous fairytale version with Ferris wheels and Lipizzaner horses. What these people knew about the real world you could write on the head of pin.

He moved deftly through a crowd of people who were watching a man eat fire to a bizarre medley of Strauss. He pulled up his collar and cursed the northern hemisphere as the autumn wind came off the Danube and whipped through the cobblestone streets of Leopoldstadt. How anyone could live here was beyond his comprehension. The sooner he got out of here the better, but first he had to track someone down.

He smirked as he surveyed the people around him. Umbrellas, scarves, hurrying home to get out of the cold.

1

There were many differences between him and these people, not least the fact that he was about to become one of the richest men alive, something every last one of them would crave but never achieve.

He checked his cell phone one last time as he slipped up the steps to an apartment block on an expensive boulevard with Aurora one step behind him. An old habit made him check over his shoulder before his next move, and then when the coast was clear he rang the door buzzer. Moments later a man in his seventies opened the door just a crack. He reminded him of Albert Einstein.

"We spoke on the phone," Mendoza said in heavily accented English. "You are Huber?"

The old man nodded and eyed him suspiciously through the crack in the door, which was still chained. "You have the object you described?"

"Let me in, old man. We're not discussing this on the street."

The old man was hesitant, but nodded in reluctant agreement and closed the door for a moment while he slipped the chain off. When the door opened again, the two Mexican gangsters stepped briskly inside. Mendoza pushed the old man aside and booted the door shut with his heel. He couldn't be certain how many drug cartel lords this Viennese professor had dealt with in his time, but he was sure it was somewhere around zero, and that as a consequence he would be nervous and unsettled.

Huber led Mendoza up an intricate sweeping staircase, his paper-white hand leaning down on the wrought-iron banister for support as he went. The two men made no conversation as they walked to the apartment and Soto was equally silent. When they got inside, Mendoza wasted no time in pulling a small golden idol out of the inside pocket of his jacket and holding it in front of the old professor's face. Huber's jaw dropped when he saw the ancient artefact.

"So what is it?" Mendoza said flatly.

"This... this can't be real... may I?"

Mendoza studied him for a second and then handed the idol over.

"It's real enough, old man. Can't you feel it in your hands?"

Huber looked like he had seen a ghost, and for a moment was unable to speak. "I can't believe it," he said, his hands beginning to tremble. "Where did you find it?"

"Inside the entrance to the Aztec underworld – Mictlan."

Huber looked at him sharply. "Mictlan is *real?*"

Mendoza nodded sharply. "You don't want to know more than that." He didn't like to dwell on Mictlan. Sometimes when he closed his eyes he could still see the Russian girl strapped to the altar and Wade's volcanic dagger pushing into her flesh. "Tell me – it's worth something, no?"

Huber said nothing, but collapsed in his swivel seat and pulled a red book from a shelf, entitled *Religious Icons of the Punic-Iberian Period.*

When he saw the dusty tome in the professor's fragile hands, Mendoza curled his lip. "What is this shit? I'm not here for a lecture, old man."

Huber ignored him. Instead he turned the pages of the old book until he reached what he was looking for, and then turned the book around so the impatient Mexican could see.

Mendoza gasped and took a step back. Aurora's eyes widened like saucers. They were looking at an exact replica of the idol. Identical to the one he'd snatched from under the noses of the ECHO team in the Mictlan Temple back in the Lacandon Jungle. "What is this?"

"This, my friend, is la Dama de Elche, or the Lady of Elche."

"I don't understand... what is it?"

"She is a limestone bust which was unearthed in an archaeological site near Elche, in Valencia near the Spanish coast... near Alicante."

Aurora eyed the page suspiciously. "But the idol was discovered on the other side of the world. How can they be sure the bust is from Spain?"

"Limestone is an organic sedimentary rock because it has the fossilized remains of deceased organisms within it and this helps us locate its origin."

"Maybe it's fake," Mendoza added.

"Many believed it to be a forgery, but this was conclusively dismissed when the bust was subjected to a series of x-ray dispersive spectrometry analyses by an electron microscope. They proved it was as old as the original archaeological claims and from the Punic era."

"La Dama – who is she... or *what* is she?"

"No one knows, but most academic opinion believes she is connected strongly to the Phoenician goddess Tanit – the main deity of all Carthage."

"But... it's *identical*..."

"It's *almost* identical," Huber corrected him. "There is a Nahuatl word which describes this – ixiptla, or likeness." His hands began to shake again.

Mendoza was starting to think this could be bigger than he had thought, and watched as an expression of confusion clouded the professor's face. "You look lost, old man."

"Some have speculated that the Lady of Elche is in fact an Atlantean goddess worshipped in the lost, mythical city of Tartessos – an Atlantean colony – but

4

I've always dismissed it as drivel, naturally, but now..."
He shook his head and his eyes furiously scanned the
text for just one clue. "None of this makes sense!"

He got up – the idol still gripped in his hand, and
used his free hand to rub his eyes for a moment. "It's
like I am losing my mind! How can any of this be real?
By 146BC the Carthaginian Empire was all but
extinguished. So what I want to know is how a statue of
Tanit ended up in a temple in the Mexican jungle that
hadn't been opened in thousands of years?"

Mendoza watched the old man with contempt as he
wiped a tear from his eye. He wanted to mock him for
his weakness but then he noticed something he hadn't
realized before this moment – his own hands were
shaking almost uncontrollably. He took a step closer to
Huber and the idol, slipping his hand in his pocket and
grabbing his switchblade as he went. "What does the
inscription say?"

"It's hard to tell. It's the weirdest blend of Aztec and
Punic-era Phoenician... it's *so strange*... almost
intoxicating. It's like it wants to reach out to me and
whisper the ancient truth it has concealed for so long..."

"So it's worth a lot of money, right?"

Huber stared up at him in disbelief, his old eyes
watering from the effort of straining at the strange
symbols carved into the idol. "What? Something like
this could never be sold. It's priceless."

"We'll see about that. What does the inscription say?
Does it lead to more gold?"

Huber shook his head as he stared at the strange
carving of a sun in the base of the idol. It looked like a
solar flare. He looked lost as he studied the intricate
carved shape of the base – like a seven-pointed star but
with peculiar terraces carved into it, receding in

undulations like an inverted ziggurat. "I must have this wrong because if not, then God help us all."

Aurora sighed and took a step closer to Huber. "Let the cat out of the bag, old man."

"First, there are two inscriptions. The first is a very simple symbol that refers to the sun, and is as old as the idol – but it seems to show the sun exploding. The second series of symbols carved into the back are later, without a doubt. They've been added by someone else... a later culture perhaps."

"And what do the later ones say?"

"I can't read them, not with any certainty, I'm sorry. Maybe it's some kind of ancient code – perhaps a reference to a flooded city, and then this business about the sun... You need someone else."

"I thought you were supposed to be the best?"

Huber looked up at them, insulted and embarrassed. "I am the best *public* figure, but there are others with a greater knowledge who prefer to keep a veil drawn over their activities. One in particular stands out."

"Go on."

"His name is Kruger. Dirk Kruger. He's an archaeologist, of sorts."

"Where can I find this man?"

"He's from South Africa but at the moment he's in Munich on business. I spoke with him a few days ago. He's at the Hotel Sendling."

"Business?"

"He sells... *relics.*"

Mendoza thought for a moment about the way the old man had said relics and wasn't sure he was telling the whole story. It sounded like maybe there were a few things hiding behind those relics. "And he will be able to tell me what this idol says?"

6

Huber nodded. "Yes, I think so. If anyone can, Dirk Kruger can." Once again he held up the idol of Tanit in his hands. The late afternoon Viennese sunshine flashed on her golden face and weird headdress. The old man fixed his jeweller's loupe into his eye once again. "She's the most beautiful thing I've ever seen."

Mendoza took the idol from the old man's hands. He noticed two police cars pull up outside the apartment block, followed by a third large police vehicle and cursed inwardly as he directed Aurora Soto to look through the window. Yes, he thought, this idol must be of great value if the authorities were already tracking him through Europe.

He turned to Huber. "I must thank you so very much for your help, Herr Huber. You have been of immense assistance to me. It is true what they say about you – you really are a very clever man."

"Well… I study very hard and… what are you doing?"

In a heartbeat Aurora Soto stepped aside as Mendoza took his knife from his pocket and as fast as lightning he pushed the blade against the wrinkled skin of Huber's throat. "You're coming with me, old man."

"What are you talking about? Put that knife down!"

CHAPTER TWO

Mendoza pulled Franz Huber roughly through the lobby door and dragged him down the building's stone steps. He pressed the tip of the switchblade against the professor's jugular and whispered frantically in his ear. "Tell them to get back, or you die!"

Huber hesitated, not wishing to collude in his own kidnapping, but a rough jab of the blade into his neck hurried him along. "Get back!" Huber said in German. "He says get back or he will kill me!"

"Now tell that one to throw me his gun, or you die right here."

"Er will eine Waffe!" Huber screeched at the police. "Oder er wird mich töten!"

Anxious glances between the leading officers were followed by a sentence of rapid German.

Huber twisted his neck towards Mendoza. "He says no way."

Mendoza said nothing but flicked the knife over in the air so he was holding it by the blade. He threw it at great velocity and the next time anyone saw it, it was sticking in the neck of a police officer. The young man fell to the floor, clutching his throat and screaming in panic as blood pumped from his artery.

Mendoza pulled a second knife from a holster around his leg.

"The gun, or more death."

Huber repeated the command, and this time the order was given. Another young officer reluctantly kicked his weapon across the cobblestones. Aurora picked it up and they began to walk backwards while continuing to use the terrified professor as a human shield.

Aurora lifted the police-issue Glock 19 into the aim and fired *one two three* rapid shots at a police VW Touran. The short recoil action delivered the goods when the nine mil parabellums punctured the gas tank and a shower of sparks ignited the fuel. The explosion was ferocious in its intensity, bursting out from the detonated tank and propelling a deadly burst of shredded steel across the street.

The force blasted men from the Federal Police and the anti-terror units into the air like a storm whipping dead leaves through a park. They tumbled in cartwheels and landed hard on the ancient cobblestones. Most survived, but several of the men were dead, their broken bodies sprawled on the street as a terrible testament to the gangsters' ruthless brutality.

What was a serene picture of Viennese charm and calmness just a few moments ago, was now a warzone. Noxious black smoke billowed from the gnarled corpse of the Touran and piercer sirens rebounded off the Baroque architecture and drifted high above the chaos.

Huber was crazed with confusion and fear, but he watched with something resembling hope as the surviving law enforcement men regrouped and fanned out in a new tactical assault formation. They pushed closer to him and his kidnapper, but they were more cautious now and moving slower. Officers in riot helmets and body armor spoke into palm mics and waited for orders through their earpieces.

With Aurora's Glock still pointed at the men, Mendoza was still holding the switchblade at Huber's throat. "Which way out of here?"

With fear pounding in his heart, Huber knew he had to delay the madman's escape but couldn't risk enraging him further. "I don't know what you mean..." he blathered.

Aurora's reply was a sharp pistol-whipping. "Don't play games, professor. If you want to live then get us out of here."

Huber's mind raced. He did want to live yes – he had three grandchildren and he wanted to see them grow up. Something told him the Mexicans weren't bluffing either, so he decided not to aggravate them with lies and delays. "In St. Michael's Church around the corner... you can access a network of tunnels that go all over the city."

"Do you know them?"

Huber shook his head. "Access is very restricted for everyone's safety."

"Take us there!"

With the police keeping a safe distance but never letting him slip from their sight, Huber led the Mexicans past the café terraces of Herrengasse until a magnificent Romanesque church came into view.

"Die Michaelerkirche," Huber said, with not even the terror around him diminishing the lifelong pride he felt for the eight hundred year-old church. "Go into the crypt here and you can disappear forever."

They crossed the expansive Michaelerplatz and drew closer to the church. Normally buzzing with tourists snapping pictures of the neoclassical architecture or lining up to ride on the famous horse-drawn carriages, the explosion of the Touran and the presence of a hovering police helicopter had cleared the area of civilians.

Huber led Mendoza and Aurora inside St. Michael's Church and along the impressive nave as he walked them toward the famous Michaelergruft, the enormous crypt which lay beneath the ancient building.

10

It was noticeably colder now as they hurried past the numerous marble tombs, each holding the bones of a different aristocratic dynasty. Except for the four thousand corpses, they were now alone inside the church, but the sound of the police above gave Huber a shred of hope that he would live to see another day.

"Where?"

"That door."

Aurora raised the pistol and blasted the lock open.

"Open the crypt door," Mendoza shouted.

Huber obeyed, heaving the old door open, and it wasn't until this moment that he realized his error in telling Mendoza that he had no knowledge of the tunnels. Then, as if he could read his mind, the Mexican cartel boss closed in on him.

"Wait!" Huber cried desperately, raising his hands in a pathetic attempt to stop the horror unfolding.

But it couldn't be stopped, and Mendoza rammed the switchblade up into the base of Huber's ribcage. The old man gasped and fell forward closer to Mendoza. For a depraved moment they almost looked like two old friends embracing, but then blood bubbled out of Huber's mouth and Mendoza pushed him to the floor.

"There can be no witnesses to this, Herr Huber. Please accept my most profound apologies, and gratitude."

Mendoza took the gun from Aurora and slipped it into his jacket pocket, tightening his scarf around his neck and then they descended into the crypt. He lit their way with the light on his phone and hoped the battery would last long enough to see them to safety in the world above. He'd read stories about people getting lost and dying in the famous Catacombs of Paris, but they surely couldn't be any more labyrinthine and disgusting than the tunnels beneath Vienna.

No wi-fi down here in the sewers and crypts, but Mendoza had saved the map of Vienna, and knew from his childhood in the jungles of Mexico how to count the turns and keep track of north. They trudged through the slime of the tunnel network, a left meant south so the next right was west... a gentle bend in the tunnel meant he was now walking southwest... good.

What was that noise? It sounded like it was coming from behind him. No, he was just imagining it – but there it was again. A sewer rat, maybe... trailing him in case he fell and knocked himself unconscious... He had no choice but to push on, looking for exits as he went. A few hundred meters would put them beyond the area that the police must surely have cordoned off by now. If they could reach the station all they would have to do was get on a train to Munich and then make contact with Dirk Kruger, the man who sold *relics*.

He stared at his phone. "Two hours until the next train to Munich."

"Two hours in these tunnels?" Aurora asked, looking into the darkness and shivering.

Mendoza looked over his shoulder and illuminated a sewer rat as it scuttled away into the darkness.

"Let's go," he said firmly.

*

They emerged from the tunnel system an hour later and killed more time hiding behind newspapers before boarding the train to Munich. Now, as the train rocked comfortingly back and forth on its western journey, Silvio Mendoza followed the woman's hand as it snaked up his thigh and made its way to his waistband. He gripped it by the wrist, pulled it out of his trousers and pushed Aurora Soto away. "You think now is the time for that?"

She pouted, and a look of contempt flashed in her obsidian black eyes. "A man like you should take what he can get, mi cielo."

Mendoza flashed into action, pulling his ejector knife from his jacket pocket and spinning around in the train seat. Less than half a second after her comment, he was pushing the tip of the knife into her carotid artery. "What's that supposed to mean?"

She flinched as he twirled the blade around and pushed it against her skin harder, pricking open the surface and drawing blood. "Nothing... lo siento, Silvio."

A grin spread on his face as he watched her squirm under his power. He nodded in self-satisfaction and retracted the blade. "Good. We don't know where they are – never forger that. Remember how easily they took Wade's empire apart and killed my brother, Jorge."

Aurora watched the black light of revenge play in his eyes. She had been there on Alcatraz, hiding in the crawlspace when Juana Diaz had murdered his brother. Better he believed that ECHO had done it, and so she kept the truth locked in her heart.

They crossed the border at Salzburg and watched the Bavarian landscape slip by. Not long after, the train stopped for a few moments at Rosenheim Station and then pulled away again onto the final northbound stretch to Munich and their final destination.

Mendoza saw the tiny towns and hamlets flash past the window before gradually melting into the suburbs of southern Munich – Zorneding, Vaterstetten, Haar. High above them in the sky a savage storm was gathering on the horizon and he watched as a bolt of forked lightning ripped down from the cloud base and struck somewhere in a forest to the east.

Lightning was his oldest enemy.

He was only young man when it struck him, blasting through the pungent ozone of the stormy air and tearing down his body. Using him as a conductor to reach the earth and almost killing him. He'd seen it coming – flashing down into the sugarcane fields with explosive fury. He and Jorge were out walking when the storm struck. They both ran for the cover of a barn but Jorge had all the luck that day because the gods had decided to punish Silvio.

It felt like someone had smashed him around the back of the head with a baseball bat and when he woke his body was numb. It wasn't until Jorge ran to him and gasped in horror that he knew something had changed. Jorge carried him home and that was when he saw the scarring on his face, the Lichtenburg figure, a shower of scars like electrical sparks running all over his face and neck.

Another bolt of lightning flashed on the horizon and a few seconds later a tremendous roar of thunder.

"The storm is getting closer," Aurora said, bringing him back from the sugarcane fields of his mind.

"In more ways than one," he said absent-mindedly.

CHAPTER THREE

Joe Hawke hated watching Alex Reeve as she pushed herself into the room in her chair. Her collapse on Alcatraz had almost cost her life at the hands of Aurora Soto, and now she was confined to a wheelchair once again. Aurora had slipped away in the Alcatraz night, and now they knew it was true about the elixir's restorative properties only being temporary. It also meant they needed another source of it – one they could secure permanently this time.

They were sitting in the expansive glass-walled briefing room which overlooked the cliffs on the western part of their secret island base. Beyond the tinted glass a tropical Caribbean sun was burning bright and even after so long here the former SBS operative continued to be dazzled by its beauty and isolation.

When he had first met Lea and came to the island it almost seemed like it was a dream, but he had been here with these people for long enough now that it was his previous life that seemed dreamlike. Now this was reality... turquoise seas, white sand, tropical palm trees and the best camaraderie he'd ever known.

His appreciation of paradise was shattered by the sound of raised voices as Scarlet Sloane and Ryan Bale argued about the relative merits of vodka and cold beer, but Hawke's mind soon returned to Alex as he absent-mindedly watched the surf crashing on the beach below.

"How are you?" he asked as she moved next to him.

"I'm fine," she said, a note of determination in her voice.

Hawke fixed his eyes on her. "We'll find more, Alex. I promise."

"We have other things to worry about, Joe."

He knew it was true, but it didn't matter. He glanced around the room at the others. The entire team was now there with the usual exception of Vincent Reno who had returned to the south of France after the events in the Lacandon Jungle.

Lexi was sitting with her eyes closed and her boots up on the desk, pretending to sleep but he knew she was listening to everything. Maria was arguing with someone on the phone in what he guessed was not polite Russian, and Lea was returning to the room from the veranda.

"Oh good," Eden said, walking into the room and sitting at the table. "You're all here already."

"So what's the problem?" Scarlet said, taking a seat at the far end of the table and placing not one but two chilled vodka and tonics in front of her. "Superman need his pants pulling up again?"

Ryan made a big show of checking his pants. "Nope." He smuggled something from his pocket into his mouth and started chewing.

Scarlet smirked. "What's that you've got there?"

"Nothing."

"Yeah, right." A few seconds later she was pinning his arms down and putting her hand in his pocket.

"Get off!"

"Don't say you're not enjoying this, *boy*. It can't be everyday a good-looking woman wants to know what's inside your trousers."

"Hey!" Maria said. "I'm not bad-looking!"

Scarlet didn't reply. Instead, she victoriously pulled the little paper bag from Ryan's pocket and waved it in the air.

"Give it back!"

"What have we here?" she said, peering inside the bag. "Gummy Bears?"

"I mean it, Scarlet."

"Stop whining," she said. "It doesn't become you."

"Whining is good," Ryan said. "After all, the squeaky wheel gets the grease."

"If you say so. I'll have a couple of these, thank you very much," she said, and then tipped the bag up, emptying half the contents of the Gummy Bears into her mouth. "Yummy!" she said with her cheeks bulging out.

"I got those in Acapulco," Ryan said, waiting until she swallowed. "They've been inside my trousers for days. Still yummy?"

Before she could respond, Lea clicked the outside door shut and joined them, and then Eden cleared his throat and began to speak.

"I know how you all feel about what happened in Mexico, but we need to move on. Friendly contacts within the American and Mexican Governments have extended their gratitude to me, and I'm passing it on to you. I know we lost the idol, but we took out Morton Wade and that was something we should all be proud of. You might like to know that the FBI raided his property in Texas and found another room similar to the obsidian chamber we saw in Mexico and..." he paused for a moment as he let out a long sigh. "They also found more evidence of human sacrifice so it looks like he'd had a few practice runs before getting to Mexico. You ended that, so well done."

"But like you say," Lea said. "We lost the idol."

"And that's why we're here today. Hawke – over to you."

Hawke nodded and began to speak. "As you all know, when the dust was settling at the Mexican temple, I said

I thought I'd seen the idol somewhere before – and I had."

"What are you talking about?" Lexi said.

"I thought about it a lot on the way home," he continued. "And since returning to Elysium it's been driving me crazy. I was agonizing about it because I was sure I'd seen it on TV or even read about it."

"TV's more likely in your case, surely," Ryan said with a smirk.

"*Thanks.* Anyway, after a while I realized where I'd seen the damned thing, and it was right here."

They all turned to look at him except Lea. He'd already told her.

"Less than an hour ago it finally clicked where I'd seen it, so I went to check it out and I was right." As he spoke he pulled the idol out of a bag on the floor and placed it gently on the smoked glass tabletop. It was almost identical in its design and style as the idol of Tanit, but was of a bearded man instead. The base was indistinguishable from the base of the Tanit idol, fashioned into an intricate seven-pointed star with an inverted ziggurat receding inside it.

Ryan gasped. "Oh my God!"

"Where did you get that?" asked Scarlet.

Hawke grinned. "Like I said – from right here on the island."

"But where did it come from originally?" Maria said.

"I know where he got it from," Ryan said. He looked at Hawke and the two men shared a glance for a second. "The Arctic Circle… via the Elysium treasure vault."

"Ryan's right," Hawke said, bringing everyone's attention back to the golden idol standing solemnly on the briefing room table. "It took me a long time to work it out but then the penny dropped. I'd seen it while the hoard we took from Valhalla was being inventoried, but we never got around to logging it because we were less than halfway through when Ben was murdered and Mexico kicked off."

A wave of realization rippled over the team as they understood what had happened.

Hawke looked at his friends. "This idol was in Valhalla. Small enough to be overlooked by us like much of the hoard, and waiting patiently in our vault to be inventoried."

"And it changes everything," Eden said.

"You bet your arses it does!" Ryan said. He got up from his seat and walked around the table. Picking it up, he weighed it in his hands and looked at his reflection in the shining golden contours of the ancient idol.

"Do we know who it is?" Maria asked.

"Oh my God!" Scarlet said. "Is it Father Christmas?"

Ryan sighed and rolled his eyes. "It's not Father Christmas."

"But it does look a little like Santa," Alex added, deliberately jibing Ryan.

"It's not bloody Santa."

"So who then?" Lexi asked.

Ryan replied without hesitation. "It's Búri, no doubt."

"And who the buggering hell is he when he's at home?" said Scarlet.

"A Norse god, father of Borr."

"Borr?" Scarlet said with a smirk. "Is he a relation of yours, boy?"

"Borr!" Ryan said, rolling the Rs for effect. "Not *bore*."

"Ah."

"He's Odin's grandfather if it makes it any easier for you, and this is highly significant."

"How so?" Lexi said.

"Because the idol I saw in Mictlan was a depiction of Tanit, and she was the supreme female deity of Punic and Phoenician cultures."

"Not putting the dots together," Lea said.

Alex smiled and nodded – she was a step ahead. "I know where this is going."

"Then be a doll and enlighten the rest of us," Scarlet said, pulling a cigarette out of her packet and flicking it from one hand to the other.

"They're both the senior divine figures of their religious cultures," the American woman said.

Ryan nodded, clicked his fingers and pointed at Alex. "Give that woman the star prize! Búri was the first god of the Norse, and Tanit was the supreme deity of Carthage, and now we know they each have idols fashioned in their likenesses."

"And yet those cultures were entirely separate," Hawke said.

"And the bloody Carthage one was found in Mexico," said Scarlet.

"So the same people must have made these idols?" Lexi said.

"I'm seeing where this is going," Lea said.

"Right," Eden added firmly. "It's going to a place that seems to be pointing toward some kind of parent culture."

"This is starting to freak me out," Lea said.

"Or in English," Scarlet added. "Shit's getting real, baby."

Eden frowned, but they all knew she was right. "Yes, I supposed shit is *getting real*," he said, the italics audible in his words. "Also, and with many thanks to the Mexican authorities, we now have photographs of all the symbols and pictograms inside both the Temple of

Huitzilopochtli and the subterranean complex we're calling Mictlan."

As he was speaking he switched on the plasma screen and began to swipe through a number of images of decorative pictograms and wall-carvings from inside the ruined complex. "As you can see, we have more to go on than you might think. Not only do we have the Búri idol from Valhalla, but now we also have images of these carvings and pictographs from Mictlan as well."

"So what's our next play?" Maria said.

"Our next play," Eden said firmly, "is to retrieve the idol we lost at Mictlan."

"Business as usual then," Scarlet said.

"Not this time, I'm afraid," Eden said. "This time is very different."

CHAPTER FOUR

"Different?" Lea asked. "How?"

"This time we've been hired by the Mexican Government. They want us to locate the idol for them."

"Fair enough," Lea said. "It was theirs to start with, I guess. If they want it for one of their museums then there's not much we can do about it."

"A good point well made," Eden said. "But they don't want it for one of their museums. They have agreed to sell the idol to a private collector for large sum of money and have engaged us to retrieve it."

"Because we're so brilliant?" Scarlet said.

Eden frowned. "Partly because of our previous experience with the artefact in question and partly to save them from the difficulty and potential embarrassment of deploying Mexican Special Forces overseas."

"And who is this private collector?" Hawke asked.

"His name is Otmar Wolff and he's a defense contractor."

Hawke laughed. "An arms dealer."

"Yes, but when you meet him you'll say *defense contractor*. He is one of the world's largest suppliers of landmines for one thing. He has a very substantial contract with the Mexican Government and he's made them an offer they can't refuse. He's willing to reduce the cost of a shipment of self-propelled howitzers by fifty million dollars in return for possession of the idol. He's based in Liechtenstein."

"And what do we get out of this?" Lea asked bluntly.

"Ten million dollars. Five now, five upon receipt of the idol."

"Woah!" Ryan said, totally unable to hide his excitement. "What's my cut?"

Eden looked at him icily. "It doesn't work quite like that, Mr Bale. As you well know. This island doesn't run on fairy dust, and neither do those jets."

"Gotcha, big guy."

Eden raised an eyebrow but let it slide.

"Returning to the matter at hand, Wolff has close connections with most of the royal families in Europe and is not a man to obstruct or annoy. He has expressed grave fears that if the idol is not recovered Mendoza will simply sell it to the highest bidder and he's adamant that must not happen."

"Ten million bucks?" Ryan repeated.

Eden ignored him. "On this mission, you're going to be liaising with Jack Camacho. The US wants an American agent on the mission and he has experience working with your *methods*," he said, glancing at Scarlet.

"Jack Camacho?" Lea said.

"That's right."

"Hang on," said Scarlet. "How come the bloody Americans want in all of a sudden? This is our quest."

"Hey!" Alex said. "I'm American!"

"Sorry…"

Eden continued. "Not since Mexico City and Otmar Wolff stepped in. The CIA want an inside man and that man is Camacho. I want you all on a flight to Zurich half an hour ago."

"Zurich?" Lexi asked. "I thought we were going to Liechtenstein?"

"There are no runways in Liechtenstein," Eden said. "So landing one of my jets there might be somewhat problematic. I've arranged for you to meet Vincent Reno and Jack Camacho in Switzerland and they'll drive you over the border."

"I still don't like the idea of working for a third party," Lea said.

Eden frowned. "The Consortium has discussed the issue and the consensus is that considering Mexico City has already decided the idol is going to Wolff we may as well have the money. It's not Fantasy Island around here after all – it takes hard cash to run a place like this and our missions. We're not turning ten million dollars down, so you'll find a way to work with Wolff and you'll do it with smiles on your faces."

Maria sighed. "But if Ryan's right then the idol could be the only way to find Atlantis."

"I appreciate that, but the idol isn't ours if the Mexicans are claiming it, which they are."

Hawke spoke next. "If Ryan is right, and the idol is connected in some way, we only need a look at it, right?"

Ryan shrugged. "Maybe, maybe not. For all we know this Wolff character is searching for Atlantis too."

Eden shook his head. "No, I don't think so. From what I can tell about this guy, he's big on world cultures, but there's nothing to indicate he's into treasure hunting, and certainly nothing to show he's ever expressed an interest in mythologies and legends."

"So he doesn't know what he's buying, in other words," Scarlet said.

"Maybe," Eden replied. "Either way, we've been hired to retrieve the idol for him and he wants to give you the payment in cash so we're taking the job. If we can use the idol along the way to assist in our other quests then so much the better, but whatever happens, I'm ordering you to retrieve the idol first and then find Atlantis."

A deep silence fell over the room. Hawke knew Eden had never ordered a mission as big and important as this, and he knew the ECHO team had almost nothing to go on – except the golden idol.

They'd seen the enigmatic idol for the first time back in the altar room of the Temple of Mictlantecuhtli, but not for long. The heat of the battle afforded them only the briefest of glimpses before Silvio Mendoza snatched it and fled the chaos.

Ryan had longer with it, while he was waiting to be sacrificed to the god of the dead, and his eidetic memory had burned a permanent image of the idol in his mind. Also, they now had the Valhalla idol and the Mictlan pictographs, but it was scraps around the edges and no clear signs pointing to the most elusive and notorious lost civilization in history. He didn't even know where to start.

Sudden talk of 'parent cultures' had rattled him as much as the others. They just didn't know what they were up against, and he knew from his past military experience that knowing your enemy was a serious rule of warfare that only fools ignored.

"Are we connecting the Athanatoi with Atlantis?" he said at last.

More silence.

"It's too early to say," Eden said, looking at Ryan. "Wouldn't you agree?"

"I would," added Ryan confidently. "We know next to nothing about the Athanatoi, apart from the fact they refer to themselves as the Immortals and they're probably implicated in the murder of Lea's dad."

Hawke saw the exchange between Ryan and Lea. Once married, they shared so many memories, and their pasts intertwined like braided hair. He coughed to clear his throat. "There's more I haven't told you."

Everyone turned to look at him, including the frowning face of Sir Richard Eden. This too had agonized him in the same way as the mysterious idol, and now it was time to unload the burden.

"Which is?" said Lea, narrowing her eyes.

"You all know I ended the Matheson affair."

"That's the euphemism of the century," Scarlet said.

He glanced at her but made no reply to her point. "When I took Matheson out, he told me something about himself."

Scarlet snapped her fingers. "That he's the Man from Del Monte?"

"No," Hawke said, too apprehensive to respond. "He told me that he was under the control of a man named the Oracle." He scanned the faces of his friends for a reaction, but all he saw was attentive expectation.

Lea touched his hand. "Go on, Joe."

"He told me this Oracle character had ordered Operation Swallowtail against my wife, and that chasing after him would be a fool's errand."

"Sounds like your kind of job," Scarlet said.

"In his own words," Hawke continued, lowering his voice and not even looking at Scarlet, "he also said that hunting this man would be a one-way journey, and implied heavily that he was extremely powerful – above governments."

Eden fixed his eyes on Hawke and shifted in his seat. "You're thinking this Oracle is connected to the Athanatoi?"

Hawke nodded. "Almost without a doubt. It would all just be too much of a coincidence if not, and I don't believe in coincidences, as you all know."

"I think we should see this as progress," Alex said. "We know about the Athanatoi, and maybe now we know who their leader is. We can work with this."

Eden nodded. "Yes, we can."

"There's more," Hawke said his voice almost a whisper. He turned to face Lea. "Just then when Ryan said the Athanatoi were probably implicated in your father's death – it's more than a probability. Matheson implied this Oracle bloke was connected in some way to your father. He said your father was the cat whose curiosity got him killed." He reached out and held Lea's arms. "I'm sorry."

Lea nodded, and tightened her lips, determined not to cry. "Like Alex said," she said at last. "This is progress."

"And if there's anyone brilliant enough to decipher it all then that person is me," Ryan said without the hint of a smile.

"Crazy enough, you mean," Scarlet threw in. "But yeah... okay."

Eden sighed. "So get moving."

"Not *more* running around," Ryan said with a sigh.

"What's the matter, mate?" Hawke said, pushing away from the table. "Can't keep up?"

"I can keep up with you any day of the week," Ryan said, but not very convincingly.

"Keep up with *you*, darling?" Scarlet scoffed, rubbing Hawke's stomach. "Any more down there and we'll have to start calling you Joe Pork."

They all laughed, and even Eden cracked half a smile as he switched off the TV.

"Yes... thanks for that, Cairo," Hawke said, giving his stomach a reassuring tap.

CHAPTER FIVE

The small group of men and women sat around the large conference table in tense silence while they waited for their leader to arrive. When he did, they stumbled to their feet out of respect for him until he waved a hand and indicated they may sit again.

The Oracle looked upon them with something approaching disdain. Here, in this room where he had on so many occasions been attended by various kings, queens, presidents, prime ministers, secretaries of state and leading men of the world's militaries and churches, he was now faced with the ashen faces of his closest advisors. They all swore their loyalty to him, but to the Oracle they were only as worthy as their last act of devotion to the sacred cause.

"Update," he said.

"No sign of the Mexicans."

"Did I hear that right?" he asked quietly. "Did you just tell me that all of our resources have failed to find the thief of Mictlan and his accomplice?"

The synchronized nodding heads gave him the answer he desired, but he had grown weary of their terrified, sycophantic faces so he swivelled in his seat to face out the window instead. Out there, across the raging sea that he knew so well, were so many of the answers that his enemies sought, and even a few they had no idea even existed.

But...

Not even he knew all the answers. He too was searching for something – something more ancient and profound than any ECHO team member could begin to comprehend, and his greatest fear was that those fools would stumble upon it like a drunk tripping over a kerb… like a child discovering a loaded shotgun…

And what then?

What then, if little people like that were to learn the truth? They would be shaken and scared, but that meant nothing to him. His concerns trampled over his mind like wild horses, especially at night. There was a power there, he knew it… they had concealed a great power from him and his kind but now it was his to find. It couldn't ever fall into the hands of someone like Richard Eden, even less so Joe Hawke or Lea Donovan. The very idea was absurd. *ECHO…*

"And ECHO?" he asked, the words barely a whisper.

"Most of them are on the island as far as we can tell – all except the Frenchman."

He clenched his fists and cursed under his breath. He had too many wars to fight with powers that made ECHO look like a basket of kittens, and yet their persistence was driving him insane. He took a slow, deep breath to reduce the tension in his shoulders and then stretched his head to the side to get a crick out of his neck.

He rose from the chair and strolled across the carpet to the tinted window, never once taking his eyes off the waves as they formed into white horses and then smashed down into the dark gray of the sea. Without the document he had found in the secret society's vault, he would never have been able to bring himself to believe any of this, but there it was in black and white. Undeniable, exhilarating and yet… *terrifying.*

It was time to move his fight with them to the next level, and that meant eradicating their precious island. He relished the prospect, and considered the job no more than pouring boiling water into an ants' nest. Yes, he nodded in agreement with his own thoughts – it was time to destroy Elysium and he knew just the man for the job.

*

With Zurich only a few minutes away, Lea pushed her seat back to the upright position and walked to the galley to get a glass of water. Toward the front of the plane, Lexi and Scarlet were playing poker. Hawke had fallen asleep just after the flight and was only just beginning to stir. Ryan too had fallen asleep, and was now sprawled out in his chair with his laptop by his side. Maria was beside him, and also asleep with her head on his shoulder. She had to admit that despite her doubts about their relationship, they had proved everyone wrong and stayed together longer than anyone expected.

She finished the water and after dropping the paper cup in the trash she made her way back to her seat, stopping on the way to wake Ryan and Maria. Glancing out the window she guessed they were no more than five thousand feet and touchdown was imminent so she strapped herself in and watched Zurich rush up to greet her.

As their jet descended through the cold sky above Switzerland, she thought once again about what Eden had said in his briefing. They all wanted the Mictlan idol – they had the Valhalla one after all, and they had presumed it was theirs for the taking, but that was wrong. They weren't thieves – they were the good guys, and if the Mexican authorities had already promised the sale of the idol to Wolff there was nothing they could do about it. The only play they had left was to retrieve the idol for him but ensure they had enough time to study it before handing it over.

Outside the tires screeched on the tarmac and the roar of the reverse thrusters brought her back to life. Moments later they were disembarking and once they had cleared customs they found Jack Camacho waiting for them in the arrivals area. He had flown in on an American Government plane from DC and arrived an hour before them. He gave everyone a solemn handshake except Scarlet, who Lea noticed got a hug and a kiss on the cheek.

In the car park they followed the American to a battered Land Rover Discovery with French licence plates. Lea leaned inside to see Vincent Reno at the wheel. "Bonsoir," he said with a wide grin and a friendly nod of his head.

"Monsieur Reaper here drove across from his place in Provence," Camacho said.

"Only six hours for ordinary people," the Frenchman said. "Or five hours if you drive like me." He patted the steering wheel affectionately. "I drive her hard."

"I'm not saying a thing," Scarlet said.

"Makes a change."

"At least I don't look like Hulk Hogan!" she said.

"Who the hell is Ulk Ogan?" Reaper said.

"This is almost as much fun as when we went to the Arctic!" Lea said.

"The Arctic Circle?" Reaper said.

"She means Valhalla," Scarlet said with a grin. "You wouldn't know about that Vincent because you were lazing around in a Swedish hospital bed."

Reaper gave a Gallic shrug. "And I cannot deny it."

"Just drive!"

And with that they were gone, racing out of the car park and making their way from the airport to Liechtenstein.

CHAPTER SIX

"Who knew Liechtenstein was so damn pretty?" Lea said.

"Or so damn small," said Scarlet. "Rich has got a bathroom bigger than this whole country back in his Oxford mansion."

"It's not *that* small," Ryan said.

"Are you kidding?" Scarlet said dismissively. "You can drive across it in about ten minutes. They probably share the electricity bill."

The corner of Hawke's mouth turned up in amusement as Reaper drove them south along the Bergstrasse to the tiny village of Bärg. Like everyone else in the team he had never been to Liechtenstein before and was impressed by how so many awesome mountains could be packed into such a small country.

"It's amazing how so much Alpine beauty fits into such a diminutive principality," Ryan said.

"That's just what I was thinking," Hawke said, glancing in the mirror. "Sort of."

They turned a sharp hairpin bend in the road and headed north, at once revealing a generous view of the country's capital, Vaduz. With only a little over five thousand residents in the town, it was one of the smallest capitals in the world, but it was a startlingly alluring town with its narrow roads and cathedral spire. As they pushed higher into the mountains, Ryan pointed out Vaduz Castle, the Sovereign Prince's official residence, far below at the start of the Bergstrasse.

"There it is again," he said, impressed by its 11th Century keep which peered imperiously over the entire valley below.

"And that's where the king lives, right?" Lea said.

"He's a prince, actually," Ryan replied. "His official title is His Serene Highness,"

"Ooh I *like* that," Scarlet said. "Is he married?"

"Yes, to a Czech countess," he said wryly, "but I'm sure he'd be *much* happier with you."

Onwards up the western slopes of the Alpspitz they drove until they reached Bärg and slowed to meet its fifty kph speed limit. Reaper cruised past the wooden ski chalets and neatly trimmed gardens. A bank of clouds was blowing in from the north and covering much of the country below in cool shade.

Turning into an unsealed side road they drove another few hundred yards to a set of imposing iron gates. They opened as if by magic and allowed them to cruise up Wolff's drive and park up outside the main entrance to his chalet.

Set over four storeys, the postmodern chalet was constructed out of hardwood timber, steel and glass, but boulders and stones from the mountain itself supported its base.

The door opened to reveal a man in a smart two-piece suit. He acknowledged them politely but without a smile. "My name is Brunhart. I keep the house."

Hawke and Lea shared a wordless glance as Brunhart showed them into a vast slate-floored hallway.

"Please follow me."

Brunhart led them out of the hall and they turned to walk down a long, cedar panelled corridor decorated occasionally with peculiar abstract sculptures in white porcelain. Approaching a closed door, Brunhart tapped respectfully and moments later they were standing inside a large, high-ceilinged room with white stucco walls and a vast slate fireplace. All around the room were pieces of ancient art and archaeology, and the entire western wall was an eight-metre high window which projected the most incredible view of the valley into the postmodern space. Lea felt like she was in an IMAX cinema. One of Bach's orchestral suites played quietly through concealed speakers.

"Please, wait here," Brunhart said. "I will tell Herr Wolff you have arrived."

Brunhart clicked the door behind him and a silence fell on the expansive room.

"He actually squeaks when he walks," Lexi said with amazement.

Lea rolled her eyes. "That's his shoes."

"Look at all this stuff," Ryan said, marvelling at the collection of ancient art and sculptures. "It's amazing."

"Looks like a load of crap to me," Scarlet said dismissively.

"What the hell is this?" Lea asked as she picked up what looked like a small wooden club.

"I can't be sure," Ryan said, squinting at it, "but it looks a lot like a wooden phallus from the Kabye tribe of Togo."

"Urghh," Lea said, and threw it into the air in horror.

"Ah, but this has potential," Scarlet said, catching it with one hand and winking at Ryan.

"You are something else, Sloane," Camacho said, wrenching it out of her hand and putting it back on the shelf with the rest of the collection. He looked at her and shook his head.

The moment ended abruptly when a tall, thin man entered the room not by the door Brunhart had used but by a concealed entrance behind the fireplace. He had silver, neck-length hair swept back from his face in neat perfection and wore a dark Nehru jacket. Holding his arms behind his back he approached them and introduced himself in a clipped, cultured accent. "I'm honoured Sir Richard organized things so quickly," he said with a businesslike nod of his head. He approached Ryan first and shook his hand fervently. "I am Otmar Wolff and you must be Joe Hawke! I read about your involvement in the discovery of the Temple of Huitzilopochtli and I must say this is a true privilege to meet you."

"Why, thank you!" Ryan said with a grin and returning the handshake. "I'm very…"

"Very much *not* Joe Hawke," Lea said with a disapproving look. "This is Ryan Bale, Herr Wolff, and I'm Lea Donovan. *This* is Joe Hawke…"

The man looked embarrassed for a moment before apologizing for his mistake, and then greeted everyone in turn. "Please – have a seat."

The ECHO team welcomed his offer and made use of the eclectic jumble of sofas and chairs scattered around the large fireplace, but Ryan paused to peer into the secret passageway.

"Ryan, arse on couch right now," Scarlet said.

"Oh, yeah… sorry."

"You have a beautiful home, Herr Wolff," Lea said.

Wolff nodded pensively, as if he were considering whether the statement was true or not. "It was very expensive to build," he explained. "We had to use helicopters to transport the steel up here because the trucks they wanted to use couldn't handle the roads."

"Isn't that always the problem?" Hawke said, drawing a hard nudge in his ribs from Lea's elbow.

"Your journey up the Bergstrasse would have taken you past Vaduz Castle, I'm sure, so you see my home is really very modest." He smiled and his eyes danced across their faces. "But I digress. I liaised with Sir Richard and the Mexicans to get you here because I feel we may be of mutual assistance to each other. As a serious collector in the world of archaeology, I have followed your exploits closely. I hope that doesn't make me sound like an obsessive. It is a pleasant and necessary distraction from my business life." He smiled at them warmly. "I presume Sir Richard briefed you fully about my business proposal?"

"You want us to retrieve the idol for you," Lea said.

"The *stolen* idol," Wolff corrected. "Yes."

"Of course."

"I have an extensive collection of antiquities as you can see for yourselves, and the discovery of the Temple of Huitzilopochtli must rank as one of the greatest archaeological events in modern history. The idol you retrieved from it is of particular interest to me as my primary fascination is with the Phoenician Empire. I can't begin to imagine how an idol depicting Tanit ended up in Mexico, but I know I cannot live without it. I am a greedy man, and I want that idol. That is why I have offered the Mexican Government fifty million dollars for it. You will be paid ten percent now and another ten percent upon delivering the item to me – all in cash."

As he spoke Brunhart walked into the room with a black leather attaché case and Wolff opened it to reveal five million American dollar in neat bundles.

"But fifty million dollars?" Ryan said. "It was only eight inches high!"

"I am aware of its dimensions, Mr Bale. There are other dark forces seeking that idol, and they must not be permitted to acquire it under any circumstances. I can tell you no more until you have retrieved the idol from

the Mexican thief. Only then will you be told the rest...
and get your money, naturally."

"Dark forces?" Lea asked.

"As I say, I am not at liberty to say more."

As he spoke, Ryan perused the extensive collection of
antiquities, stopping at a stone sculpture of the Lady of
Elche. Ryan's eyes widened like saucers. "I thought this
was in the National Archaeological Museum in
Madrid?"

Wolff turned to face him. "A reproduction only. This
is the genuine piece. I paid far too much for it."

"I've seen it in pictures but never up close like this.
She's incredible."

"I'm very proud of it," Wolff said.

Ryan made a circle around the sculpture and studied
the intricate carvings with care. What had once been an
impressive piece of Phoenician sculpture now took on an
entirely different perspective thanks to what he had seen
in the depths of Mictlan.

"It's made of limestone and was discovered over a
hundred years ago near Valencia," Wolff continued,
noting his interest, "but the truth is we know very little
about it. There are many sculptures of Tanit in the world,
but la dama de Elche has always captivated me."

"Naturally," Ryan said, still peering at the convoluted
carvings in the headdress. "The idol I saw in Mexico
looked like this one, and precisely so, as well."

Wolff rose from his seat. "Am I right in
understanding you also found the Treasure of the Sad
Night?"

Ryan nodded. "The Aztecs were storing it inside the
Temple of Huitzilopochtli so we know they were using
the place up till the conquest era but they never took it
inside Mictlan itself. We know this because we found it
dumped outside the gates of the underworld and we

know the Spanish never went inside because it was sealed shut. But the idol itself came from Mictlan."

"We can't say much more," Camacho said stepping forward, "for reasons of national security. I'm sure you understand."

"Of course," Wolff said.

"So now we know who you are and what you want," Hawke said, "what part will you be playing in all this, except for paying a shed load of cash for the idol?"

"My part in all this is to supply you with whatever armaments you may feel necessary to achieve your mission. As you will no doubt be aware, I have access to the very latest weapons technologies in the world and you are welcome to use any you deem appropriate in order to secure the idol for me."

"All my Christmases have come at once," Scarlet muttered.

"My warehouse is in a secure facility on the outskirts of Vaduz, but I took the liberty of having a selection brought here to my home. Please, won't you follow me?"

Wolff led them through the secret passageway and along a dimly lit corridor. "This goes through the heart of the house," he said solemnly. "If you'll please follow me down these steps."

"Are we sure this is Liechtenstein?" Ryan whispered to Maria. "What if we took a wrong turn and it's Transylvania?"

She playfully slapped the back of his head and told him to shut up.

They approached another door which gave way to a short corridor with breeze block walls and a cement floor. "It's just down here." He opened a second door and they entered a small storage facility. "This is the vault."

Inside the climate-controlled vault, Wolff made a sweeping gesture with his hands and revealed the largest cache of weapons Hawke had ever seen outside of any military arsenal.

"This is incredible!" Scarlet said.

Wolff smiled, beaming with pride. He tipped his head forward in a courteous and courtly bow. "And yours for the taking, my dear."

CHAPTER SEVEN

After selecting their weapons, Hawke, Lea and Lexi rejoined Wolff who was now wearing a thin, silk scarf and taking Orange Pekoe tea on the balcony overlooking Vaduz. The others remained inside by the fire while Ryan returned to the bust of the Lady of Elche and studied her headdress.

Scarlet watched Ryan tracing his fingers over the statue's face. "Do you two want a room?"

"This is fascinating," Ryan said, crouching once again to get another look at the sculpture. "I've stared and stared at these carvings but they're just not making any sense. Another thing that's bothering me as that I'm seeing pictographs and echoes of so many cultures it's starting to freak me out. This here looks Aztec but this one is obviously Punic – and then again over here is a hieroglyphic that quite frankly looks like Early Dynastic Egyptian. It must be an historical first. I'm speechless."

"And that makes two historical firsts," Scarlet said.

"Amazing!" Ryan said, too excited to catch the jibe. "It really is amazing."

"I was being sarcastic, *boy*," she said.

This time he turned to face her. "Are you ever anything else?" he said. "While I'm here appreciating this ancient art you're making smarmy comments and staring at Camacho's rear end."

"I am not!" she said.

"Was she?" Camacho said, and then turning to Scarlet: "Were you?"

"Absolutely not!"

41

"Touched a raw nerve…" Ryan said.

"I'll touch some raw nerves in a minute," Scarlet snapped. "Like the ones in between your…"

Camacho looked at her with a sly grin. "I don't know if I'm buying that denial, babe. You're kind of blushing there."

Scarlet put her hands on her hips. "I bloody well am not!"

"She is – look at her!" Ryan said.

"I think so too," said Maria.

"The lady protests too much, methinks," Camacho said.

Ryan sighed. "Actually when Shakespeare wrote that it meant to make a vow, not like today when it means to make a false denial."

"Thanks a lot, *darling* – oh, look out – captain's on the deck."

Wolff showed the others back inside the warm and Brunhart appeared from nowhere with a silver plate full of Valle Dulcis chocolates and glasses full of Reisetbauer schnapps.

"Please, help yourselves – if it's not too early for you."

"What's the time, Mr Wolff?" Ryan said, deadpan.

Scarlet rolled her eyes.

Lea sighed.

Maria turned to suppress a smile and pretended to watch an imaginary bird flying outside the giant window wall.

Wolff surprised them all by pulling a solid silver pocket watch out of his jacket. "Time we toasted to your success, I think!"

Everyone helped themselves with the exception of Ryan who had now moved on to the Venus de Milo. "You know, I'm certain this is a fake."

Wolff took a step closer and squinted at the stonework. "Nonsense! I bought it directly from the Louvre!"

"No, I'm sure I'm right – this looks like deliberate distressing here, and here."

"I see," Wolff said, his words heavy with scepticism. "You expect me to believe this statue is a fake?"

"Pretty much," Ryan said without looking up from the smooth curve of her upper thigh.

"And he's never really wrong," Lea said.

Scarlet rolled her eyes. "True, but bloody annoying."

"But you'll be pleased to know," Ryan said, standing up to face Wolff, "that your Tanit is without a doubt the original and a wonderful depiction of a goddess of Atlantis."

"What did you say?" Wolff said, suppressing a chuckle.

"He said Atlantis, darling."

Wolff shook his head and took a step back. "Is this some kind of a joke?"

"No joke," Lea said. "Ryan doesn't joke about things like this."

"It's true," Scarlet said. "The only funny thing about Ryan is the length of his…"

"Yes, thank you, Scarlet," Hawke said.

Ryan gave Scarlet a sideways glance but didn't rise to the bait. Instead he turned his attention to Wolff who was now looking surprised.

"You mean to tell me you seriously believe in Atlantis?"

"Well…"

"I have studied ancient cultures for decades!" Wolff said. "Atlantis is a myth, and not substantiated in the least beyond a few short words from Plato. A myth! That is the opinion of every academic and curator who

43

has ever studied the subject. The mere suggestion is absolutely ridiculous and makes me question your credibility. Atlantis is nothing more than a legend!"

"Maybe, maybe not," Camacho said. "But we can't take any risks. I'm sure you would have said Mictlan was a myth but now we know it's real."

"I want the idol, Mr Hawke, not some ludicrous search for Atlantis. Is that clear?"

"Clear as crystal," Lea said, but Hawke could see she was biting her tongue.

"Good," Wolff said, and called Brunhart to the room. They exchanged a few words and then he turned to face the ECHO team and Brunhart locked the attaché case back up. Wolff slid it off the table and handed it to Lea. "Here is your five million dollars. The other five will be transferred when you retrieve the idol."

*

Driving back to Vaduz Airport, Lea called in to report their meeting with Wolff to Eden. After a brief conversation they decided to Skype and moments later she was watching Eden, Alex and recently-arrived Kim Taylor in the Elysium Briefing Room.

"Any luck?" he asked.

"Not much – we're still in Liechtenstein."

"And how was Herr Wolff?"

"He should be called Big Hair Wolff," Ryan said. "Talk about a mullet."

"It wasn't a mullet," Lea said, rolling her eyes. "He gave us plenty of toys to play with in the hunt for Mendoza but he's not sold on the idea of Atlantis. He was very clear about that when he handed us the five mil in cash."

"As we thought," Eden said "And I've got something else you all need to know."

He leaned forward in his seat and picked up the remote from the glass-topped table. "It's about the idol." As he spoke, he selected some more files on the plasma screen and closed the electronic shutters, plunging the room into darkness.

"Ooh, cosy!" Scarlet said.

"Don't tell me – Silvio Mendoza?" Lexi said.

"The very same," Eden said with a heavy sigh. "As you know, after he fled into the jungle I put the word out among my MI5 contacts – gave them a description and some of his more recent mugshots given to me by Enrique Valles in Mexico. They poked around a bit..."

"Translation," Scarlet said. "Did more hacking than a Canadian lumberjack..."

Eden gave her a look. "They *looked into it* for me and handed it to Six who in turn pushed it out to some of their global assets. An hour ago Europol contacted MI5 with a positive match."

Eden tapped some information into his iPad and Mendoza's face was projected on the plasma screen behind his head.

"Urgh," Scarlet said. "I had no idea how much of a bastard he looks until you blew his face up like that."

"I'd like to blow his face up, all right," Lea said.

"Yes, quite," Eden said, changing the image. "The picture you see here is one of Silvio Mendoza and Aurora Soto exiting Vienna International Airport a few hours ago."

"Vienna?" Hawke said. "What the hell are they doing there?"

"We know he took the idol from the temple complex in Mexico," Ryan said. "Maybe he's trying to find out more about it from one of the museums. There are dozens of them there."

"Or maybe he fancied a trip on the Wiener Riesenrad," Scarlet said, her voice heavy with sarcasm, referring to the famous Ferris wheel in the Prater amusement park.

"He didn't want any ride on a fairground ride," Eden said flatly "And if you listened to the briefing you'd know why."

He put a third and final image of Mendoza up on the screen. This was a grainy black and white still from some CCTV footage showing the Mexican drug lord. "They caught the train from the airport and arrived in Vienna shortly afterwards. This is our man walking along the western platform of the Vienna Praterstern train station in Leopoldstadt. After this they were tracked west on CCTV across a bridge spanning a tributary of the Danube."

"And then?"

"They visited a Professor Franz Huber, formerly of the Vienna Museum of Ethnology, who just happens to be…"

"A world-famous expert on Aztec artefacts?" Maria said.

"A dead expert to be more precise," Eden said with a sigh. "We don't know exactly what happened inside Professor Huber's apartment, but when he tried to leave the apartment block the Vienna police were already surrounding the building. They had followed him there using the same information I am now telling you. Mendoza reverted to form and used Huber as a human shield until he was safely out of sight. After a shootout they managed to get away. They found Huber's body in a church less than an hour ago. Either Mendoza or Soto had stabbed him through the ribcage in what the local police have described as a frenzied attack."

"Which means they must have already got all they wanted from him," Hawke said.

"The latest?" Lexi said.

"Vienna has a maze of subterranean tunnels and cellars running underneath it dating from ancient Roman times. They disappeared into them from the crypt and for a while the police thought they'd lost them."

"What is it with this bloke and tunnels?" Ryan said. "Maybe it's a Freudian thing?"

Eden flashed him a disapproving look. "According to the Viennese police they connect up with the modern sewer network and he used them to make his way undetected to the train station where he caught a train to Munich."

"Munich? What's there?"

Eden sighed heavily before he spoke. "A former associate of mine named Dirk Kruger. Think of him as my nemesis... *I* do."

"Dirk Kruger?" Ryan said with a smirk. "Did you just make that name up off the top of your head, Rich?"

"I did not, funnily enough. Dirk and I went to university together and were friends a long time ago – when I went into the army he went into archaeology. He's no lover of the ancient though and in it purely for the looting. We haven't spoken for decades. Today it looks like he's hosting a little soirée for our Mexican friends."

"How do we know all this?" Lexi asked.

"Mendoza was tracked to a hotel used by Dirk in Munich about two hours ago. The Hotel Sendling. Dirk has a room booked there."

Eden raised his wrist to check the time. "So here's the plan. We're formally engaged by Mexico City to retrieve the idol for Wolff, but I'm sure you'll all agree with me that Atlantis is the real prize here."

"The idol and Atlantis are linked anyway, I just know they are," Ryan said distractedly. "I don't care what old Wolff says."

"Well," Eden said. "We need Mendoza in custody at the very least, and more than that we need that idol. We can analyse it in depth before returning it to Wolff, and we just cannot allow someone like Mendoza to have anything that could lead him to Atlantis." He lowered his voice and fixed his eyes on them. Lea noticed he looked more anxious than usual. "I'll warn you now that Dirk Kruger is ruthless, and worse than that he's lucky. In fact he's the luckiest bastard I've ever known."

He cut the call just as Reaper steered the Discovery into Vaduz Airport.

"Rich did say Munich, didn't he?" Scarlet said smiling. "It's the Oktoberfest right now, isn't it?"

"Sounds good to me," Lea said. "I've always wanted to go to Munich."

CHAPTER EIGHT

The South African stared at the Lichtenburg figure on Silvio Mendoza's creased face with unconcealed fascination. A man like Dirk Kruger had never worried about the views and opinions of others and he wasn't about to start now. The veins of scar tissue ran up from beneath the cartel boss's collar and crawled all over the left side of his neck and face like the baby boomslang snakes Kruger had tormented as a child in Cape Town.

Kruger's heavy South African accent filled the otherwise silent Munich hotel room as he raised a finger full of gold rings and pointed at Mendoza's face. "How did you get that?"

"Lightning strike," was all the Mexican said, and Aurora took a step closer to him.

Kruger nodded pensively as he twisted one of the many rings on his gnarled, tanned hand. A man in a snakeskin jacket beside him sniffed hard and jammed his hands in his pockets.

"Why are you here?" Kruger asked.

"I have a business proposal," Mendoza said in poor English.

Another nod, but this time more suspicious. "My business is antiquities, Silvio. You don't mind if I call you Silvio, do you?"

Mendoza and Aurora exchanged a glance. "Of course not, *Dirk*."

"But you can call me Mr Kruger."

An awkward moment of silence followed until Kruger laughed. "I'm joking, Silvio. It's just a joke... as

I say – my business is antiquities – and precious stones. In particular I hold a deep fascination for diamonds."

"That's what I was told."

"So people talk about me behind my back – you hear that, Willem?"

The man in the snakeskin jacket nodded dully and cracked his knuckles as Mendoza reached into his bag. In a heartbeat Willem drew a gun and told the Mexicans to freeze.

"Take it easy, Silvio," Kruger croaked. "My associate is under the impression you have something nasty in your bag. If you pull out a gun or knife you'll be dead a second later. Know that."

"It's not a weapon," Aurora said.

Mendoza pulled out the golden idol and watched Kruger's eyes sparkle like black diamonds. The South African looter extraordinaire was in his element now and squeezed the arms of his chair as his eyes danced all over the idol. Carthaginian, he thought at once... Tanit... gold. He wanted to study it in greater detail in a big hurry but he knew from his poker days not to show too much interest this early in the game.

"I found it in Mexico," Mendoza said.

Kruger leaned so far forward in his chair he nearly fell out of it. Now, this looked more than interesting. If he'd found it in Spain or North Africa that would be one thing, but Mexico was an altogether different kettle of galjoens. If an object like this was unearthed somewhere in Mexico then the possibilities could be infinite in their wonder. He beckoned for Mendoza to bring the object closer.

"Give it over."

Mendoza and Aurora shared a glance but knew they had no choice. It had taken them almost seven hours to get from the tunnels of Leopoldstadt to Kruger's hotel room and when they arrived the South African had been elsewhere attending to business and made them wait another hour. They were weary, hungry and entirely in the palm of Dirk Kruger's hand. Mendoza stepped forward and handed it to Joh Van Zyl, and he in turn handed it to his older brother Willem. Neither man spent long looking at the thing, and soon it was in the boss's hands.

Kruger weighed the idol in his hand. Yes, gold for sure. There were some out there who would spray tungsten because it had such a similar mass and feel to gold, but not this. This was *art* and he had never seen anything like it, not even in the finest museums. Her face was... almost toxically bewitching, and wait a minute – what the hell were those markings on her back? He wanted to say Egyptian hieroglyphics but that wasn't quite right. And where on earth did those diamonds come from?

"Where exactly did you find it?"

"In a temple in the south."

Kruger's black eyes fixed on the Mexican. "You found *this* in a Mexican temple?"

Mendoza nodded.

"But this writing is... what is that – Punic script, maybe?"

"Huber spoke for a long time about Carthage and the Phoenician Empire."

"That's Franz. How is the old bastard?"

"He's... fine, I guess," Mendoza lied.

Kruger looked at him sharply. "What do you mean, 'you guess'? Franz does a lot of work for me – I hope you treated him with respect."

"We really only spoke for a few short moments," Mendoza said quietly.

But Kruger was once again staring at the idol, and the Mexican's words drifted away into the awkward silence. It was captivating without a doubt, and Kruger was drawn to it like a magnet. He cradled it in his arms and leaned over it as if he were holding a baby. It was enthralling him. "And what did he say in those few short moments?" he said with casual indifference.

"He said you were the man to bring this to, and that perhaps you would be able to translate the symbols. He said it could be an ancient code."

An ancient code... it might hold water, Kruger thought. Huber was brighter than he was and he knew it, but he had zero experience in the real world and the South African knew that in this life, paper never beat rock, no matter what the game said.

He held the symbols up to the light and after a moment of quiet concentration his eyes suddenly widened. "Willem! Get me a map of the world."

Willem Van Zyl, Kruger's Number One, returned a moment later with an iPad and called up Google Earth. Kruger bit his lip with anticipation as the 3D model of the planet spun around under his finger's control. He chuckled. "One day the real world will dance to my tune."

Mendoza and Soto shared a glance while the South Africans huddled around the iPad. Kruger was holding it, while the Van Zyl brothers were peering over his shoulder as their boss navigated the model around to Morocco. "It's got to be here somewhere." He watched the landscapes zoom past as he flicked around to the north of Africa.

"Why there?" Van Zyl said.

"This symbol refers to a western kingdom."

"What's that?"

"The Western Kingdom is a reference to Morocco, you domkop."

Van Zyl nodded but said nothing as his boss hurriedly zoomed in on the African state. He stopped and stared at the idol again, and then his eyes lit up for the second time. "Get me my briefcase!"

Willem Van Zyl fetched the tattered case from beside the desk and handed it to his boss. After a few moments of rustling papers Kruger returned his face to the light. "Roses!"

"Huh?" Willem said.

Kruger pointed aggressively at the symbol. "This means roses, and this means valley. So the next step is obvious."

"Where?" Van Zyl asked, the confusion spreading over his face once more.

"The Dadès Gorge," Kruger said, sighing and shaking his head. "Are you really that thick, Willem?"

Van Zyl made no reply, knowing only too well what happened to men who gave Kruger any backchat.

"Look here – this is the place!" He pointed a heavily suntanned finger at a stretch of the Dadès River. "It's identical."

"You're sure?" Aurora asked.

"Yes, I'm bloody sure! The symbols on this idol cannot lie. Whoever carved them into her was making a trail for us to follow all the way to the Dadès Gorge. It's as clear as day."

Van Zyl zoomed in on the area on Google Earth and sighed. "It looks like it's just a desert wilderness."

Kruger got up in his face. "Not any bloody more, it isn't – not with this!" He threw the idol into the air and caught it again. "So I'm in... but I'll need to round up a few old boys first. Can't go after something like this without a small army, and I happen to know just where to find one."

*

With their own jet back in Zurich, it was only thanks to Otmar Wolff's generous offer to let them use his private helicopter that they escaped more of Reaper's haphazard approach to negotiating busy traffic. On board the chopper, the journey to Munich was short and pleasurable. The Eurocopter EC145 was a nine-seater business helicopter with a luxury interior and gave all of them some idea about Wolff's success in the international arms business.

"This is the life," Lexi said as she peered out of the chopper and drank in the view of the mountains below. They stretched out along the eastern horizon and faded into a haze somewhere along the Austrian border.

The Eurocopter crossed the border at Oberstdorf and as they moved further into Bavaria the mountains reduced in size to rolling hills. By the time they passed over Schongau it was mostly flat, agricultural land peppered with crystal clear lakes and sporadic carpets of dark green forestry.

They spoke briefly of Otmar Wolff's haircut, but more about his ten million dollars, and then his dismissal of their Atlantis ideas. Hawke was undeterred and underlined to the team that despite Wolff's employment of them to find the idol, Atlantis was their main priority.

"But he was explicit about not wasting our time on a wild goose chase looking for Atlantis," Lexi said.

"What he doesn't know can't hurt him," Hawke said. "And he might not believe in Atlantis, but it's pretty obvious to the rest of us that it exists and that it's linked somehow to Mictlan and the idol. Anyway – here's our stop."

The Eurocopter swooped down over the center of Munich and landed in a park west of the Oktoberfest. Thousands of people were milling around the beer tents below enjoying the buzzing folk festival and Hawke looked at the peaceful men, women and children with increasing anxiety as he imagined what could so easily go wrong if Mendoza or Soto started to panic.

As soon as the chopper's tires were on the neatly trimmed grass of Bavariapark they were climbing out and meeting the head of GSG-9, the German special police. Hawke cast a wary eye over the hubbub around the beer tents as introductions were made and with the tropical paradise of Elysium now on the other side of the world, he warmed his hands as he walked into the temporary police HQ. The others followed behind and moments later they were introduced to Polizeihauptkommissar Holtz and his immediate subordinate Polizeiobermeister Schmidt.

According to their intelligence, Silvio Mendoza and Aurora Soto were still inside the Hotel Sendling at the north end of the beer park. The man the Mexicans were meeting was confirmed as Dirk Kruger, the South African tomb raider with a penchant for diamonds who was known to be extremely unpredictable.

"No evacuation order?" Hawke asked.

Holtz cast a concerned eye in the direction of the festival and he looked like a troubled man as he addressed them. "The authorities don't want to alarm anyone without cause."

"Any more details?" Lexi said.

"Our intel shows they are in the Hotel Sendling. It's a luxury hotel near the beer festival so we're keen to make sure the problem is contained, as you can imagine."

Hawke nodded. "I understand this Kruger is based in Salzburg, so why is here in Munich?"

"Intel is a little sketchy on this but we think he's meeting a Qatari named Al-Hajri with a view to selling him a quantity of unknown ancient artefacts."

"And this Qatari – you tracked him into the country?"

Holtz shook his head. "He entered the EU in Hungary and after hiring a car in Budapest he disappeared."

They exited the HQ and walked closer to the Hotel Sendling. The four-lane Theresienhohe which ran around the western edge of the Theresienwiese fairground was now empty of traffic and they easily crossed it on foot. As the Polizei München cleared the last few cars in a detour and stopped pedestrians from wandering out of the festival and getting too close, Hawke took cover behind the GlaxoSmithKline building and monitored the hotel. Schmidt finished talking on his radio, jogged up to Holtz and saluted.

"We have the back covered," he said calmly. "He's still checked in and not due to leave until the morning."

Holtz nodded. "And Berlin has just issued a no-fly zone over the city so no helicopters to whisk them away either."

Hawke looked up at the hotel room and readied himself for a fight. "Looks like I finally caught up with you bastards."

CHAPTER NINE

Aurora Soto was beginning to wish she had stayed in Mexico. Ever since she had arrived in Europe she'd had a very bad feeling about how things were going to turn out, and tonight the company of Dirk Kruger and his weird entourage of treasure hunters wasn't helping the situation.

She didn't know what that damned idol was, or what it meant. She was pretty sure Silvio had no idea either, but she didn't like the way it seemed to captivate whoever held it in their hands... whoever glanced upon it. And she especially didn't like the way it stared back at people, silent and inscrutable.

She walked across the room and pushed the curtains aside to watch the street for a few moments, and it was then that serendipity introduced her to the next chapter in her life. "We have company," she said quietly.

Kruger's head snapped up from the idol and he stared at her, his eyes widening with anger. "What did you say?"

"She said we have company," Mendoza said, taking a protective step toward Aurora.

The South African leaped from his chair, the idol still gripped in his hands like a weapon. "And who might that be?"

"Looks like our friends from the jungle," Aurora said. She and Mendoza exchanged a worried glance.

"What friends?" Kruger said as he padded to the window and looked at the force gathering in the street.

"They're called the ECHO team," Mendoza said, recalling the research he'd done on the flight to Austria. "They're some kind of independent group loosely connected to the British Government but that's all I could find out about them. The main man's called Hawke and they had something to do with stopping the kidnap of President Grant."

"Jesus," Van Zyl said.

Mendoza continued. "No one knows anything about them – not where they're based, or what their agenda is. All we know is they're dangerous – they destroyed Morton Wade's operation in a matter of hours."

Kruger turned to face Mendoza his face suddenly all business. "These pricks out here are the people who brought Wade down?"

Mendoza nodded. "With some help from American and Mexican forces, and by the looks of things they're with some heavily armed police as well."

"And you led them right to me, you fucking idiot?"

"I…, well, I…"

Aurora wanted to run a knife across Kruger's throat just to teach him not to speak to Silvio Mendoza like this, but now wasn't the time. Perhaps that time would come later… perhaps not. She had learned to roll with the punches, but she had a hunch Dirk Kruger might not make it to the final curtain.

She stepped out of her daydream about cutting his throat only to see he was still ranting about ECHO. "You have any idea how many people want to sink their claws into me? You have any idea how many enemies I have made? There are hundreds of men who want Dirk Kruger's head over their fireplaces and you bring this lot right into my life."

Van Zyl stepped over to the window. "Looks like they mean business, boss."

"Where are there?" Kruger asked.

"At the end of the street."

Kruger contemplated for a moment. "If this idol has the attention of so many governments, then I'm not letting her out of my sight. This could be the hoard I've been waiting for all my life."

"What about ECHO?" Mendoza asked.

"Forget those stupid bastards," the South African snapped. "They have a big surprise coming to them."

*

Hawke gave a quick nod as he smacked a new magazine into the housing of his Heckler & Koch MP5 and followed Holtz into the hotel lobby. ECHO and the local police worked well together as they fanned out and began to climb the service stairs to the top floor. Moments later they were gathered in the corridor outside Kruger's room.

After a quick signal from Holtz, the police swiped a keycard in the lock and burst into the room with their submachine guns raised into the aim. Hawke and Maria were a step behind and quickly saw the suite was empty.

"Nothing!" called a police officer through the comms.

"Clear!" called another from the bathroom.

Hawke lowered his gun and sighed. "Damn it all!"

"So where the hell are they?" Maria said.

"We had good intel they were at this hotel,' Holtz said, his voice rising with frustration and anger. "Good intel."

"Obviously not good enough," Hawke said. "Looks like they played you with the oldest trick in the book. Kruger must have hired out this room and then hired out another one under a false name."

"But where?"

"Nearby, for sure."

"How do you know?"

"Because he'll want to know if anyone's rumbled him or not. That means keeping an eye on this place. He'll already know we're in here, and…everyone get out!"

Hawke screamed at the others to get out and he turned and pushed Holtz and the others through the door but at that second an RPG tore through the balcony door windows and exploded in the room. The savage detonation of the high-velocity warhead ripped through the plush hotel room and exploded a lethal fireball into every corner.

It blasted Hawke out of the room and into the corridor where he landed with a crash on top of Maria. Above them, the fireball ripped over their heads and ignited the paint on the ceiling. He covered her with his body to shield her from the blast and felt the searing pain on his back as the explosion burned out and turned to hot smoke.

The Russian looked up at Hawke, now on top of her, their lips no more than an inch apart. "You seem to have a habit of doing this."

Hawke opened his mouth to reply but instead of speaking he rolled off her and helped her back to her feet. Further down the corridor Lea and the others were dusting themselves down, and Hawke was now scanning the area outside the window for any signs of the assassin.

The calm peace of the Munich evening was now a chaotic mess of screaming and smoke alarms. Outside the shockwave of the RPG explosion had set off half a dozen car alarms to add to the sense of manic turmoil and now they heard emergency service sirens wailing in the distance.

They got themselves together and retreated along the corridor. Hawke kicked open the panic bar on a fire exit and a second later they were outside in the cool night air.

"What the hell was that?" Holtz yelled.

"Rocket-propelled grenade," Hawke said. "Fired from over there." He pointed to another hotel on the other side of the street.

"So I guess we know where Kruger's other room was," Maria said, dusting herself down and sliding a round into the chamber of her gun.

"An old trick," Lea said.

Scarlet cursed and kicked the kerb. "Sod it... how could that have happened?"

"The intel was good!" Holtz insisted, but the others weren't so sure. Hawke thought it more than likely Kruger had an inside man at the hotel but that was small potatoes when measured up against the mission to retrieve the idol and something local police could deal with later. All that was bothering him was how they knew ECHO were going to be there.

"Any sign of the bastards?" Camacho said staring up at the hotel on the other side of the street.

A second of stillness until Reaper pointed to a side street adjacent to the second hotel. "There they go!"

Across the street Kruger, Mendoza and the other targets were fleeing from their hotel, using the carnage unfolding in the Hotel Sendling for cover. Hawke guessed they had clearly hoped to kill the Qatari with the RPG in what had been a carefully planned action and ECHO had gotten the sharp end instead, but they had failed. Now they turned on their heels and sprinted across the Theresienhohe toward the enormous beer festival in the fairground at the end of the street.

Some of Kruger's men turned and fired blindly over their shoulders. Their shots rang out in the night but the haphazard and hurried aiming meant the bullets missed their targets and Hawke and the others used the cover of a line of parked cars for protection as they closed in on them.

Lexi took a shot, and her razor-sharp aim hit its target and picked off one of the goons at the rear, but then they were gone – scattering into the fairground and blending into the panicking festival goers, now rattled by the RPG explosion and fearful of a terrorist attack on their city.

"They're getting away," Holtz said. "Using the festival crowd for cover."

Hawke peered into the crowd and saw Kruger and his thugs trying to blend into the crowd. Mendoza and Aurora were nearby with their arms around each other's waists trying to look casual.

"All right, let's make sure they don't get away again."

They fanned out, with Lea moving to the north. Soto sensed the danger and broke away from Mendoza, opening fire on her. In response, Lea sprinted for the cover of a cab parked up in the north entrance of the park, but it was further than she thought and a close-run thing. She just managed to dive behind the car and was still sliding along the muddy verge as the Mexican woman opened fire on her with the machine pistol for the second time. The rounds punctured the Merc's front wing and door panel before blasting into the windshield and spraying the inside of the cab with shattered glass.

The terrified driver turned the key and fired up his car, skidding out of the Theresienwiese a moment later leaving Lea totally exposed once again. Aurora Soto grinned and fired at her again. Lea scrambled to her feet, slipping and sliding on the wet mud and fallen leaves in her bid to find more cover. That came in the form of one of the oak trees surrounding the Theresienwiese, and when she got behind the trunk she tried to slow her breathing before spinning around and returning fire. She was surprised to see Soto hadn't retreated to safer cover but was now thundering toward her with her gun raised.

"She's like the sodding Terminator!" Lea muttered, squinting into her sights as she prepared to take the kill shot. "And she just will not bloody die!"

"She needs a long kiss with a piece of two-by-four," Scarlet said. "And I'm just the gal to make it happen."

But then Soto broke away and retreated. It looked like they had decided to run.

"Look!" Camacho shouted. "They're splitting up!"

The CIA man was right. Mendoza and Soto were branching off to the left and skipping down the steps to the Theresienwiese U-Bahn station while Kruger, the Van Zyl brothers and their remaining thugs were desperately trying to weave their way further into the Oktoberfest crowd.

"They're trying to break us up!" Holtz said through the comms.

"Fine with me," Hawke called back.

"Et moi," Reaper said. "I'm closest to the Mexicans so I'll go after them."

"Right with you," Hawke said as he and the former legionnaire took off after the fleeing Mexicans.

Hawke felt the cold air in his lungs as he and the French merc pounded along the street and pushed pedestrians out the way as they pursued Mendoza and the idol. In a full-on sprint now to close the gap, Hawke was aware of the dangers to the public if Mendoza felt cornered, but there was no option other than to follow him into the station and down the steps. He descended into the U-Bahn tunnel and readied his weapon for a shootout.

In the beer-soaked heart of the Oktoberfest, Lea, ECHO and the rest of the Munich police were struggling to contain the panic as thousands of people began to stampede to the exits of the festival, bundling out of the beer tents and falling over each other with Pilsner glasses still gripped in their hands.

"What a waste," Scarlet said

Lea desperately scanned the crowd. The people had been happy – half-cut on the finest range of beers in Europe and a good time was being had by all... but now terror was spreading like floodwater and things were getting out of control. Somewhere among the chaos was Dirk Kruger and the rest of his gang of looters.

And then they saw them.

They rushed forward, weaving in and out of the fleeing crowd and never taking their eyes off Kruger's gang as they moved deeper into the Theresienwiese fairground. In the lead now alongside Scarlet, Lea saw she had a clear shot and raised her gun into the aim.

Kruger was clear in her sights as he, his Yes Man Van Zyl and a couple of other goons punched their way aggressively through the crowd and headed for the main beer tent.

"He's over there!" Camacho called out.

"I have him!" Lea cried back, focussing through her gun sights.

"Do try and get the aim right this time, darling," Scarlet said, raising her own gun.

"Get stuffed, Cairo."

Gripping the Heckler & Koch MP5 in her hands, Lea unleashed a salvo of bullets into the walkway between two lines of beer tents. She took out one of the men in the rear but the others split and vanished inside one of the giant tents. More screaming now and overhead a police chopper began searching the crowd with a spotlight while someone inside was barking orders to calm down and leave the area calmly.

Lea cursed. Kruger and the Van Zyl brothers were once again lost in the shadows.

CHAPTER TEN

The U-Bahn was busier than Hawke expected, and by the time he and Reaper had run down the steps he was desperately searching over the heads of the travellers for the fleeing figures of Silvio Mendoza and Aurora Soto. He saw some movement to his left and they followed it just in time to see the Mexicans darting into the crowd waiting along the platform.

They weaved further along the amber-colored station, lit from above by a bright strip-light which ran the length of a gracefully curved ceiling. At the far end of the platform Mendoza and Soto were clambering onto a train that was pulling away from the station.

"Freeze!" Hawke yelled.

"They're gone…" Reaper said.

Hawke's mind was racing with ideas, but there was only one possible play.

Bloody hell..!

With his options restricted to jumping on the train or losing Mendoza in the Munich underground he started running along the platform. The train was nowhere near full speed and its doors were closing, so he knew he had only one chance, and when there was only one chance the only thing you could do was grab it with both hands and never let go.

He heard a burst of gunshots as Mendoza fired at him from further up the train and one of them nicked Reaper's shoulder. He dived for cover but Hawke ran forward. The Mexican had jammed his foot in the door to give himself a gap through which to fire on the

Englishman, but when the train started to slow in response to the open door alert he cut his losses and pulled his boot back in, allowing the door to close and the train began to gain speed again.

Almost level with the rear of the train as it accelerated away from the platform and prepared to vanish into the tunnel, Hawke leaped into the air with all his might and grabbed hold of a steel handle on the rear cab's door. He felt a violent and powerful jerk on his shoulder as the train pulled away and had seconds to swing himself tight against the side of the carriage before the train blasted into the tunnel.

The stench of ammonia and brake dust blasted in his face as the wind in the tunnel buffeted him and almost forced him to release his grip on the door handle. He clung to the thin bar with all his might as the train gained speed and the noise in the tunnel escalated to a deafening roar.

You're getting too old for this, sunshine.

To his horror, the train now swung around a sharp right hand bend and was now running at high speed alongside a second set of adjacent tracks where two lines came together.

He blinked the dust out of his eyes and stared down at the tracks while he got his breath back. *Who knew hanging on to a moving train required such strength,* he thought. At least there wasn't a train coming on the other line because that would really screw up his day.

And then another train appeared on the adjacent tracks.

He pulled his gun from his belt. A risky move but it was all he had… he turned his face away from the cab's window and fired three shots into the glass. He looked at his work and saw the pane of glass was still in the frame but it was shattered into thousands of pieces, so he took the butt of the gun and smacked it hard into the window until the force of his strikes bent a hole in the pane and then finally knocked the pane out of the frame.

It landed with a smack on the floor of the driver's cabin and he had to make a snap decision. The train on the other tracks was racing toward him, so his best chance was to be inside the cab, but that meant heaving himself away from the side of the train in order to swing his legs inside, or diving inside head first and kicking his legs out, leaving them exposed to the other train.

He breathed out hard with the effort of the struggle and wondered exactly what his cut of the ten million dollars would be until he recalled Eden's words to Ryan... *it doesn't work quite like that, Mr Bale*...

The idea of getting hit with a collision force of the combined speeds of the two trains brought him into the moment, and it appealed to him about as much being fed alive to sharks. On the other hand, the idea of clinging to the side of the cab while the other train raced past seemed even less enticing. He took the risk and heaved himself up until his waist was level with the smashed window and then pushed his body out while he raised his legs to slide them inside the opening.

The train driver on the other tracks had seen him now, and slammed on his emergency brakes and sounded the horn but he was too close to stop in time. Something told Hawke this wasn't the sort of scenario that came up too often in the day to day life of a Munich U-Bahn driver, but he wasted no time and hurled himself into the cab as fast as he could, landing with a hefty crunch on the shattered safety glass all over the floor.

He jumped to his feet just in time to see the horrified face of the other train's driver and then those of the passengers as they flashed past. He paused to give them a wink and a cheery wave and then opened the driver's door, heading into the main carriage with his gun raised.

*

In the main hall of the Oktoberfest, Dirk Kruger fired on the police and one of his bullets struck Schmidt in the shoulder and knocked him back as if he'd been punched. He fell down, howling in pain but quickly scuttled away behind one of the upturned beer barrels. He had dropped his weapon and by the look of the bloodstains all over the floor he'd hit an artery. Moments later he died and Holtz ordered a savage onslaught to bring the perpetrators to justice.

But the vicious fire fight didn't last long. At seven hundred rounds a minute the submachine gun magazines were empty after four seconds if fired on full automatic, and it wasn't long before things devolved into a desperate fist-fight. Now, in the chaos of the temporary beer halls, the South Africans were heading to the exit in a bid to escape.

Camacho darted after them in pursuit, and immediately felt a heavy blow on the back of his neck that nearly knocked him out. He staggered around and saw one of the younger South Africans. He was pulling his fist back for another go.

The American grabbed the man's shoulder, spinning him around and then planted a hefty punch in the center of his face. The man tumbled backwards and fell down onto the wet grass. Behind him, Lea and the others were now in pursuit of Kruger, the Van Zyl brothers and the remaining goons but they were already disappearing into the night through another exit behind the bar of an adjoining tent. Kruger slipped through first, but before

Willem Van Zyl made his departure he turned and fired blindly all over the tent.

Camacho dived to the floor as Van Zyl continued to fire with the machine pistol, spraying bullets through a line of beer barrels and ripping the tent behind them to shreds. Seconds later great jets of beer burst out of the bullet holes and began spraying high into the air, soaking anyone within their range.

Scarlet rolled behind a long trestle table in the center of the tent, ducking her head down to escape the shower of splinters and lager jets and then leaned around the edge of a chair to fire back. She hit one of the goons in the back but he slipped through the opening after the others who were now all gone.

"Where'd they go?" asked Scarlet.

"Behind the tent," Camacho replied.

"I think I got one of them," she said.

*

Outside the tent, everyone had scattered into the chaos. Kruger quickly found the man Scarlet had shot, but there was no sign of anyone else. He looked at the panicking young man from Pretoria, his face now pale and covered in a thin film of sweat. "What happened to you, Joh?" he snapped. Joh Van Zyl, Willem's younger brother looked stricken as he pulled a blood-drenched hand out from beneath his jacket.

"I got hit, Dirk… the bitch got me."

All around them now were the sounds of chaos – police sirens, screaming, helicopter rotors – and Kruger was starting to feel like a trapped hyena.

"I got hit…" he said again, starting to cry with fear. "Please… don't leave me."

Kruger curled his lip as he looked at him. "I'm sorry, but I don't carry dead weight." He fired three shots into his chest and killed him on the spot. Without a second glance at him he stuffed the gun in his belt and began to retreat. Leaving the bloodbath he had created behind him, he began to pull back into the city to the north of the Theresienwiese, but before he got out of the park, he heard someone calling his name.

"Is that you, Dirk?"

The South African turned to see Willem Van Zyl hiding in the trees just beyond the tents. "Yes."

"Where's my brother?" he asked. "Did he escape?"

Kruger planted a heavy, gnarled hand on the treasure hunter's shoulder. "Sorry my friend, but they got him. He's dead."

"Dead?" Van Zyl's eyes narrowed. "Who killed him?"

"That English bitch – I saw it with my own eyes."

Van Zyl's heart filled with rage and he vowed revenge on the Englishwoman. He and his brother were close. They'd grown up together on their father's farm and life hadn't been easy but they had always stuck together. No one was going to take him away and get away with it, least of all the same bunch of bastards who were now hunting him like a jackal.

"Come on, you stupid bastard!" Kruger yelled. "We have to get out of here."

But Van Zyl was starting to look like he had bitten off more than he could chew. "Where?"

"Into the city – lose them in the backstreets. We get a car and then we get out of here – to Salzburg. I have a little turboprop parked up there that we can use to get to Serbia."

Van Zyl watched the ECHO team through the trees, fanning out and making their way toward them. "What the hell's in Serbia?"

"Never mind about that, Willem – all you need to know is we're going there."

"And where the hell are the Mexicans?" Van Zyl asked, desperately searching the chaos for them.

"Who gives a damn?" Kruger said. "We have the idol. Let's go."

Kruger and Van Zyl made their way north through the city, pursued for over a mile by the local police before they finally saw their way out at the north end of Albrechtstrasse. Turning their machine pistol on the enormous glass facia, they blasted a man-size hole in the front of Lamborghini München and made their way inside.

"The Aventador," Kruger said with a smirk. "Just like my baby back in Cape Town." He stroked the hood adoringly. "I'll get the keys."

Kruger searched the office for the keys while Van Zyl blasted the wheels of the other cars to shreds. Seconds later they were inside the luxury Italian sports car and driving at full speed through the remains of the facia window. He skidded the car out into the street in a dazzling shower of smashed safety glass and burned some serious rubber as he took off out of the city.

Several minutes later Lea Donovan and the rest of the ECHO team plus several shattered police officers lumbered up to the garage. Camacho darted inside the garage and paused for a moment to give a gunmetal-gray Lamborghini Veneno an admiring glance before booting open the internal door and searching the office. He returned and shrugged his shoulders. "Nothing."

Holtz barked commands into his palm mic and a chopper thundered over their heads but the young

Irishwoman knew immediately the chase was over. The Lambo was long gone and would be out of the city in seconds. "They've gone."

She holstered her gun and closed her eyes for a few seconds, praying Hawke and Reaper were having more luck in their pursuit of Silvio Mendoza and Aurora Soto.

CHAPTER ELEVEN

Silvio Mendoza had seen *The Terminator*, and for a second he thought he was reliving the movie in real life when the door at the far end of the carriage slammed opened and a man in black appeared. They were at the front of the U-Bahn train, and sharing the carriage with only two other people, a young couple in business suits. But now someone else was in the carriage, and walking toward them with determination.

Mendoza peered over Soto's head to get a better view of the man. It couldn't be the Englishman, could it? They had left him behind at the U-Bahn station, and maybe even shot his friend. There was no way he could be on board this train, so maybe it was an official of the company, he thought. No, not dressed like that – black jacket, old scruffy jeans... Mendoza narrowed his eyes and reached inside his pocket for his gun.

Maybe it was an off-duty policeman... no – not the way he was looking at him. He didn't know and wasn't taking any chances. It was bad enough that in the chaos of the attack back at the hotel Kruger had kept hold of the idol, and now this.

"We've got company – don't turn around."

"Who is it?" she whispered.

He shook his head. "I'm not sure, but whoever he is, he's seen me before."

"How do you know?"

Mendoza ran his fingertips over the scar on his face. "I know when someone sees me for the first time, believe me."

The man in black introduced himself by pulling a sleek pistol from inside his jacket.

"Get your hands where I can see them, Mendoza!"

Up close now, and with the accent, neither Mendoza nor Soto had any doubts about the identity of their assailant.

Hawke.

But how?

Mendoza reached for his gun and Hawke began firing at them. The shots rang out loudly in the small compartment. "Stay where you are."

Mendoza thought not, and he fired back forcing the Englishman to dive for cover behind some seats at the back of the carriage. A second later he was returning fire, and the bullets ripped through Aurora's seat and shattered the safety glass window. Hot, diesel-air rushed into the carriage and the roar of the train in the tunnel was almost deafening. At the far end of the compartment, the business couple leaped to their feet and tried to run, but Mendoza spun around and killed them both with two well-aimed rounds before turning back to Hawke at the other end of the carriage.

"Hawke!" Mendoza hissed. "You will die for killing my brother!"

"Your brother was killed by Juana Diaz, Silvio."

"Lies!"

"Just hand over the idol and all you will face is custody."

Hawke looked into their panicked eyes and wondered if they would ever give themselves up, but the two fresh corpses on the compartment floor told him all he needed to know.

"You want the idol?" Mendoza said. He started to laugh nervously and then began firing indiscriminately at Hawke's end of the carriage. Overhead the ghostly white light began to flicker as the train swung around another corner.

Hawke returned fire. He fired over their heads, still hoping to take them alive, but then a bullet from Soto nearly hit him and he knew he had to take them out. He fired again and struck Aurora's shoulder. It ripped through her jacket and she screamed as the round grazed her flesh and buried itself in the wall behind her head.

"You bastard!" Mendoza screamed. "First my brother and now my woman." He felt the rage rise in him as the smoke drifted out of Hawke's muzzle. Who was this man to hound him and try and kill everyone he loved? Who was this man to threaten him and take pot shots at his woman? The smell of burnt gunpowder mingled with the scent of Aurora's perfume.

"All right, fine…" Mendoza said. "I'll get the idol for you."

"Drop the guns." Hawke kept his cover and they all swayed with the turns in the tracks. "And make it slow."

The Mexican cartel boss nodded as he and Soto lowered their guns and then he reached into his pocket. Aurora's eyes flicked over to him. She knew what was about to happen and a second later her hopes were proved right when Mendoza pulled the switchblade out of his pocket and threw it at Hawke. Its aim would have been deadly in its accuracy, with the high-velocity blade burying itself in the Englishman's neck were it not for a violent jerk in the train as it ran over some points and turned just as the blade left his hand.

The knife missed Hawke's throat by an inch and struck the wall behind him, clattering to the floor beside his boots.

"Playtime over, Mendoza," Hawke said, bringing his gun into the aim.

"Run!" Mendoza screamed in Spanish, and kicked open the door behind them.

Aurora obeyed, darting through the compartment door a step ahead of the cartel boss. Mendoza turned to follow her but Hawke rugby tackled him to the ground and they landed with a crash on the hard floor. The Englishman raised his gun, but the Mexican grabbed his wrist and smacked it down on the floor in an attempt to knock the weapon out of his hand. In the struggle they rolled over and now Mendoza was on top and didn't intend on losing the advantage again.

Hawke retained his grip on the gun, squeezing the weapon so hard he pushed the blood out of his knuckles, but Mendoza didn't give up, smacking his hand down a second and third time. The former SBS man released the gun but brought his other hand up and punched the Mexican in the jaw at the same time. Before he could recover, Hawke brought his knee up and wedged his boot in Mendoza's stomach, forcing him back and kicking him away.

Hawke scrambled to his knees and reached for the gun but Mendoza caught his drift early and sprinted forward again, powering a ruthless kick into his face, blasting him back and almost knocking him out.

Mendoza kicked the gun away but snatched up his knife. This one was for gutting, he thought, and leaped over to the Englishman, blade raised above his head. And it wouldn't the first time he had gutted someone, either.

But Hawke was fast, rolling over and jumping to his feet. He snatched up his gun and Mendoza knew better than anyone that you never brought a knife to a gunfight so he darted out of the compartment, and found himself in the gangway connection dividing two of the carriages. He opened the door and clambered outside.

Hawke saw him go, and he followed knowing he had the upper hand. The Mexican was on the run. He watched him sliding along the outside of the train with the deft agility of an acrobat, and then climb up onto the roof.

He knew it meant more of the damned tunnel, but Hawke stuffed the gun in his belt and followed the man up to the roof. Outside the high-pitch roar of the diesel engine mixed with the *ka-chang-ka-chang* sound of the wheels flying over the rails' fishplates and created a confusing chaos. Hawke's hair whipped around madly as he climbed up to the roof, but his journey nearly ended when Mendoza kicked him hard in the face. He was lying on his back because of the height restriction caused by the roof of the tunnel, but he was able to bring his boot forward with enough force to deliver a solid strike to Hawke's face.

Hawke fell backwards, gripping a ridge of steel running along the top of the train with his right hand as the force of the wind rushing past him pulled his left side back and clawed at his grip. He fought the velocity of the rushing air and brought his left hand back to the ridge, but now Mendoza brought the heel of his boot down on his fingers. Hawke released his hand with the pain still throbbing in his fingers and immediately swung backwards with the force of the air blasting into him.

With no warning the tunnel opened up and they were racing into a large station. Mendoza clambered to his feet ready to deliver the final blow to Hawke but the Englishman was ready for him. He fired at the Mexican one-handed while hanging on to the train with his other hand, and struck him in the shoulder.

Mendoza stepped back, reaching up to check his wound. He grinned like a devil as the cold air of the station whistled around him, flicking up his black hair and rippling his shirt. He heard Aurora yelling, and turned to see her at the other end of the carriage, climbing onto the roof.

Hawke was dimly aware of the barking tannoys and then travellers running from the platforms to the exits, but his attention was on the two targets in front of him.

Mendoza rushed him but then the game changed in a second as a bullet tore past him and right through Aurora's neck, spraying an arc of blood and flesh into the freezing air. She had pulled another knife and tried to throw it at Hawke, and he had ended the threat the way his training told him.

Her eyes widened with terror as she reached up to the wound, but then she started to sway as the blood pressure dropped and she tumbled off the roof of the train and crashed down over the side of the carriage. Her body fell into the dark space between the train and the edge of the platform and she was gone.

"That's for Alex," Hawke said.

An enraged Mendoza looked up to see the English SBS man still holding the gun that had killed his girlfriend. Before his next heartbeat the gun fired again and he felt the bullet bury itself in his shoulder. He howled in pain as the hot lead clawed at him from deep inside. Seconds later he was on his knees, swaying back and forth on the carriage roof as the train was slowly gliding to a stop.

Hawke looked up and saw the sign on the platform: München Hauptbahnhof.

"Looks like your final destination, Mendoza," he said.

Mendoza saw a second bright muzzle flash as the Englishman fired again, striking him in the throat. The Mexican released his grip on the carriage and flew back off the roof, tumbling over in the air like a rag doll. The

79

last second of his life was spent watching the train tracks race toward his face at a terrifying velocity.

CHAPTER TWELVE

After filing various reports with Holtz, the ECHO team gathered in a hotel to drink coffee and brief each other on their missions. The team reacted well when Hawke explained about the deaths of Silvio Mendoza and Aurora Soto, but less well when he told them that a search of what was left of their bodies and the surrounding area revealed they were not carrying the idol when they died.

Lea's report about Kruger and Van Zyl getting away went down even worse, especially when they figured out that the South Africans must now be in possession of the idol and could be anywhere.

"Wolff won't be pleased," Lea said.

Hawke finished his coffee and set the cup down on top of the TV. "So we don't tell him. The mission's not over yet anyway, is it?"

"No, but…"

"Come on – where's your spir…"

"Don't say it."

"Sorry."

He wandered over to the window and sighed heavily. At least the view was good. The room offered a spectacular view of the Königsplatz, the city's famous square which was modelled after the original Acropolis. He breathed out slowly and rubbed his shoulder. He had smashed it hard a couple of times back on the train and it was starting to give him problems, but he was distracted from the pain when Lea's phone rang. She cupped her hand over it and whispered *Rich* to everyone and then she took the call out to the other room.

Hawke rubbed his eyes and wished he had more coffee. His eyes settled once more on the view outside the window of their room. He had never been to Munich before but considering his first trip here had involved the destruction of the Oktoberfest and thousands of euros' damage on the U-Bahn he thought it would probably be his last trip. Still, it was pretty, and now his eyes were studying across the square where the National Collection of Antiquities was located.

He tried to make a joke about things but the rest of the team was all too concerned with Lea's telephone call to Sir Richard Eden to pay any attention to him or the outside world. A few moments later, the former Irish Ranger returned. "Rich just had a briefing with the Munich police. Using facial recognition technology and the images we were able to provide them, they think they know where Kruger is."

"Where?"

"He boarded a private Beechcraft King Air and flew out of Salzburg Airport less than an hour ago. A flight-plan was filed for Belgrade."

"Belgrade?" Ryan asked.

"Serbia."

"I know where it *is*," he said sharply. "I'm saying – why the hell would he go to Serbia?"

"According to Rich's MI6 contacts he's been communicating with Dragan Korać."

"Who?" Ryan asked.

But Reaper knew. "I know him. I'm not proud of it but I worked for him many years ago."

The others looked at him, stunned. The Frenchman didn't share their horror, and dismissed it with a Gallic shrug. "I was much younger then, and it was only one job."

"Tell us about him," Hawke said.

"Dragan Korać is a former Serbian commander who fought in the Balkans conflicts. He's a brutal warlord who now uses his military skills and experience running one of the largest mercenary armies in Europe."

"I don't like the sound of that," Maria said. "I've had a lot of trouble in Serbia."

Hawke heard the word again.

Serbia.

Of all the places in the world the former SBS man had served his country and now fought in for ECHO, nowhere had come as close to killing him as Serbia. It was on a mission in Serbia that Alex Reeve, known to him back then only as Agent Nightingale, had saved his life by talking him safely out of the worst nightmare of his life. He hadn't been there since then but now he was going back.

"So what's the plan?" Lea asked.

"I can make some calls," Reaper said.

"To what end?"

"To get me on the inside."

Everyone stared at him like he was insane. "Are you crazy?" said Maria. "Dragan Korać sounds like a total psycho, Vincent! You can't go in alone."

"It's the only way," Hawke said firmly. "And he's not going in alone. I'm going in too."

"Now I've heard it all," Lea said. "As if one of us getting killed by this nutcase wasn't enough you want to go and make it two!"

"Listen," Hawke said. "We know Kruger's going to Korać for mercenaries and at such short notice that means Korać will have to go on a recruitment drive. Neither Reaper or me ever got close enough to Dirk

Kruger for him to recognize us, and Dragan Bloody Korać has never seen me before either, so it's an opportunity we just can't afford to turn away."

"I don't like it," Lexi said. "It seems reckless, and that's *me* saying it."

"I hear all your concerns, but it's the only way. If we can meet with Korać and convince him we're mercenaries looking for work he'll snap us up and we'll be on the inside."

"And by the sounds of it, if he works out who you really are you'll be inside out," Camacho said.

"Non... it could work," Reaper said with an evaluating nod. "I've worked as a mercenary for a long time. I know these people. I know how they think. Our story will be convincing enough, and better if there are two of us."

"So let's get going," Hawke said, cheerily rubbing his hands together. "But everyone else stays in back-up."

Lea sighed. "Jet's in Zurich," she said flatly. "So an hour till it's here."

"A whole bloody hour?" Scarlet whined, turning to Jack Camacho and opening the top button of his shirt. "*Whatever* are we going to do in that time?"

Before he had a chance to reply, she hooked her finger through his belt and led him out of the room.

"Where the hell are they going?" Lexi asked.

"His choice – maybe another room," Ryan said. "Her choice – the janitor's cupboard will suffice, and may even be preferable."

A chuckle went around the room.

'Don't laugh," Hawke said without thinking of Lea. "I've been there and that's the sad truth."

Lea gave him a look and he immediately wished he hadn't said it. "Sorry."

"Forget it... unless doing it in cupboards is something you want to talk about."

"It was all her," Hawke said, relieved she had taken it as a joke.

"I bet she's done it everywhere," Ryan said, glancing over his shoulder to make sure Scarlet had left the room. "In fact I think I heard a rumor about her and a Dunkin' Donuts car park in California."

"Really?" Lexi said.

"Yeah, just Scarlet, a Dunkin' Donuts car park and half the US Pacific Fleet."

"Now I know you're lying," Lexi said. "Scarlet would never settle for just *half* the fleet."

CHAPTER THIRTEEN

Hawke hadn't opened his eyes since the Gulfstream had roared off the runway back in Munich. His mind was busy enough without adding more sensory input to it, and even the sound of his friends talking among themselves was distracting enough. Reaper was the loudest – his gravelly laugh filling any silence in between the moments of silence.

Half asleep now, he heard Lexi speaking Mandarin – or was it a dream? Maybe she was on the phone, or talking in her sleep. The gentle sing-song words leaped from her lips like exotic birds, and he started thinking about Han, the Shaolin monk he had fought alongside against Sheng Fang in China. Han and his secrets – Khan's secret treasures, Qin's immortality quest, and maybe even some missing idols...

Lea and Camacho were talking about Dublin. The American was describing a vacation he'd taken there with a girlfriend who wanted to visit because her grandparents had been born there. Camacho had a solid, deep laugh that projected his honesty to the world.

Ryan was nowhere to be heard, and he guessed he was busily engaged in his laptop as usual... earbuds keeping the wild world at bay and some kind of crazy ancient conundrum keeping his polymath mind whirring all the time.

Closer to him, at the table, Maria was sitting opposite and now he sensed Lexi join her. He was sure they thought he was asleep as neither had spoken to him since takeoff.

"We know you're not asleep," said the Russian voice. Hawke didn't move. Kept his eyes shut. He tried to focus on getting to sleep but with every passing second he knew it would be impossible. Under the table, one of them gently kicked his shin, but he was ready for it and pretended not to feel it.

"You're not fooling anyone," said a second voice – this time it was Lexi, backing up Maria's initial salvo.

He heard Maria sigh. "So open your eyes, Joe."

"And stop pissing about it," Lexi said flatly.

Despite the effort not to, his lips cracked into a smile and he relented, opening his eyes and focusing on his two friends. "Did someone say something? It's just that I was asleep."

Lexi rolled her eyes. "The world of comedy missed out big when you joined the army."

"Marines."

"Does it matter?"

"Not to idiots."

Lexi also tried to suppress a smile but failed.

"Anyone want a drink?" Maria said.

"I thought you'd never ask," Lexi said. "That phone call was me arguing with my mother."

"It sounded *ferocious*," Scarlet said yawning and turning over on the couch. "At one point you almost raised your voice to a whisper."

"Go back to sleep, *honey*," Lexi said.

She turned to Hawke and smiled warmly. It was true he and Lexi had slept together, and it had been good. It was also true that he found her attractive, not that he would ever tell her that. Giving her information like that would be like giving your worst enemy your most secret attack plans. But despite all that he loved Lea. He wondered if he had ever told the Irishwoman that. He didn't know. Maybe he had and maybe not. Did it matter?

It would matter to Lea, but she would never let on. She wasn't that kind of woman. She was too independent.

Did she feel the same? He thought so, but couldn't be sure. In their quiet moments she talked about a man called Danny Devlin a little too often and with maybe a dash too much admiration. Maybe it was nothing. He didn't know exactly who this Devlin was, but he sounded like he might like him. As long as he didn't get too close to Lea Donovan.

Hawke looked toward Maria in the galley. "Where's that drink?"

Maria returned with three beers and they relaxed into their seats once again. Outside, forty-thousand feet below, the Austrian Alps gave way to the more gentle hills of Slovenia and northern Croatia as they raced closer to their destination. Hawke looked at the flight display on the partition wall and read the names as they slipped by: Ptuj, Varaždin, Zagreb.

He sipped his beer and started to put together a plan for the attack on Korać when he was interrupted by the sound of his phone ringing.

Alex.

He picked up the call. "Hello, the Regent Cocktail Club. How may I help?"

Without hesitation Alex said: "How do you make a Jungle Bird?"

"I really don't know."

"In that case it looks like your little joke fell flat on its ass."

Hawke smiled. "You could say that."

"For future reference, it's Bacardi superior, Campari, lime juice, pineapple juice and sugar."

"I'll bear that in mind."

"Or just answer your phone like a normal human being."

"Or that, yes. How can I help, Agent Nightingale?"

"I'll get right to it. Are you sure this is a good idea?"

"If you mean Reaper and me going off the grid and infiltrating Korać's private army to get closer to Kruger, then yes. It's the only way we can be sure the idol doesn't vanish into the night."

"I'm not so sure."

"Out with it."

"You need me to say it?"

"Well, *I'm* not going to."

"Come on, Joe. Serbia was a big deal for us both. It was the first time I'd ever had to save someone's life and you nearly died in there."

"I hate to break it to you, but I've nearly died lots of times." He winced as soon as he said it. Bravado bullshit like that wasn't something real Special Forces operatives talked about, at least not any of the ones he knew.

"Fine, if that's your attitude."

He softened his tone. Alex Reeve was one of his oldest friends, and it was true that she had saved his life. In fact that was how they met. He cared about her, and he felt responsible for the fact she was back in her wheelchair. He had supplied her with the elixir in the hope she would walk again, and instead it had done nothing but give her a taste of freedom. Now, its absence mocked her, and he had failed to secure her another source of the precious liquid.

"I know you're concerned, Alex, but we have no choice. Korać has powerful connections and as soon as he gets his army together we will be massively outgunned. If we're going to stand a chance of getting close then it's now, before he can organize his forces."

"I'm not convinced, Joe. This could be dangerous."

He resisted the urge once again to tell her that nearly everything he did was dangerous. "We're not going to get close enough unless we get on the inside and this is the only way to do it. It makes perfect sense and I've got Vincent to hold my hand if that makes you feel any better."

But he knew it wouldn't. He knew what she was going through, confined once again to the wheelchair and trapped on Elysium when everyone else was in the chase. Now she'd just found out he was going into the monster's lair with the minimum of backup, and they would both be forced to relive that day in Serbia all those years ago.

"Fine, but don't say I didn't warn ya."

He smiled again. "You take care of yourself over there Agent Nightingale."

"Me? I'm on Elysium. What could possibly happen to me?"

*

Minutes after touching down in Nikola Tesla Airport they were escorted to an ancient Serbian Army FAP 2026 transport truck and a round of quick, professional introductions was made. Eden and his contacts had called ahead and deals were struck. Elements of the Serbian authorities were keen to terminate Dragan Korać's mercenary business and now they had the pressure of Eden's contacts in the British Government to push them along.

The ECHO team hurried through the frozen air and climbed into the back of the truck and moments later they were crossing the Sava into the old part of the city.

Following behind them an original, battered, mustard yellow 1983 Lada Riva driven by one of the soldiers. Korać's compound was built on the site of a medieval fort in a village eight kilometres southeast of

Belgrade, nestled in the wooden hills near Kaluđerica. When they reached the woods Hawke and Reaper would take the Riva into Korać's compound.

Hawke peered out the back of the FAP at the 1.3 litre Lada with more than a dash of scepticism. "Is that really the best they could find?"

"At such short notice, yes."

He turned to see Captain Jelena Karapandža scowling at him. She was the ranking officer of the small army contingent the local authorities had offered to escort them to Korać's compound. She was beautiful, with sparkling brown eyes and blonde hair discretely tied up and tucked away beneath her beret, but the Englishman guessed cracking a smile on those red lips would be like climbing K2.

"It's just that if we have to make a break for it and Korać and his men give chase, they could catch us with a ride-on mower."

"Then you'd better hope they have very long grass at the compound," Jelena said with no trace of a smile.

"That's of great reassurance to me," Hawke said. "Thank you so much."

"You're welcome," she said. "Now, what is all this about? My colonel told me only that we were to take you to the Korać compound at Kaluđerica."

"Korać is meeting with a South African archaeology looter and diamond smuggler named Dirk Kruger. We think Kruger's going shopping for some mercs and if you know Korać then you'll know he only does business face to face."

"Korać is a very dangerous man," Jelena said. "Anyone in the army here knows all about him. He was an incompetent army officer who turned to brandy after the war and then after that he degenerated into a ruthless warlord. Not a man to play with. This *Kruger* I have never heard of, though."

Hawke shook his head. "Me neither – not until the last few hours anyway. He was contacted by a third party, a Mexican cartel boss called Silvio Mendoza who's now out of the picture. Now Kruger is looking for some muscle to take on a treasure-hunting expedition. I can't say much more, sorry."

She shrugged. "I understand, naturally. We all have our secrets."

And there it was – the first hint of a smile, but then she turned away to cadge a cigarette off one of her soldiers and Hawke drifted away as they made their way through the southern reaches of Belgrade. It was somewhere here, in this labyrinth of broken-down streets and former Soviet housing projects that he'd almost died all those years ago. It was here where he had gone dark and infiltrated a small band of Serbian radicals and their assorted Mafia cronies.

Beside him, Lea felt her fate looming ahead of her as the truck raced through the busy streets of the Serbian capital. From here, in the safety of the speeding vehicle, she watched the traffic and pedestrians as they flowed through Senjak like blood in one of the city's most important arteries.

She closed her eyes. She didn't know what it was, but life was starting to feel heavier these days. It felt like every day she was dragging more and more baggage around behind her and it was just slowing her down and stopping her from getting where she wanted to go. She sighed and opened her eyes again to see a different street, but the same faces and cars... the usual blur her life had become.

Less than half an hour later they left the city behind and entered the wooded hills south of Kaluđerica. They were getting closer to Korać and his hidey-hole now, so Jelena banged on the back of the truck's cabin and the driver pulled over to the side of the road. Behind them the little Lada Riva followed suit and parked up on a muddy verge.

"This is it then," Maria said, uncertainty coloring her voice.

Using a pair of powerful army field binoculars they monitored the compound for anything unusual. They saw only the regular comings and goings of a few vehicles and a handful of bored-looking men who were clearly supposed to be on guard duty but seemed to spend most of their time smoking cigarettes and joking.

No sign of Kruger yet.

Hawke watched the scene with care as he pieced together the final parts of his strategy for the operation. It was true, the place reminded him of the location in Zemun where he had almost died, but he shook it off. Memories could only bother you if you dragged them up to the surface. Nevertheless he double-checked his comms signal to Alex back on Elysium.

"You reading me, Agent Nightingale?"

"Gotcha safe and sound, Joe."

"Good stuff, Alex. We're going in soon, so I'm signing off."

"You're keeping the comms, right?"

"No can do, Alex. If we're searched and they find earpieces we're dead on the spot."

Hawke popped out the earpiece and handed it to Maria. Then he gave Jelena the word and she ordered her soldiers to take up their positions around the compound's outer perimeter but to keep well back and out of sight.

It was up to Hawke and Reaper now, and they handed over their side-arms before climbing into the Riva and firing the tiny engine up.

"Monique's hair dryer has more power than this," Reaper said, casually flicking his tattooed hand toward the engine compartment. "It would be quicker if we got out and pushed it."

"Our mission is simple, Vincent," Hawke said. "Get in the compound and infiltrate Korać's private party. Then we can get close to Kruger, secure the idol and take him out before things get out of control. All we need the hair dryer for is to drive us into the compound."

"If you say so," Reaper said, his voice heavy with doubt. He lit a cigarette and inhaled deeply as he tossed the match out the window and wound it up against the cold air. "How many did Jelena say were in here?"

"Korać has a regular force of around a dozen or so men here usually, so now Kruger's here with Van Zyl we're looking at no more than maybe fifteen, absolute max."

"Us two versus fifteen?" the Frenchman said with an evaluating nod. "Doesn't seem fair – on them."

Hawke smiled but said nothing. Even though he had distrusted him at first, he liked Vincent Reno. He respected the French Foreign Legion but Reno's work as a mercenary, especially in Fallujah and Sierra Leone had made him wary when he'd first met him. But that was a long time ago – they'd done so much that it felt like forever – and because of all the battles they'd fought together he now trusted him with his life. Whether or not the feeling was mutual was hard to tell. Reno wasn't the kind of man to share his feelings.

They drove along a series of winding lanes, flanked either side by heavy Serbian spruces until eventually turning onto the main approach to the compound. Up ahead they saw the main gates and seconds later two men with rifles swung over their shoulders ambled casually toward them and gave them a hand signal to stop. Something about the way they moved told Hawke they would make pretty slovenly soldiers, and he hoped all of Korać's men would be the same.

As Hawke gently pressed the brake, a powerful spotlight from the top of the wall over the gates swung around and shone into the Riva, blinding both of them and forcing them to cover their eyes.

One of the men pulled his weapon from his shoulder and tapped the driver's window with the muzzle. He spoke in Serbian, the incomprehensible words tumbling from his mouth like crumbs.

Hawke spoke to the man in his own language, the words carefully rehearsed on the flight. "We're here to see Korać."

The man nodded but narrowed his eyes with suspicion as he peered inside the car at Reaper. The Frenchman raised his hand and pretended to rub his face, but Hawke knew the intended purpose was to show the burning grenade tattoo of the Foreign Legion to the guard.

The man gave an appreciative nod and shouted a command at the other soldiers. Up ahead Hawke and Reaper watched the main gates swing open to reveal the inside of the Serbian warlord's fortress.

ROB JONES

CHAPTER FOURTEEN

Dragan Korać took a long look at the two unemployed
mercenaries standing before him and drummed his
fingers on the edge of a table laden with meat and fruit.
His eyes shone dully in the low light as he pronged a
piece of rare lamb with the point of his knife and raised
it to his mouth. As he chewed he revealed a missing
canine tooth from the left side of his upper jaw. There
was a dark, evaluating glint lurking in his eyes.

"You," he said, pointing the knife at Reaper. "Now I
see your face I remember you. You worked for me in the
Congo."

"That's right."

"You were very good," he said, slowly chewing on
the bloody lamb.

"We're the best," Reaper mumbled.

"It's easy to say, my friend," the Serbian drawled. He
raised a glass of red wine and guzzled it down, sloppily
wiping the trickles from the side of his mouth with his
sleeve. "But in this business action speaks louder than
words." He belched loudly.

"Of course," came the reply.

Korać nodded his head, but no smile. "We'll see
about that. I have a reputation to think about – ah!" He
stopped mid-sentence when Dirk Kruger and his men
walked into the room. "Kruger, I trust you are refreshed
after your flight?"

Kruger looked at Hawke and Reaper like they were
stray dogs and then returned his attention to his host. "I
am. You show great hospitality, Mr Korać."

96

Korać twisted in his chair, his mouth full of meat once again, and while still chewing spoke through the lamb. "Please – these men are offering themselves to me as mercenaries. If they're any good they will join my regular army. Business is good, and I take new recruits all the time but they must work very hard to prove themselves or they're out the door. If they're lucky, that is."

Kruger gave Hawke and Reaper a second cursory glance and returned his attention to Korać. "I hope the financial terms I offered were acceptable," he said.

Korać waved his hand to indicate ambiguity, and then smiled broadly. "We talk about the money after we eat, but first you must all be very hungry. Please – sit down and join me. We will talk about your plan."

Hawke, Reaper, Kruger and Van Zyl joined Korać at the thick wooden table and began to eat, but Hawke knew the real purpose of the meal wasn't to sample the local delicacies of pljeskavica beef patties and veal schnitzel washed down with lashings of plum brandy. The real reason was to talk about Kruger's mission and study him and Reaper for their reactions. From Korać's point of view there was no harm in including two strange men in the discussion – either they would be determined as trustworthy and included, or not, and killed.

"Tell me, Dirk," Korać began. "Why the need for my army?"

"Treasure."

Korać stared at him, his smile fading and then returning. His eyes crawled over Hawke and Reaper for a moment before settling on the bottle of brandy in front of him. He poured a glass for himself and smacked the bottle back down on the table. "Treasure, you say?"

Kruger nodded, clearly uncomfortable with saying too much in front of so many people. "Treasure – diamonds... gold. Lots of gold."

"You want my men to break into Fort Knox, like Mr Goldfinger?"

A low laugh rippled around the tense room.

"No," Kruger said sharply. "The gold I want isn't in Fort Knox, Dragan."

"So where is it?" The earlier hint of a smile on Korać's face was now totally gone and an even grimmer atmosphere fell over the room like a dark, suffocating blanket.

After a pregnant pause, Kruger fixed his dark eyes on the Serbian commander and spoke one single word. "Atlantis."

For what seemed like eternity, silence hung in the air like cannon smoke, but then Korać burst into laughter and his men followed suit. Hawke and Reaper joined in but Kruger remained steely-eyed and straight-faced.

"You..." Korać struggled to get the words out through the laughter. "You're not serious, Dirk?"

"I bloody am serious," Kruger snapped. "And I don't like being laughed at, man!"

In a heartbeat, Korać pulled a srbosjek blade from his belt and thrust it into the wooden tabletop before sweeping the brandy and bowls of fruit aside with his arm.

"Watch your tongue, Professor Kruger! I do not take kindly to people talking to me like this."

Not expecting such a reaction, Kruger recoiled awkwardly in his seat and almost fell backwards on his chair. He saved himself from going back and landing with a smack on the flagstone floor, but he was clearly rattled. Across the table from him, Korać wrenched the knife from the table and studied the blade for a few moments.

"I'm sorry…" Kruger said reluctantly.

Korać slipped the knife back into his belt and offered a smile to the South African. "Let's try and get along from now on. I'm sure we can be friends, but friends don't lie to each other."

"I'm not lying. I have spent many years looking for Atlantis and finally I have evidence it exists."

This time, Korać didn't laugh. "You better not be playing games with me, Dirk. My army has a very solid reputation from fighting in wars all over the world from Chechnya to the Congo. If you make me look like a fool chasing after mermaids you will pay for it with your life and the lives of your family."

"No one's talking about mermaids," Kruger said regaining some of his cool after the unforeseen outburst a few moments ago. "I already said I'm looking for diamonds. All my life is about diamonds, Dragan. The legend of Atlantis was written by Plato, and he was very clear about it being an island full of gold and silver not to mention endless other precious stones and metals – including diamonds."

"But you already said the word – *legend*. It's nothing more than a legend."

"I thought that until a few hours ago when I saw this." Kruger pulled the golden idol from his bag and gently set it down on the table. The smooth golden edges sparkled in the dim light of Korać's pretentious candelabra.

The Serbian's eyes were glued to the idol. "What is that thing?" he said, nudging his chin at the ancient statuette.

Hawke saw it now up close for the first time. It was beguiling, beautiful, and yet flawed – covered in strange carvings as if someone had tried to tattoo her, and it was in a much poorer condition than he'd imagined too – with chips and gouges cut into her here and there. It was in a much worse condition than the Valhalla idol, but he noticed that the base she stood on had the same peculiar seven-pointed star configuration.

"You seem very interested in it..."

Hawke looked up to see Korać staring at him grimly. He hadn't realized that he'd been so fixated by the idol. He shrugged his shoulders. "I don't even know what it is."

"It belonged to an associate of mine," Kruger said, moving it away from Hawke and closer to Korać. "He gave it to me for the purposes of getting you and your army on board our project. He was very reluctant to let it out of his sight, I can promise you."

Korać picked it up and gave it a contemptuous look. "But what *is* it?"

"It's a likeness of a Phoenician goddess named Tanit who was worshipped in North Africa three thousand years ago. She's made of gold and there are diamonds embedded in her as well."

"How do you know this?" Korać asked Kruger, still not lifting his eyes from the idol.

"I'm a leading archaeologist in the field," Kruger replied haughtily. "I've dedicated my life to uncovering some of the greatest archaeological sites of the ancient world."

Yeah, Hawke thought. *And looting them for your own benefit.*

Korać was equally as unimpressed with the South African's grandstanding. "So, what is special about her? There is not that much gold on her."

"She was found in a temple in Mexico which was sealed long before the Spanish or any other Europeans arrived – ah – I see now I have your interest."

Korać had finally raised his eyes off the idol and was now burning two holes in Dirk Kruger. "You may continue."

Hawke saw a flash of hatred in Kruger's eyes, and guessed not many people spoke to him like this, but he and Van Zyl were clearly playing the long game as far as Dragan Korać was concerned.

"No one knows how the hell this thing ended up in Mexico, but it is my opinion that this little idol is identical to a statue in Madrid that many believe is an Atlantean goddess who was worshipped in Tartessos, a colony of Atlantis. For me the possibility of a link is too great to ignore. She was found in Mexico, but she came from Atlantis originally."

Korać gave a long evaluating nod and leaned forward in his chair, elbows on the table. He shovelled more of the lamb in his face and released another violent belch into the room. "It is true you have intrigued me, but my army is not cheap. Where will we be deployed?"

"Morocco."

Hawke and Reaper shared a silent glance.

Korać whistled. "This is not an easy thing to do, as I am sure you will appreciate. It takes a great deal of logistics to move my men around the world, although we are more than a little familiar with Africa."

Kruger shrugged. Hawke could see he was relishing having the upper hand again. "You tell me your men are the best private army in the world, so I came to you with this. My expertise tells me that the signs are pointing to the Atlas Mountains, so that is where I need your army. Either you can do it or you can't."

"The Atlas Mountains?" Korać was shocked. "You think there is some kind of link between the Atlas Mountains and Atlantis?"

"Yes. They have a strong connection to the legend, but to find the truth we will have to go there."

"Where exactly?" Korać asked.

Kruger looked around the room at the other men and lowered his voice. "There's a gorge near the Valley of Roses. The symbols refer to it. I think that's our location."

"You say she is from Atlantis originally – how do you know this?"

"This inscription starts with the symbol for the ancient Persian god Apam Napat – the god of the sea – and ends with the Valley of the Roses. It reads: from Apam Napat's Kingdom to the Valley of the Roses. A beginning and an end. It's written almost like an obituary."

"An obituary? I thought you said Tanit was a goddess?"

"I'm just telling you my opinion."

Another long silence and slow nod from Dragan Korać before he turned to Hawke and Reaper. "What do you two think?"

"We follow the money," Reaper said.

The Serb nodded once. "A good plan, I'm sure… and now my men will take you to the courtyard." He gestured for Hawke and Reaper to join him, and then standing between them he placed a paternal arm over each of their shoulders. "We have business there."

Hawke met his gaze, and pulled his arm off. He didn't want to let the idol out of his sight but there was nothing he could do without giving himself away. "Business?"

102

"Yes, business! Come... join me. You won't be disappointed."

"Lead the way, boss," Reaper said.

They moved through the lower floors of the fort until reaching a set of large timber doors reinforced with heavy iron bolts and hinges. A merc moved ahead and respectfully opened one of the doors, quickly moving out of Korać's way, and a second later they stepped out into a broad cobblestone yard.

The low autumn sun was coming down at a strange angle through a slit in the clouds and an ominous, crimson light was filling the yard. When his eyes had adjusted to this, Hawke saw another group of men in fake leather jackets and black jeans standing around in a huddle in the corner a few yards from a Mighty Bucky bull-riding machine. This was an unexpected sight to see inside a fortress run by a Serbian warlord, but he kept his surprise concealed and focussed on the men. They were smoking and grumbling, and one of them flicked a cigarette to the ground. Another coughed loudly and stared up at the sky with his hands jammed in his pockets. He looked bored.

When another of the men saw Korać approach, he flicked the other around the shoulder and pointed. With tangible terror on his young face, the first man reached down for his cigarette butt and crushed it in his hand before putting in his pocket and scuffing the soot mark off the cobblestones.

A second later the group broke up to reveal two older men on their knees in the corner of the yard with their hands on their heads. One had a full beard and the other had a thick moustache. The one with the moustache was visibly shaking but trying to control it. Hawke didn't like the look of it one little bit.

"What is this?" Hawke said.

Korać pointed to the bearded man. "His name is Čanak. He attacked my daughter and she barely got away with her life." With a flourish, he now pointed to the other man. "And his name is Dačić. He lied to me to give his friend an alibi and get him off. Today, Čanak and Dačić are being executed for their crimes against my family."

Reaper glanced at the Englishman. "So give them to the police..." he said.

Korać and the other men fell about laughing. "I know two things about you now," Korać said though the chuckling. "You do not know the Serbian police, and you do not have daughters."

Hawke and Reaper remained silent while the former Serbian commander settled his men down and approached the prisoners. "Old Serbian proverb – God gave himself a beard first, my friends," he said, slapping the bearded man around the back of his head.

"What does that mean?" Reaper said.

"You help yourself before you help others, no?"

"What are you saying?" said Hawke.

"Yes," Reaper said. "What has this got to do with us?"

Korać turned to Hawke and gave him a ghoulish smile as one of his men handed him a heavy antique Ottoman sword. In turn, Korać gave it to Hawke. "You are their executioners and if you don't kill them, then my men will kill you."

CHAPTER FIFTEEN

Richard Eden was in Elysium's Memorial Garden with his eyes closed and his mind whirring. Situated in a quiet part of the island to the south of the complex it was a serene place guarded by a ring of palm trees and the name plaques of their fallen colleagues rested peacefully in the sun-dappled shade. From behind the safety of his sunglasses, his eyes settled momentarily on the latest three additions – Ben Ridgeley, Alfie Mills and Sasha Harding. It was hard to believe they were gone and now rested alongside Olivia Hart and Sophie Durand.

He came here from time to time to contemplate things when life grew too painful, or when ECHO business started to climb all over the top of him and make him feel like it was crushing him. Now was one of those times. The Mexican affair had proved costly – three of their own brutally murdered in the jungle and two more – Maria and Ryan – coming perilously close to being sacrificed in Mictlan by the lunatic Morton Wade.

Everyone in the team knew the risks but it still made him uneasy. He had come a long way since his army days – working hard to climb the ladder from senior officer to Member of Parliament and then finally his work in MI5. He had meticulously ticked boxes, crossed Ts and dotted Is all the way along and it hadn't been easy.

With the exception of a few quiet chats with Lea Donovan, he never spoke about his personal life to any of the team members. It was need-to-know as far as he was concerned and they didn't need to know. They didn't need to know about his wife who had died, mercilessly taken from him by illness after so many years together. They didn't need to know about his children – adults now and living their own lives. They didn't need to know about his private life and who he was dating.

And they certainly didn't need to know about the Consortium which had bought Elysium and set up the ECHO team. That was such a long time ago, he thought with a fading smile. He wished the years didn't pass so quickly. They seemed to be piling up behind him faster than he could count them and the stockpile of future years ahead of him was growing ever smaller. He knew he had to make them count.

His eyes drifted from the tropical ocean horizon back to the plaques. He sighed, removed his sunglasses and gently rubbed his eyes. Maybe – just maybe, he considered – he was getting too old for all this. Right now, his mind was split in too many different ways and it was starting to get stressful. A desperate, clawing stress he hadn't felt since his exam to get into Sandhurst and was trying to prove to his father he could make it as an officer in the Parachute Regiment.

As of right now, the team was heavily engaged in the search for the idol. At least they had a chance to redeem themselves in the eyes of the Mexican authorities by retrieving the idol, but the mission was a dangerous one and had just got a whole lot more unpredictable with the sudden deaths of Silvio Mendoza and Aurora Soto in the Munich U-Bahn.

The local German news was already reporting it as a failed mugging gone horribly wrong and maybe the public would buy that. But now the idol they'd stolen from Mictlan was in the hands of Dirk Kruger and that worried him more than anything. Eden had known

Kruger decades ago when they were both young students. He'd always shown more interest in archaeology's potential to make him rich than bringing light to world history.

Dirk Kruger. Hidden in the shadows while he learned his trade, and then exploded onto the scene in grand style when he looted the golden Dacian bracelets unearthed at Sarmizegetusa Regia in Romania. He followed the starter up with a very rich main course when he flew into Iraq after the war and looted dozens of valuable artifacts from sites like Umma and Aqarib.

Dirk Kruger, the man who told Eden to his face that he was luckier than a dog with two dicks and he meant it too – he was the luckiest bastard Eden had ever known, except for the night his luck nearly ran out in Iraq when a team of Dutch soldiers caught him raiding trenches in a site at Babylon and nearly blew his head off.

Dirk Kruger, a man entirely without ethics and a lethal triple obsession – wealth, power and diamonds.

And now he had the idol. The idol everyone wanted… he closed his eyes and turned his mind back to Mexico.

Deep beneath the Temple of Huitzilopochtli, Mictlan had been sealed since long before the Spanish conquistadors arrived in Mexico and that idol simply should not have been there. Ryan Bale and Alex Reeve had both assured him that it was impossible for it to be in Mictlantecuhtli's sacrificial chamber and that meant questions he wanted answered.

That the Consortium wanted answered as well.

At least the team were on it, and he was confident that thanks to his contacts in the SIS, Hawke's infiltration into Korać's army should hopefully result in the return of the idol and the arrests of Dirk Kruger and the Serbian, but it was still early days.

He sighed and replaced his sunglasses, rising from the bench and slipping his hands in his pockets. For a few moments he wandered along the secret island's South Beach as he tried to gather his thoughts, and then Alex called his cell phone.

"Anything new on Kruger?" he asked.

"Lea just called. They're in."

"Good, I think."

"I don't think it's good," Alex said. "I think it's a stupid idea. Korać is a former commander in the Yugoslav People's Army and after that the Serbian Army. He used to serve under Ratko Mladić, the former Bosnian Serb military commander. He's dangerous."

"I know all this, Alex. Hawke knows how to look after himself."

"I'm not so sure, Rich. Korać is unpredictable. When he's not drunk on Rakia in Belgrade strip clubs he spends his time coordinating one of the biggest private military companies in the world! Joe and Vincent could be in deep shit."

"Let them do their job."

Eden cut the call and let out a deep, long sigh. Maybe he really was getting too old for this. Maybe it was time to step aside and let someone else lead ECHO. He turned into the breeze and closed his eyes. At least the warm wind was stopping the mosquitoes from wreaking their usual havoc on his elbows and ankles.

Thank the heavens for small mercies, he thought, and headed back toward the ECHO compound.

CHAPTER SIXTEEN

Hawke weighed the sword in his hand and looked at the desperation on the old men's faces. No, there was no way he could kill either of these men in cold blood – not even to prove his loyalty as a mercenary, but an unemployed mercenary seriously asking Dragan Korać for work wouldn't hesitate, so if he failed to do as Korać asked then his cover would be blown and they would both be killed on the spot.

He looked around the yard and time seemed to slow down. The odd, crimson light was fading to a regular gray and a cold wind was whipping fallen leaves around the cobblestones. Behind Korać, Dirk Kruger and Willem Van Zyl were eagerly waiting for the show to start. Kruger even checked his watch, a chunky Omega Seamaster in burnished titanium.

A quick headcount of Korać's men and Kruger's goons only made him even surer that death would be certain if he failed to execute the men.

"What are you waiting for, man?" Kruger boomed as he strutted forward and kicked the old man in the stomach. "You want him to send you a bloody invitation?"

The men laughed, including Reaper who knew that if Hawke got caught out and killed then the mission would be down to him. It was a cold thought, but that was the nature of his work.

Hawke lifted the sword, his mind still racing with options when he was stopped by the sound of a man entering the courtyard and speaking with Korać. They spoke for several minutes before the Serbian commander nodded and dismissed his underling.

He turned to the others. "The execution will have to wait – my guests are here. From what I hear they would want to see this."

Hawke breathed an inward sigh of relief as Korać and some of his men turned to greet his guests in the hall. Moments later they returned, and that was when he realized the game was up.

Standing beside Dragan Korać was Mr Luk and Ekel Kvashnin, otherwise known as Kamchatka, or Kodiak. For a few heart-stopping moments Hawke wondered if they had recognized him. Kamchatka had seen him much less, but Luk was up close and personal for far too long as he'd prepared to slash him to death in Sheng Fang's boat shed back on Dragon Island.

But that was some time ago now, and maybe Luk had killed so many people Joe Hawke simply didn't stand out to him. He watched as the two men spoke quietly with Korać for a few minutes. "These two bastards tried it on with my daughter," he said to the two new arrivals, repeating the speech he had given a few moments earlier. "Can you believe that? Now we have two new men in our army and they are going to prove to us all that their hearts are with us by executing them." With a grim smirk, he turned to Hawke, who had now realized that neither Luk nor Kamchatka had recognized him. "And you're not going to let us down."

Hawke was out of options, and raised the sword above his head when Korać suddenly stopped him and grabbed the sword. "Who taught you how to use a sword? This is not how you swing it."

Korać took the sword and began an elaborate demonstration of how to swing a sword down against the bare neck of a man awaiting his execution. With each slash of the blade the terrified men flinched and whimpered in fear. "This is how you do it – Mr – what was your name again?"

"Slade," Hawke said.

"Slade – of course. Only, my friend here..." he tipped his head to a now-grinning Luk. "He seems to think your name is Joe Hawke, and you work for a Western intelligence agency by the name of ECHO." He pushed the tip of the sword into the soft flesh of Hawke's throat. "Is he right or wrong?"

"He's right," Reaper said, and followed his words with a devastating right-hook into the side of Korać's face. A terrific crunching sound emanated from his mouth and the Serbian staggered sideways, dropping the heavy sword.

Then all hell broke loose in Korać's compound.

"We need to get the fuck outta here!" Reaper screamed.

"You think we're rumbled then?" Hawke said with a grin.

Reaper gave him a look and the two men scrambled across the courtyard as Korać staggered to his feet and after spitting blood onto the flagstones he screamed at his men to kill the two runaways.

A second later a dozen Serbian mercenaries opened fire and filled the courtyard with a savage blaze of nine mil rounds. The two ECHO men only just evaded their bullets by darting into one of the doors in the cloister on the western edge of the courtyard. A second later and they were inside Korać's compound.

Hawke paused and stared up and down the long corridor in a bid to remember which way led to the front of the sprawling property where their car was parked. The corridor was filled with magnificent and obviously stolen works of modern art wherever he looked – this was where Korać wined and dined his potential clients and this grotesque display of wealth and crime was clearly what it took to swing the deals in his direction.

"Quite the collection," Reaper said, getting his breath back. Everywhere the Frenchman's eyes settled they fell upon a famous work of art. "Rothko, Basquiat – and *mon dieu* – this is a Matisse. These must be worth millions of dollars."

"You can admire the art later, Vincent – we have work to do."

They hurried through to the main hall where Korać had shown his guests his twisted brand of entertainment and picked up some of the Serbians' weapons.

"Lucky he didn't have more of his men here or we'd be toes by now."

"Toast, Reaper. It's toast."

Hawke checked the mag and slid a round into the chamber while Reaper smashed open one of the windows and opened fire on the men in the courtyard. Hawke joined in a second later from the next window down and soon the men outside were dancing like fools as they darted here and there to evade the bullets.

Hawke's mind was racing with the unfolding chaos. He was good at absorbing shocks to the system and prided himself on moving on past them and not letting them get to him but the arrival of Luk and Kamchatka in Korać's courtyard had taken him by surprise. He had no idea what either of them were doing here, but at the very least it meant he had two more people to fight – two people with a serious grudge against him and the rest of the ECHO team.

They fired at the men to keep them pinned down. Across the other side of the yard their bullets smashed out windows and tore Korać's Mighty Bucky bull-riding machine to hundreds of pieces, but now the mercs and

Kruger's goons worked out where the fire was coming from and split into two to fight back, with a backup unit forming a second front on the west side of the house.

Hawke grabbed Korać's candelabra and set fire to the drapes either side of the main entrance to his hall and seconds later enormous white-hot flames were licking up the curtains and crawling all over the wooden support beams on the ceiling. The room filled with a noxious black smoke which poured from the shattered windows in thick columns before blooming up into the cold Serbian sky.

Korać screamed in response, waving his men forward into the fray with his gun hand, but making sure to keep at the rear with Kruger as they began to close in on the English soldier and the French legionnaire.

Hawke kept up the barrage, never flinching and not even considering retreat. He tore through his magazine and smacked his second and last into place before taking out another of Korać's men who had left himself exposed in the corridor.

And then Korać changed tactics.

"He's telling his men to pull back!" Reaper screamed.

"They're all getting out of here," Hawke said. "Including Kruger."

"If they go up to the main road they'll run straight into our people."

"They're not that stupid," the Englishman replied. "They're going out the back of the courtyard where Alex said he had a second garage block. Jelena's men are all around the perimeter!"

"Let's get after the bastards," Reaper said.

They crouched low and made their way out of the burning room toward the courtyard where they heard the sound of multiple engines roaring to life. "Quick!" Reaper said. "To the Riva!"

113

They sprinted to the front of the house where their car was parked, and Hawke looked from Reaper to the Riva and back again. "Do we have to?"

"Mais, oui… it's our only chance."

Hawke pushed his reluctance aside and clambered into the Russian car, twisting the ignition key and revving the tiny engine as the Frenchman climbed in beside him and slammed his door shut. Hawke trundled the car around the side of the house as the Frenchman scanned the horizon for the fleeing enemy.

"There they go!" Reaper said, pointing through the rear archway of the courtyard. Speeding away from the compound was a Cadillac Escalade and a Jeep Wrangler. They skidded out of the garage block in a blaze of exhaust fumes and burning rubber before chewing up clods of dirt from the side of the road and spraying the earth up in a wild arc behind them.

"Go!" Reaper said.

"I *am* going," Hawke said flooring the throttle. He rammed the Riva's gear stick into first and spun the front wheels so fast he almost burned through the rubber. He released the clutch and the tiny car jolted forward. As the underpowered sedan belched and farted its way out of the compound, something told him this was not going to be the easiest pursuit he had ever given.

"Call Lea and the others and get a team in the fort to save those men."

Reaper nodded and made the call as Hawke steered the car through the brown Serbian countryside which now stretched out before them as they speeded down the hill in pursuit of Korać and Kruger. A quick glance in the wobbling rear view mirror at least gave Hawke the satisfaction of seeing the Serbian warlord's compound burning to the ground, including his precious art collection.

Hawke struggled to power the ageing Lada forward but at least for now they were racing down the hill on which the compound was built. Ahead of them the Escalade and the Wrangler were making short work of the rough tracks stretching away toward the forest.

"They're getting away!" Reaper screamed.

"I think that was a forgone conclusion, Vincent," Hawke said as he stamped on the throttle once again and made the engine howl like a scolded cat. Another series of engine farts followed and more fumes billowed out the rear of the Riva.

"It's Reaper!" he said, sighing. "On missions my call sign is Reaper!"

The trucks ahead turned a sharp right into the woodland and disappeared from sight behind the thick, dark trunks of the Serbian spruces.

The same turn was coming up fast, and Hawke spun the flimsy wheel heavily to the right and for a second he thought he might snap if off the steering column, but instead the Lada responded and screeched around the bend, spraying up a shower of gravel chips and filthy mud.

The tiny car had a good turning circle, but at this speed not so much, and now Hawke struggled to keep the car under control as it smashed up a bank on the left-hand side of the new lane and nearly tipped over. He powered on, steering wildly to the left to stop it tipping but then one of Kruger's goons appeared in the back of the Wrangler and opened fire on them with a submachine gun.

"I could be working as a security guard right now," Hawke said.

"Pfft," Reaper said.

Hawke flicked at glance at him as he brought the Lada back into the lane but swerved it violently from left to right to avoid the hail of automatic fire pouring out the back of the Jeep. "What the hell does that mean?"

"What?"

"Pfft."

Reaper gave a Gallic shrug. "Don't ask me."

"You were one that said it!"

"Is that a bridge?" Reaper said.

Hawke peered ahead in the gloom. "I think so – a wooden one... Great."

As he spoke, the Escalade ripped over the bridge, followed sharply by the Wrangler which then slowed as soon as it was on the other side of the river.

"What are they doing?" Reaper asked.

"They're not stopping for a picnic – I know that much."

The goon who had fired on them leaned out the back of the Wrangler and hurled a grenade at the bridge.

"What now?" the Frenchman said.

"Never give in and never give up, is what I always say."

And with that Hawke increased speed and aimed straight for the bridge.

"Are you crazy?" Reaper said. "You don't know what kind of fuse that thing has on it?"

"Six seconds on average," Hawke said, increasing speed as they raced toward the bridge.

"So yes, you are crazy. I see that now."

Hawke slammed the throttle and Reaper yelled: "Merde!"

"Shit!" Hawke screamed.

"C'est exactement ce que j'ai dit!" Reaper said, shaking his head.

A couple of seconds later they hit the bridge and ripped across it just as the grenade exploded. Only a second ahead of the shockwave they felt pieces of shrapnel slam into the back of the Riva, puncturing the rear panel and blasting the window in. They ducked as the shattered glass sprayed forward with the force of the explosion and Hawke checked the mirror as the detonated bridge exploded in a giant fireball and returned to earth as thousands of pieces of charred matchwood.

No time to think about what just happened, Hawke looked ahead to see the trucks making slower progress along a twisting stretch of the track. They were now deep in the woodland and the giant black spruces towered over them blackening the sky. And then the Wrangler got stuck in the mud of a flooded ditch.

The engine howled as the driver stamped on the gas but it was the worst thing he could do and only drove the Jeep deeper into the mud. Now at a stop and with the Escalade racing away into the heavy forest, it was the chance Hawke had been hoping for and he drove the Riva on another hundred yards before pulling it to the side of the track behind the cover of a line of spruces. They got out and made their way forward with their side arms.

"Things a bit more even now, n'est-ce pas?" Reaper said.

"I don't think so!" Hawke yelled. "Run, they've got a sodding mortar!"

The men in the Wrangler fired the mortar at them and Hawke and Reaper dived for the safety of a muddy ditch as their Lada exploded like an old dustbin loaded with firecrackers.

Hawke cursed as pieces of twisted Russian automobile fell back to earth through the spruces and landed with deep squelches in the rain-filled grooves on the track. Ahead of them, the men had gotten the Wrangler free and were pulling away into the forest.

Hawke watched them disappear with a frown on his face. "Absolutely arsing fantastic, as someone I know would say. Let's get back."

"It's several kilometres, mon ami."

"Now's the time to start then."

CHAPTER SEVENTEEN

"We're on!" Lea said, slipping her phone in her pocket and drawing her gun. "Joe and Reaper say there are more mercs at the fort and also some hostages."

Lea's team raced down the track toward the fort with Captain Jelena Karapandža at the wheel of the army truck right behind them. Seconds later they smashed their way through the front gates and skidded to a halt in the front drive. The truck piled in behind them in a roar of stinking diesel, mud and gravel chips. The tailgate slammed down and the soldiers filed out the back ready for action.

The small contingent of Korać's men who had stayed behind to guard the fortress took two of the soldiers out right off the bat, their bodies tumbling down from the back of the truck and falling into the shallow ruts created by their own vehicle.

Ahead of the Serbian soldiers, Lea's team thundered on relentlessly, but Jack Camacho received a stark reminder of his age when he quickly found himself bringing up the rear behind Lea and the others – even Ryan Bale edged ahead of him in the sprint for cover. He knew that meant more gym time when he got back to the States.

"I'm getting too old for this!" he yelled as he changed his magazine.

He watched as Lea and Scarlet covered each other in their advance toward one of the side-entrances, but Korać's men pushed them back with superior firepower. When he caught up and joined the fight they finally

119

turned the tables on the Serbs outside, pushing their way through the entrance and getting inside the inner sanctum.

Inside now, Korać's goons were at the end of a long corridor, but the smell of fear was starting to rise from them. They were consolidating and trying to hold a defensive line but ECHO and the Serbian soldiers were slowly pushing them back. Then a handful came out of nowhere, rounding the basement stairs and dragging the two hostages up along the corridor from the courtyard the garage block.

Face to face with the enemy at last, the man leading the Serbs screamed at his men to kill Camacho and the ECHO team at all costs, and their response was to loose a barrage of gunfire at them and send the American and the others scattering for cover in rooms either side of the corridor. Bullets flew like firecrackers on a Chinese New Year, but whoever they were, Camacho thought, they weren't professional. Their firing was aggressive but undisciplined and it didn't take long for him and the others to exploit their weak cover and poor timing and take out nearly half of them. They worked their way up the corridor using the various rooms as cover until they were almost upon the men, who then turned and fled at the last moment in a bid to stay alive.

"They're taking the hostages into the garage!" Lea shouted through the comms.

"Got it!" Scarlet said.

Camacho and the team followed them into the garage block only to see them piling into the back of a double-cab Hilux. He was horrified to see what looked like a light machine gun set up on the flatbed at the back. He was even more horrified when the Hilux skidded away in a wild roar of revs and exhaust fumes, slowing on a shallow bend to dump two dead bodies out one of the side doors.

"Jesus," Ryan said, looking at the two corpses as they slowly tumbled to a standstill in the ditch. "That's just terrible."

"I'll say," Scarlet said. "They've got an M240 on the back of that flatbed."

"A what?"

Scarlet rolled her eyes. "A crew-served, air-cooled, fire-spitting monster from Fabrique Nationale."

"Is that bad?"

"I'd try not to get in the way of it if I were you."

As she spoke, Camacho sprinted to the front and fired up the FAP 2026 truck, bringing it around to the rear so everyone could pile in. He took off after the Toyota but it was clear right from the start that the Serbs had no concerns about using them for target practice with the GPMG. Just minutes into the chase Camacho was forced to swerve the old military truck violently from side to side to avoid the standard chambering seven mil bullets as they punched the air all around them.

Empty bottleneck cartridges flew out the ejector port and rained down on the gravel track as the Hilux speeded along the lane on its way to the forest. The weapon was designed as a crew-served GPMG so two of the mercs had the pleasure of operating the gun as the Hilux tore through the Serbian countryside. Red-hot lead roared out the muzzle, smashing into the gravel in front of the FAP and ricocheting all over the lane.

In the distance, they heard the Hilux's wheels squealing as the Serbs took a corner so fast they nearly tipped over. "We're losing him, Camo!" Scarlet yelled.

"Have a little faith, would ya babe?" said the burly American.

He slammed his boot down on the FAP's accelerator and did a little wheel-squealing of his own. The truck jolted forward leaving a cloud of blue-gray rubber smoke and exhaust fumes in its wake, not to mention a number of bemused cows in a neighboring field.

Scarlet smacked a fresh magazine into her Glock and slid a round into the chamber. With her trademark enthusiasm for the hunt, she leaned out the window, spat her cigarette out, and started firing on the Toyota. "It's open season on arseholes!"

Back inside the truck, Lexi leaned closer to Ryan. "Does she have any friends?"

"Only victims," the young man said, but in his heart he felt nothing but admiration for her as she unloaded a magazine of nine mil bullets. She had been the one cradling his head when he nearly died in Valhalla, after all.

Now Reaper made the same turn that had nearly sent the Hilux to the scrap-yard, but the FAP had a higher center of gravity than the pick-up. It made the turn with considerably less grace, and for a second before he straightened the wheel he thought they were going over.

The Hilux went in a different direction from the Escalade and Wrangler and soon they were zooming into a large town somewhere south of Belgrade. Seconds later they were all aware of a screaming siren behind them. Reaper flicked his eyes to the rear view and saw the blue and white stripes of the Serbian Police BMW F10 as it gave pursuit. "Shit!"

"What is it?" Lea said, turning in the back seat to look out the window. She saw the Beamer and sighed. "Shit!"

For Lea Donovan, she knew the hunt had started once again, and things were getting up-close and in her face. As Camacho hammered the FAP around another corner they saw he was making progress closing the gap between them and the Hilux, but now the Serb thugs were speeding along the A1, a straight highway south of the Belgrade suburb of Kumodrž. As they powered the FAP along the motorway the goons on the back took advantage of the long, straight road to open up the M240 on the flatbed and seconds later carnage exploded on the highway.

Innocent commuters and other travellers skidded left, right and center to avoid the lethal barrage of ammunition as the rounds ricocheted off the tarmac and punctured the steel panels of their cars.

On the back of the Hilux, one of the goons was still firing the GPMG as another fed more and more bullets into its firing chamber via the one hundred-round bandoleer in his hands. The metallic split-link ammo belt was designed to disintegrate as the machine gun swallowed the rounds and spat them at the enemy, but it still took the second member of the crew to feed more bandoleers into its hungry jaws.

Camacho reacted the same as the regular punters, skidding hard to the left and right in a bid to make it harder for the gun crew to hit the FAP, but this wasn't impressing Scarlet who was still hanging out the window and trying to cause some havoc with her handgun. As they swerved hard to the right the GPMG chewed up the police car and sent it flying off into a ditch.

"For fuck's same, Camo!" she yelled, and banged on the roof. "Can't you keep this thing on the straight and narrow for five seconds?"

"Keeping you on the straight and narrow is hard, but this is impossible!"

She rolled her eyes and sighed as she raised her Glock into the aim and put the crosshairs over the top of

Mr Bandoleer. It was a two man crew and the first target was the guy behind the gun but he was obscured so she settled for second best. She squinted her eye and gently squeezed the trigger, but just before she fired the FAP swerved without warning to the right and her shot went high and wide.

"Are you doing this on purpose?" she screamed.

"For fuck's sake, Cairo!" Lea shouted. "He's making sure we don't get..."

Before she finished her sentence the M240 successfully ploughed dozens of rounds into the front of the FAP and punctured the grille, giving Camacho half a second to get out of the way before a line of bullets smashed into the windscreen and tore through them in the front seat. "Holy Bloody Mary – that nearly hit me!" Lea screamed.

Up top, Scarlet rolled her eyes again and shook her head. "It's always about Lea Donovan isn't it?"

"Eh?"

"I'm the one on the outside of the sodding truck!" And with that she took a second aim and fired. This time Mr Bandoleer got it right between the eyes, with a couple more in the chest as a goodwill gesture. Scarlet nodded with pride at a good job done as he tumbled over and fell over the Hilux's tailgate, smashing face-first into the asphalt.

The final bandoleer he had fed into the GPMG was now gone, and the gunner had smacked it out of frustration before pulling a handgun out of his jacket and using that instead.

"At least now you're even!" Ryan shouted.

"Even?" Scarlet shouted. "Don't be silly, *boy!* He's a man. We're nowhere near even. Have to feel sorry for him, really."

She punctuated her comment with a series of rapidly-fired bullets, striking the gunner in the throat and smashing the rear window of the Hilux's double cab behind him. The pickup swerved wildly to the left and right and then skidded toward the crash barrier in the center of the highway.

It smashed straight through it and crossed the path of a DAF truck hauling timber. The DAF hit the air brakes and the massive vehicle violently juddered and jackknifed. The weight of the timber on the semi-trailer spun the truck around as the driver fought to maintain control, but the DAF's cab just clipped the rear of the fleeing Hilux and sent it smashing over onto its side.

The surviving Serbian mercs struggled to release themselves from their belts as the timber-laden truck ploughed into them and crushed their Toyota to no more than a metre wide. The carnage was total, and soon the traffic was backed up in both directions as drivers rubbernecked to see what had happened. Somewhere in the distance they heard the sound of sirens as the emergency services raced to the scene of the accident, but the ECHO team were still staring in disbelief at how much the timber had compacted the Hilux down to almost nothing.

As she surveyed the damage, Scarlet winced. "That's not nice at all."

"Neither were they," Camacho said.

"Seconded," Maria said.

"Thirded," said Lexi.

"Can you say fourthed?" asked Lea.

Ryan cleared his throat, unable to look at the terrible mess captivating the others. "Guys… I think we need to get out of here unless we want to spend the next ten years in a Serbian prison."

"The boy's got a point," Scarlet said.

They climbed back into the battered FAP and slowly dissolving into the gridlock, they pointed the car in the direction of Belgrade.

CHAPTER EIGHTEEN

Hawke checked the hotel car park one last time before strolling across the room and perusing the takeout boxes. They were stacked in a messy jumble on the telephone table at the foot of the bed beside some beer cans. Wherever Kruger and Korać were, it wasn't here. His first guess was they were already gathering their forces together and preparing to leave the country. His next guess was that Luk and Kamchatka were busy briefing their new friends on all they knew about him and the rest of the ECHO team.

He was sharing the Chinese food with his ECHO compatriots and Vincent Reno, but Vincent had looked at the food with disgust and chosen instead to make a cup of coffee from the complimentary jar beside the small kettle. He took a tentative sip, nodded his head with meaning, and then poured the contents of the cup into the pot of a plastic bonsai tree on the windowsill.

No one was saying much and the atmosphere in the room was tense at best. It was true they had gained valuable information from their infiltration of Korać's compound, but things had gone badly wrong when Luk and Kamchatka had walked back into the picture, and the ensuing chaos had resulted in the compound being torched and some of the enemy taken out, but the main players had escaped.

Mendoza and Soto were out of the game, but Luk and Kamchatka were back in it, and not only that but the Mexicans had managed to pass the idol to Dirk Kruger, the only man who Eden considered worthy of the word *nemesis.* Kruger always meant business, but this time was more serious than ever because he had forgone home-grown amateur muscle for the much tougher brand available for hire in the Balkans and hitched the notorious war criminal Dragan Korać to his looting wagon.

His phone rang. He looked at the screen and saw it was Alex.

"What gives?" she said.

"We cocked up and lost them *and* the idol. You?"

"They lost Kruger?" Eden's voice, in the background.

"Let's just say he's expanded his fighting force," Lea said.

Hawke sighed and ran a hand through his hair. "Bastard surprised us with a shitload of hoodlums."

"Hood*la*," Ryan called out from the bathroom.

Lea sighed. "Oh, fuck off, Ry. You know what he means."

"Seriously," Alex said. "Korać had that many men?"

"Uh-huh," Camacho said flicking through the TV channels.

Hawke shovelled some cold noodles into his mouth. "Including our old friends Luk and Kamchatka."

"You get anything from them?" said Alex.

"Yes, we think they're heading to a town called Kalaat Mgoun in the Atlas Mountains. Kruger was more than certain. A place in Morocco called the Valley of the Roses."

Ryan emerged from the bathroom. "Which means I was probably right about my Atlantis theory. No one go in there for at least half an hour by the way."

A look of disgust crossed Lea's face as she slammed the bathroom door behind her ex-husband. "What were you doing in there, opening a drain?"

"All right," Hawke said, opening the window and giving Ryan a suspicious glance. "We need to focus."

Lea sighed. "We don't know about Atlantis, but we *do* know that what we have is basically dozens of mercenaries belonging to Korać's insane private army, now hired by a South African tomb raider and gold lover…"

"You mean a chrysophilist…"

"Fuck off again, Ry. You know what I mean."

"He's a diamond lover actually, not bloody Goldfinger," Hawke said.

Scarlet got up from the bed. "Everyone who wants to flush Ryan's head down the toilet he just defiled, raise your hand!"

Everyone's hands went up except Maria's, who shook her head and mumbled something about behaving like stupid children.

"This is an abuse of democracy!" Ryan said.

Lea looked at him. "I once read that the definition of democracy was two wolves and a sheep voting on what's for dinner."

"Or Scarlet, Lexi and Ryan voting on who gets the coffee," Camacho said with a smirk.

Hawke stepped in, setting the phone on speaker so everyone in both locations could hear the conversation. "All right – recap. What we have here is simple. A Mexican drug cartel boss found an ancient idol and was way over his head. He spoke to an antiquarian specialist in the field and before he murdered him he found out that Dirk Kruger was the only man who could help him. Kruger in turn spoke to Korać because he knows he's going to need a lot of aggressive manpower for the mission."

"So right up our street," said Scarlet.

"Maybe, but this is getting darker now," Hawke said. "We've never faced anyone with their own army for one thing – especially an army of hired mercs with a lot of experience."

Reaper stubbed out a roll-up and sighed, breathing the smoke form the cigarette through his nostrils. "And Korać can call on people all over the world. He knows mercs in many, many countries."

Hawke nodded. "Plus we now know Luk and Kamchatka are back on the scene, and they both have a major score to settle with us so it's personal."

"In other words," Scarlet said, "we have enemies coming out of our ars..."

"Yes, thanks, Cairo – we get the picture," Hawke said. "And while we certainly *do* have enemies coming out of our arses, I want everyone to understand Kruger is our main target now. He's payrolling everything."

"How come you get to say arses and I don't?" Scarlet said.

Hawke looked at her and shrugged. "Just the way it is."

"So what's next?" Lea said.

"Easy," said Hawke. "We have to get our backsides to Morocco as fast as possible because Kruger has a major head start on us. We need the time to organize a proper strategy against these guys or we could easily lose this one."

"Agreed," Lea said.

"All right, so we know where in Morocco thanks to Joe and Vincent – The Valley of Roses in the Dadès Gorge," Camacho said. "But what's bothering me is what Kruger thinks he's going to find there. No one can seriously believe Atlantis is in the middle of the Moroccan desert."

"That's why we're chasing him, Jack," Lea said.

"So we're just winging it?" the American asked.

The ECHO team looked at each and replied together: "Yeah!"

"Because we're *that* hard," Scarlet said, and cracked the lid off a bottle of chilled Niška.

*

Moments after their jet tore off the Belgrade asphalt, Scarlet was still in close dialogue with the rest of the beers she'd stolen from the minibar back at the hotel and her mood was starting to show it. She yawned and stretched her arms. "I'm getting too old for this."

"What is it now?" Ryan asked. "Forty-five?"

"I'm not a day over thirty-something," she said, her hands cradling a chilled beer.

Ryan looked at her over the top of his glasses. "You're having a laugh!"

"Look at my face Ryan. Does it look like I'm having a laugh?"

"In all fairness, it actually does *not* look like you're having a laugh, but you might want to pitch your fake age within more realistic parameters next time."

"Look, it works like this." Scarlet said, taking a pen off the small table. "You will shut up or I will sign my autograph up your arse."

"You know what, *Cairo?*" Ryan said, fronting up to her. "Why don't you take those stupid mirrored sunglasses off so we can see the real you, or are you too hungover?"

"Bugger off."

"And what is it with those things anyway?" he said. "A tad eighties, don't you think?"

131

Scarlet sighed. "Coming from a fully-grown man in a Green Lantern t-shirt I hardly think you're in a position to make comments about fashion."

"They're back in fashion, anyway," Lea said matter-of-factly from across the cabin.

"What?" Camacho said, "Green Lantern t-shirts?"

"No, mirrored shades."

"Well, they look ridiculous," Ryan said.

"Settle down, everyone," Hawke said. "We've got enough shit to deal with without turning on each other."

Hawke grabbed a coffee from the galley and went back to his seat. He checked his watch and cursed Kruger's head start. Eden had been right when he talked about the South African's luck. He sipped the coffee and hoped that his luck was about to run out, but he knew that in this world a man's luck never ran out. It had to be taken from him.

CHAPTER NINETEEN

"They just left Serbia, sir,"

The Oracle heard the words as if they had travelled miles to his ears. As was often the case, his eyes were closed and his mind was in another time and place. Now, he was thinking about the day he had discovered what had been concealed from them for so long... the day his long life had changed forever.

He hadn't even been looking for it, but instead searching for other records in the Athanatoi vaults deep beneath Rome. It wasn't even as if it had been his first time in the vaults, either, and yet there he had found it – the ancient text, the oldest records, a damning truth that had shocked him to his core. It had set his old life on an entirely different path the way two comets might collide out in the furthest reaches of space.

When he'd found those ancient documents his heart had almost stopped. For so long the secret society of which he was a member had spoken in hushed tones of all this but there was never any proof – just rumor, and then just like that the mythological vapor had condensed into reality for the first time, and he knew it was true.

The witless ramblings of the old priests had been real after all, and there was a higher source, and ancient power. It was if someone had handed the Pope undeniable proof of the existence of Adam and Eve themselves. The whole thing had been a terrible shock.

That was where conceit got you, he'd thought.

The conceit that he, as the Oracle, had known everything there was to know about the world, but he should have known better.

Much better.

The world was far too great for a single man ever to know, even a man with his reach and power, and that day taught him more than he had simply been ignorant of the true depth of it all. It also taught him humility. And it gave him an insatiable urge to rip his way though the layers of deceit the way a hungry lion's lethal jaws tear through the flesh of a trapped gazelle.

Yes, the whole thing had come as a shock, but then the possibilities began to present themselves and his mood began to change very much for the better.

Somewhere in front of him the man was speaking again. He was saying something about the ECHO team leaving Serbia, but his words were hard to hear over the sound of the Mozart which was playing so loudly in his study. Rosina Almaviva was singing about her grave and now the whole thing was being ruined by Joe Hawke.

"Sir?"

"What?" the Oracle snapped viciously.

"They just left Serbia, sir."

Serbia. He had the vaguest recollection of when Serbia won autonomy from the Ottomans, and a fine piece of diplomacy it was, too. But now the ECHO team was there sniffing about like truffle hogs in the dirt and fungus of antiquity in their pathetic search for a truth they would never be able to accept.

"What should we do, sir?"

The Oracle raised a withered finger to indicate that silence was required, at least from the man, if not the singing Countess, and turned his thoughts inward once again. Their journey to Serbia was a confusing one but he would follow their quest until the very end. Were they working for someone else besides Eden? So many wanted the idol.

"Nothing, just monitor. And get out."

The old man watched his underling leave the room and then he pulled a cell phone from his pocket. A few seconds of static and someone picked up the call.

"Hello?"

The Oracle sighed. "Davis, we have trouble."

Davis Faulkner, the head of the CIA, took several seconds to think before replying but when he did, it was as cool as usual. "Go on."

"The Mexicans are dead and Kruger has the idol."

"Grave news."

The Oracle watched a line of whitecaps rise on the sea before crashing back down into the ocean in a frothy, milky white foam. "I've waited a long time for these idols, Davis. Many forces want to get their hands on them. I can't let anyone take them from me. Not Kruger, and certainly not the damned ECHO team. You hear what I'm saying?"

"Yes, sir. You know I will do anything for the cause."

"Of course, and now you have an opportunity to show me just how committed you are."

A long silence. "Anything, sir."

"I'm told the ECHO team have a secret hideaway somewhere – a little island."

Another silence, and the exhalation of cigar smoke. "Yes."

"I presume you know its location."

"Yes. It's a former French naval facility in the Caribbean."

"Good. I want it destroyed, and everyone on it is to be killed. Is that clear?"

"It could take some time to…"

"I'm not interested in details, Davis. You're the head of the CIA. If you want to play with some hardware in the Caribbean Sea and use an unknown island for target practice then you can do it."

"Yes, sir."

"Don't be too hard on the infrastructure – I'll add it to my portfolio once your pest control teams have done their work."

"As you wish."

This time it was the Oracle stretching the silence as he watched an ocean storm gathering strength to the north. "Don't let me down, Davis. You of all people know what's at stake."

CHAPTER TWENTY

Eden's private Gulfstream cruised to Marrakech high above the Mediterranean Sea and not for the first time Joe Hawke realized he was thinking not only about how all of this was possible, but also about how long any of it could last. Beside him, Lea slept. He watched her eyelids fluttering as she dreamed, and gently swept her hair away from her face.

"How you doing, you old tosspot?"

He turned to see Scarlet Sloane hovering menacingly above him with an unlit cigarette hanging off her lip and a half a bottle of Stoli in her hand.

"You can't light that thing in here, Cairo."

"Who says I was going to light it?"

"That's normally what you do with cigarettes."

Then Ryan turned to face her. "With all the alcohol fumes around you I'm surprised you've never ignited yourself with that Zippo of yours."

"Bugger off," she said, and shrugged her shoulders. She slid the cigarette behind her ear. "Wee nip?" She held the bottle up and shook it.

"Not for me," Hawke said, truly amazed by her tolerance for alcohol.

"Suit yourself."

"I hear you and Camacho are sharing more than fighting tactics these days."

Scarlet grinned, but quickly suppressed it. "What can I say? I am irresistible to men." She chased the words down with a swig of the Russian vodka and sighed as it went down.

Across the aisle Ryan saw her and shook his head slowly.

"Problem, *boy?*" she said.

"I have no problem," he said, glancing at the bottle.

She noticed his glance. "You have to run an engine on something."

"First the man takes a drink," he said smugly. "Then the drink takes a drink, and then the drink takes the man – or in your case, the woman."

"Oh great," Scarlet said. "Now we have our very own pontificating prat to tell us how to live our lives."

Ryan smiled and shrugged his shoulders. "It's an old proverb I thought you should know. That is all."

Camacho stepped up. "Someone being mean to my babe?"

"You let him call you his *babe?*" Hawke said, a grin breaking out on his face.

Scarlet rolled her eyes. "I'm still in the process of training him, all right?"

"Did you say you're still in the process of *straining* him?" Ryan asked, bobbing his head up once again from behind his seat. "What the hell goes on in your boudoir, Cairo?"

"*Training* him, I said, you pathetic little social outcast."

"Hey!" Maria said. "He is not pathetic or little!"

"Ouch!" Lexi said.

"And what is that terrible noise?" Scarlet asked, leaning over Ryan's seat to see what he was watching on the iPad.

"I was thinking about learning the pibgorn," he said awkwardly.

"The what?"

"It's an idioglot reed aerophone used in traditional Welsh folk music."

Scarlet simply stared. "I... I just don't... I don't know where to start with you. I thought you were researching the mission and instead you're listening to an idiotglot. Whatever it is, turn the bloody thing off, it sounds awful."

"Cairo's got a point, mate," Hawke said. "It sounds a bit like someone's choking a duck, and maybe your time might be better spent briefing us on what we need to know about Atlantis."

Ryan turned the iPad off and turned in his seat. "We'll start with Plato."

"Why him?" Scarlet said. "I thought he was an old Greek duffer?"

"Yes, he was, but the reason we'll start with him is because just about everything anyone knows about Atlantis starts and ends with Plato."

"Really?"

He nodded and once again failed to conceal the grave disappointment he was feeling for his friends' ignorance of the classical world. "You all know that Plato wrote the classic dialogues Timaeus and Critias, right?"

"Er, yeah," Hawke said.

"Er, *no*," said Maria, staring at Hawke. "Do please tell us what they are."

"Critias is the important one because it's in there he talks about Atlantis. Many claim it's the first reference to the place but there are some older ones if you look hard enough. The important point is it's in Plato's Critias where we get just about everything we know of Atlantis. It's pretty much where the entire story starts."

"So he's to blame!" Scarlet said.

"It's in Critias that Plato describes Atlantis in size and even a few hints about location but no one has ever been able to use the text to track the place down, not least because if it ever existed we all know it doesn't exist any more, at least not as a functioning civilization."

"Right," Camacho said. "If there was an island in the middle of the Atlantic supporting a sophisticated population I think our satellites might have found it by now."

"Exactly," Ryan said pushing his glasses up the bridge of his nose.

Scarlet sighed. "God that's so *annoying* when you do that."

"What?"

"That thing you always do with your glasses. Can't you get contact lenses like everyone else?"

"I never really thought about it."

"Well, do."

"Piss off, Cairo," Lea said, stretching her arms as she woke up. 'If you hadn't noticed, Ryan is once again saving our arses."

"Thanks, Lea."

"Well get on with it then!"

"Ah, yes… sorry. Anyway, Critias is pretty 101 stuff but of more interest to us is where Plato got that information from. According to Herodotus, the Greeks learned everything they knew about many of their gods – including Poseidon…"

He stopped while a big groan went up all around the cabin until Hawke intervened "Go on, mate."

"They derived their knowledge on Poseidon from the ancient Libyans who also used to worship him as their god of the sea. There are some theories that hypothesize that Poseidon was the God of Atlantis as well, while others claim it was Tanit, but either way, the knowledge from Libya is among some of the most ancient in the world. In fact that entire part of Africa has some of the oldest records of humanity, like the cave art of the Hoggar Mountains in Algeria for example."

"You're swerving off course again," Scarlet said. "That's even more annoying that the thing you do with your glasses."

"It's not off course," Ryan said. "If Plato and the Greeks got their knowledge of Atlantis from the Libyans, then it stands to reason that the cultures of north Africa had that knowledge first, and that Atlantis was known to them before even the ancient Greeks got hold of it. Knowledge has to pass down from an older culture – it's the only way we can progress. Usually we know where the knowledge comes from, and sometimes we don't. Just take the Dogons."

"No thanks," Scarlet said. "I've already eaten."

Ryan rolled his eyes and sighed. "The Dogon people," he said with a glance at Scarlet, "live in Mali, just south of Morocco and other Berber lands. They have a legend going back thousands of years about the star Sirius and how it had a companion star that was invisible to us here on Earth, which is weird because it wasn't until 1862 that astronomers actually discovered it for real. How did an African tribe know about Sirius B thousands of years before modern science?"

"They made a very good guess?" Scarlet said.

"Impossible odds. When you look at Sirius you see one star, but it's an illusion – there are actually two stars there. It's a binary system."

"So how did they know?" Maria asked.

"The only way they could have known about Sirius B is if another more advanced people told them about it," Ryan said.

"Like the Atlanteans, you mean?"

"Maybe," Ryan said with a shrug. "No way to prove that at the moment though… and then that raises another question – if the Atlanteans were real and *they* knew about Sirius B, then who told them?"

"I give up."

"I think we all give up," Lea said, laughing.

"The Dogons claimed that ancestral spirits called the Nommo came to the Earth from the Sirius system."

"Warning," Lexi said. "Mind Melt Alert."

Camacho and Reaper both laughed, but Scarlet scoffed. "Bullshit alert, more like."

Ryan grinned. "I'm just saying that what we really do when we find these ancient relics is find information, and where it comes from, and if you ask me there is definitely a strong link between Plato, his writings on Atlantis and this part of north Africa. I'm guessing that whatever Kruger hopes to find in the Dadès Gorge is obviously something he hopes is going to lead him to Atlantis."

"So it's still on?" Scarlet asked, eyes finally widening with excitement.

Ryan nodded. "Is it on? It's on like Donkey Kong in a thong!"

*

Hawke smiled, pushed back in his seat and closed his eyes. Despite the banter, he could sense a real feeling of tension in the air. Korać's worldwide army of mercs was serious business, and Kruger's obsession with archaeological loot would drive him to any lengths to locate the treasures to be found in a place like Atlantis. Throw in Kamchatka's sniper skills and Luk's psychopathic tendencies and this was the mission from hell. A mission, he suddenly thought, that they would be lucky to all walk away from.

Scarlet stepped to the galley to get a fresh glass and after tweaking Ryan's nose on the way back to her seat she collapsed into the soft leather and sighed.

"Do you believe all that bollocks about Dogons and stars?" she asked Hawke.

He shrugged his shoulders. "These days, living my life is like hanging on to a raft so there's no time for questions."

She sighed and sipped her water. "You know, I'm thinking about making this my last mission."

Hawke turned to her but didn't know what to say.

"Does that surprise you?" she said.

"I never know with you, Cairo. Why the sudden change of heart?"

"It's not sudden at all. I've been working for Rich for a long time now and since I started seeing Jack I've been questioning why I spend my life flying around the stratosphere fighting nutcases."

"Troposphere," Ryan called out from the back. "You're not in a spy plane."

"This is a private conversation, gomer."

"Sorry, but I can't help correcting ignorance."

"Leave it, Cairo," Hawke said, gently pulling Scarlet back down into her seat. "You were saying?"

"It was nothing, really. Just rambling... Being with Jack has just made me start to see what I've been missing all these years." She glanced over the headrest in front to where Camacho and Reaper were chatting to the pilots. "And don't you bloody dare tell him any of this or I'll kick your balls to Mount Olympus."

Hawke shifted uncomfortably in his seat. "But you really think you could bail out of ECHO and leave all of this behind?"

She never answered – simply shrugged and walked away leaving him to his thoughts. He looked silently out of the window for a few moments and saw nothing but the ocean stretching to the horizon. He wondered just how far ahead Kruger and the others had gotten in their search. He visualized them crawling all over the Dadès Gorge desperately seeking the next clue that would lead them to Atlantis.

Maybe this time they were just too far behind, and now Scarlet was talking about bailing out as well. Things were going to start changing fast, he thought.

Maybe a little too fast.

CHAPTER TWENTY-ONE

They landed at Marrakech airport and walked across the apron toward a Royal Moroccan Air Force Eurocopter whose rotors were already whirring and ready to go. Between Alex and her father, the US Secretary of Defense Jack Brooke, they had organized a small back-up force of a dozen members of the Royal Moroccan Army who were now climbing in right behind them.

"So who are these men?" Sergent-chef Chabat asked.

"An assortment of international mercenaries and treasure hunters," Lea said.

"But what do they want with the Dadès Gorge?" Chabat asked.

"We don't know exactly," Ryan said, "but it could have something to do with the search for…"

"That's classified, Sergeant," Camacho said firmly, giving Ryan a sideways glance. "We can't talk about it. All you need to know is we're looking at a force of around twenty heavily armed men, mostly Serbians but also some Russians, and they have considerable fighting experience. As such, they represent a serious terrorist threat to the vital national security of the United States and your country too so it's our job to take them out, got it?"

"Of course," Chabat said. "I'm certain my government knows what it has to know."

The Eurocopter made short work of the flight east to the Dadès Gorge, and as they approached their destination, Hawke was able to get a dazzling tourist's eye view of the Dadès River as it cut through the enormous desert canyon below. It was an incredible sight, like a ribbon of steel in the middle of the desert, held in place by the towering walls of the rocky gorge and shining brightly in the bright Moroccan sun. The town of Kalaat Mgoun slipped beneath them as they crossed the Valley of the Roses, named after the famous flowers grown here, but they zoomed over the top of as they made their way further east.

Ahead he saw a large mesa in the center of the river as the chopper flew over the tourists' lookout point. It spun around and flared its nose for landing on top of the western plateau of the mesa's lower side. They didn't need any help finding Kruger and his team – the western section of the meander was now home to three jet boats lashed to the trunks of some walnut trees with mooring rope.

The team climbed out of the chopper and were joined by Chabat and the rest of his soldiers. Without speaking they set off down the path which twisted its way down to the base of the mesa where Kruger's team had left the boats. Summer was long gone, but the sun here was still fierce and burned hard in the vast Moroccan sky. The Dadès River was impressive, and flanked with countless wadis stretching off toward large ravines on both sides of the canyon. Reaper felt it on his neck as he picked his way down the rocky track.

"At least you won't need to top up your tan this year, Reap," Scarlet said.

"But maybe you should work on yours, no?" came the immediate reply. "You have the English pastiness."

"Hey!"

As they descended toward the Dadès River and carved their way deeper into the canyon, the desert floor began to tower above them. Reaper had never been here before and was inwardly amazed by the place. The feeling of vastness was almost overwhelming and the silence of the landscape was eerie. Nowhere on earth had ever made him feel more insignificant.

"This place is nearly one hundred miles long," Ryan said from the back of the team. "They call it the Road of a Thousand Kasbahs."

"I used to know a place like that when I was at uni in Oxford," Lexi said.

"Really?" Ryan said, stopping in his tracks with amazement.

"Oh no – wait," she said, pausing a beat for effect. "That was Road of a Thousand *Kebabs*."

"Oh yes, very good!" Maria said. "I knew a road like that in Moscow."

"It wasn't very good at all," Ryan said. "It was a terrible joke."

"That was a joke?" Scarlet said.

They pressed on, banter flying between the ECHO team but Chabat's soldiers mostly silent. The limestone rim of the canyon was now high above them, and Lea was staring up at it when she tripped on a loose rock and tumbled forward, crashing into the back of Hawke.

"Steady as she goes, Lea," he said with a wink.

"Anyone see where they went yet?" Scarlet called out. Deep in the gorge now there was no longer any need to shield her eyes from the sun as she peered down the track at the jet boats.

"I think so," Maria said. "The track from the boat dies out over there but not far beyond it is a split in the mesa."

They tracked away from their path now and hiked north to the track Maria had found. It was turning into a tough slog now and their weapons began to weigh heavier with each step. They pushed on and were encouraged when they found broken branches on the bushes either side of the fissure in the western edge of the mesa's rock face.

"Something's come through here for sure," Hawke said. "And look down at the path – it's obvious a number of people have been through here recently by the footprints."

"And whoever it was, they were carrying something heavy," Reaper said.

"How can you tell?" Ryan said.

"Forensic track analysis isn't rocket science," the former French Legionnaire said as he crouched down and pointed at the tracks. "Look here and you see they are deeper and further apart and also at a slightly odd angle. The fact that there are two tracks parallel to each other with these features suggests that two men were carrying something from the boat all the way into the cave."

"There's been an explosion here recently too," Hawke said, running his hands over freshly blasted rock at the mouth of the tunnel. "Kruger widened this entrance."

"So, what now?" Ryan said, peering inside the gloom.

"Now, we go pot-holing," Hawke said.

As they were expecting, the temperature dropped rapidly when they ventured inside the mesa and suddenly the atmosphere changed from casual banter to one of imminent danger. There was so sign of Kruger or Korać and his army yet – not even a trace of a glow stick, which meant they were probably using some pretty chunky Maglites to light their way inside the mesa caverns.

Hawke did the same thing and switched on his flashlight. "Looks like we're going up this time," he said with surprise as he shone his flashlight up an incline.

"Great, more sodding climbing," Ryan said.

Reaper joined Hawke at the front while Chabat and his men took up the rear and they began to climb the incline inside the mesa. After nearly thirty minutes of twists and turns they found their first evidence of Kruger – and more evidence as to why whatever was hidden here had remained untouched for so long. Ahead of them, another part of the tunnel had been blown out with explosives and what had been solid sandstone was now a few piles of shattered rocks and gravelly dust lying around at the newly-formed entrance to a second tunnel.

They shifted inside and noticed yet another drop in temperature as they went deeper into the mesa, only this time part of it that had been off limits to the rest of humanity for countless centuries.

They continued on their way, each of them thinking about the dangers ahead but never considering failure, and then they found a shaft which descended from a rock ledge. They gathered around it, and Hawke was the first to spot the gentle glow of artificial light as the silver Maglite beams of Kruger's team bobbed about down at the bottom of the shaft.

He hushed the team and got down on his stomach to listen and instantly recognized the voices of Kruger and Korać. He felt a surge of hope as he realized he had another chance to redeem himself after his failure in Serbia.

He jumped back up to his feet and lowered his voice to a gentle murmur. "Looks like the whole Groovy Gang is down there."

"So what now?" Chabat asked.

"We go down, of course," Hawke said, and with that he jammed the Maglite in his belt and started to climb down into the shaft.

CHAPTER TWENTY-TWO

From his new vantage point inside the shaft, Hawke saw it wasn't as deep as he'd initially thought and that explained how Kruger and his men had managed to descend it without the use of abseil lines, but he could see scratch marks where they had lowered down a serious quantity of explosives.

He used brute force to hold himself level in the narrow tunnel as he moved himself down, and then after listening carefully to make sure the coast was clear he lowered himself out of the shaft and dropped gently to the sandy floor, instantly retreating against the wall and gripping the Maglite in his hand like a club in case Kruger had left guards behind.

He levelled his flashlight and scanned the cavern. It was not a large space and, as it happened, the place was empty. Most of it was nothing more than hollowed-out bedrock, but intricate, carved columns stood like silent sentinels every few yards. Kruger had obviously decided the chances of anyone being clever enough to follow him were so unlikely he hadn't left any men behind to guard his way back out. Not guarding your logistics trail was a cardinal error in warfare, and this only showed what an unpredictable amateur Dirk Kruger was, but the fact Korać had made the same mistake surprised him.

He gave the rest of the team a signal with his Maglite and they followed him down the shaft and soon they were all gathered together in the new cavern.

"The lights I saw have long gone," Hawke said, pointing down a long twisting tunnel. "But they must have gone down there because it's the only route."

They followed the tunnel but it wasn't long before they started to find more evidence of Kruger and his team by way of angry shouting and then more lights bobbing about up ahead. Moving forward along the final stretch, it didn't take long before they had caught up with the enemy who were now gathering in a much larger chamber, clearly built to strike awe into anyone trying to approach whatever awaited them.

Kruger was running his hands over what at first looked like a flat stone wall until their flashlights uncovered the faintest of slits running directly down the center. Both sides of the stone door were covered in the same peculiar symbols they had seen in Mictlan.

"This is the entrance!" Kruger yelled over his shoulder.

Van Zyl whistled in amazement and shook his head. "Must be fifty tons of rock here."

"Which is why we brought the drill and the explosives," Kruger said, and then turned and gave Korać his instructions.

Chabat and his team finally joined Hawke, rifles gripped in their hands and anxious expressions on their faces. Hawke guessed crawling through ancient tunnels not seen by man for countless millennia wasn't part of basic training for the Royal Moroccan Army.

"I do not like this place," Chabat said, glancing over at the ghostly glow of Kruger's flashlights up ahead. He passed a hand over his sweaty forehead and swallowed. "How many did you say there were?"

"We thought around twenty," Camacho replied.

Hawke nodded. "And judging from the jet boats out on the river I'd say there couldn't be much more than that."

"So what are we waiting for?" Scarlet said. "The quicker we get this over and done with the quicker I get a smoke."

Kruger stood beside the giant rocky entrance while Korać ordered his men to assemble the rock drill and ready the C4 explosives. Moments later the hidden ECHO team heard grunts and heavy lifting as the men rigged up the drill and then Kruger gave the order. When they fired up the enormous rock drill, the cavern was filled with the deafening sound of drilling.

"They're drilling holes for the explosives," Hawke said over the shrill noise. Another sequence of drilling was followed by yet more grunting as they hauled the drill out of the way.

"They're not going to blow up the entrance?" Ryan asked, hurriedly pushing his glasses up the bridge of his nose.

Scarlet rolled her eyes. "They're not going to rub through it with tea towels, are they?"

"But what about the symbols?" he replied with genuine concern on his face. "They're an invaluable archaeological find just by themselves, not to mention they could contain any amount of information leading to hidden knowledge."

"I think that ship has sailed," Camacho said. "They're pushing the C4 inside the drilled-out holes... jamming it in good as well."

Hawke carefully watched the men as they prepped the door for the detonation. "They're not taking any chances, that's for sure."

"So you'll just have to suck it up, in other words," Scarlet said.

"Those symbols could also lead to treasure..."

Scarlet stared at him. "Hang on a minute – we can't let this wanton destruction of priceless archaeological petroglyphs go on!"

"Your conscience is thirty seconds too late, Cairo," Lea said.

Scarlet's eyes narrowed. "Eh?"

"Ear plug time," said Hawke.

"But I didn't bring any ear plugs!" Ryan said in a panic.

"Fingers, numbnuts," Scarlet said with a roll of her eyes.

And then a tremendous explosion as Kruger blasted his way through the wall with the petroglyphs on it.

The blast struck one of the Serbian mercs who was too close and smashed him hard against the rocks behind them, cracking his skull and instantly killing him. Korać and Kruger barely glanced at him, the South African especially now utterly fixated by the progress they had made.

"We did it!" he yelled, his heavy accent hanging in the air with the smoke and dust. "We broke through!"

The men cheered but Kruger yelled at them to shut up when he saw part of the roof had been damaged and was now crumbling down dangerously into their path. "Look out!"

They staggered back and waited until the rock-fall had settled, allowing a clearer view of the wall once again.

"They were only supposed to blow the bloody doors off!" Scarlet said, glancing surreptitiously at Hawke who simply rolled his eyes in response. "If that accent was supposed to be Michael Caine, I actually feel sorry for you."

"They're going inside!" Lea said.

"So let's get after them," Camacho said. "Why should they have all the fun?"

As they progressed they discovered Korać's men had cleared the piles of detonated rocks away from the entrance. The left-hand side of the stone barrier was still standing with only a deep fissure running through the center of it where the C4 had tried and failed to break it open, but the stone to the right was now no more than smouldering chunks of rock and the occasional misshapen boulder.

ECHO proceeded with caution through the smoke and dust until they reached the end of a short tunnel and stumbled upon the top of a broad set of stone steps leading down into an imposing catacomb.

"They must have gone down there," Ryan said, pointing at the glow of the Maglites as they bobbed about along the wall at the far end of the catacomb.

"Do you think?" Scarlet said turning to face him. "Are you still Captain Obvious or have they promote you to Major Obvious yet?"

They continued pursuing Kruger until they reached a large chamber constructed of perfectly hewn granite blocks.

"It's like the chambers in the middle of the pyramids!" Ryan said.

The South Africans and Serbians swarmed all over the chamber, and then Ryan saw it first at the far end.

"Oh my God!" he said. "That's a statue of Tanit!"

"Are you sure?" Maria asked.

"I can see the resemblance," Lea said.

"And it's in some kind of shrine," he continued. "This must be her tomb!"

Kruger approached the shrine and then pulled the idol from his canvas back. Flanked by his goons, he held it in his hands for a few seconds while savouring the moment.

154

"What's he doing now?" Lexi asked.

"Taking a shit," Scarlet said. "What does it look like?"

"Now, now," Hawke said. "There's no need for nastiness."

Kruger pushed the star-shaped base of the idol into a slot in the base of the shrine and the far wall began to grind open. Behind it was a small chamber filled with an intricate sarcophagus and another statue of Tanit looming above everything. Kruger placed the idol back in his canvas sack and moved forward.

"The idol's a key!" Ryan said. "I knew it!"

Hawke looked into the final chamber and saw Korać's men were arranging their flashlights on rocks to act as mini spot lights as they circled the magnificent sarcophagus carved out of the limestone itself. Stacked up all over the tomb was not gold, or gems, but books.

"That's amazing!" Lea said. "Looks like something out of Lord of the Rings."

"A bit like Ryan's ears," Scarlet whispered, keeping her eyes fixed dead-ahead on the chamber.

"What the hell is that supposed to mean?" Ryan said.

"They're just a bit pointy, that's all."

"I do not have pointy ears!" he said.

"No, he doesn't have pointy ears," Maria said, coming to his defense, but Ryan was now compulsively checking his ears with his fingers.

Kruger ordered his men to raise the lid of the sarcophagus and a moment later he was trembling as he peered over the rim into the inside. "It's here!" he yelled. "We just took another step closer to Atlantis."

"You were right, mate," Hawke said as he gazed at the ancient lock-and-key combo. "About Atlantis, I mean."

"One of the side effects of *always* being right, I suppose," Ryan said, but was quickly cuffed across the head by a fast-moving back-slap delivered courtesy of Scarlet Sloane's right hand. "Ow!"

"Arrogant twat," she said, but leaned forward to kiss him on the temple.

"What the fuck?" Ryan said, as stunned as everyone else.

"It's for all the times you've been right in the past, and all the times you'll be right in the future, so you're only getting the one."

"I don't know what to say," he said.

"Well that's a first," she said, and gave him another slap. "Right, let's move on."

Silently they watched as the men circled the sarcophagus like vultures.

"There's that little bastard Luk again," Hawke said, gritting his teeth.

"Let's not forget that weasel Kvashnin who tried to kill me in Germany," said Lexi.

"Two nutcases led by the not-so-funny double act of Kruger and Korać," Scarlet added.

"And all four of them caught in flagrante delicto," Ryan said.

Lea sighed. "Say caught red-handed if you mean caught red-handed."

Then Kruger pulled something from the sarcophagus and a cry went up among the men. It was a stone cylinder of some kind. "We have what we need... move out!"

"They have it," Hawke said.

"What?" Chabat said.

"The latest Network Rail timetable," Scarlet said under breath. "What do you think?"

"What does she mean?" Chabat said, confused.

"We don't know *exactly* what they have," Ryan said. "It looks like it could be another key but we'll need to get hold of it for a better idea. Whatever it is, we know we don't want them to have it."

"You think?" Scarlet said, the unlit cigarette still bobbing about on her bottom lip.

"They're moving out!" Camacho yelled.

"And they're coming straight for us!"

The fireworks started when Chabat ordered his men to open fire on the Serbs and seconds later the cave was filled with a brutal strobing effect as his men's carbines lit the semi-darkness with savage muzzle flashes.

Kruger's archaeological genius was no longer enough to lead the mission, and a split second after Chabat's assault, Dragan Korać took charge, ordering his army of mercenaries to take cover and return fire. They all knew what was at stake here, and no one was playing games.

"They have to get through us to escape back to the boats," Maria said.

"Apparently not," Reaper said as he fired on Van Zyl. "Look!"

Dirk Kruger was now climbing inside the sarcophagus and calling the others over to join him.

"I read about how they got fourteen people in a phone box but this is just ridiculous," Scarlet said. "You wouldn't think they had the time for world records."

Ryan sighed. "Duh! It's an escape tunnel…"

Scarlet looked at him and pursed her lips. "You think?"

Van Zyl was the last man to climb into the sarcophagus and before he vanished he turned to give a final burst of submachine gunfire at the ECHO team. Ten seconds later a deep roar emanated from below their feet and then the sarcophagus lurched heavily to one side and sunk into the floor.

"They blew the sodding tunnel up,' Hawke said. "They're going back to the boats so I'll lead a team back the way we came and cut them off." He turned to Ryan. "I need you to stay here and go through this place looking for anything that can help us. Kruger has the key but there has to be something else."

Ryan and the others began the laborious process of sifting through the rubble in their search for anything that might help them work out what the South African had looted, while Hawke, Lea, Reaper and Lexi sprinted back along the tunnel in a bid to head Kruger off before he got to the river.

CHAPTER TWENTY-THREE

Clambering back up the vertical shaft took longer than Hawke had allowed for, and when they reached the fresh air of the outside world Kruger and the others were already emerging from a pile of scrub-covered rubble at the bottom of the mesa's northwest slope.

"They took a hell of a risk going into that second tunnel," Reaper said.

Hawke nodded sharply, exhilarated by the hunt. "Eden said he was the luckiest bastard alive, and I'm starting to believe him."

They jogged down the hot, rocky mesa, occasionally slipping on loose scree but making good progress until they reached the bottom of the slope and took cover behind a number of juniper trees growing around a small oasis. They were now on the same level as Kruger, who was totally exposed as he and Korać ordered their men into the boats.

"We can't let them get away," Lea said.

"She's right," Reaper added. "If they get into the boats they'll be out of sight in seconds, and it's a half hour hike up to Chabat's Eurocopter."

Hawke's response was to bring his Glock into the aim. For a second he heard nothing but the gentle desert breeze as it whistled through the thick leaves of the date palms and juniper canopies above his head. In the distance was the splashing sound of the river as it moved west though the deep gorge.

Softly, he squeezed the trigger…

Gunshot crack, puff of smoke... one of the mercs clutched his throat and dropped into the muddy bank beside the boat.

Korać and the mercs reacted with speedy professionalism, moving into defensive positions while Kruger and Van Zyl fired up the front two boats.

Hawke fired again, and the second shot gave away their destination tucked away in the oasis. A second later another gun battle revved up to full speed as the Serbs defended their position and prepared to retreat with the column-shaped stone key.

With the superior cover afforded by the shady oasis, Hawke and the rest of the ECHO team made short work of the exposed Serbian mercenaries, so the second Kruger and the key were secured, Korać ordered his men into the boats and they pulled out into the center of the coffee-colored river, guns blazing off the sterns the whole time.

Thanks to the ECHO team's assault, they had taken out a good handful of the mercs available to Kruger and forced them to leave one of the jet boats behind.

"Looks like we're going white-water rafting!" Hawke said. "Anyone up for a splash with me?"

*

As the smoke began to clear, Ryan was able to get a better look at the detail inside the inner chamber. He spent a few moments shining his Maglite on various parts of the tomb and was amazed by what he was seeing. "Some of this stuff is unbelievable. Problem is that the cylinder Kruger and the others got was obviously the main attraction and without that there's much less to go on."

"We're going to need more than that," Camacho said gruffly, and turned to Chabat. "Call for back-up and get what's left of this place secured. This location is now a major archaeological site and potential international security risk and I want it quarantined."

"Yes, sir," Chabat said, and walked along the tunnel to get a signal on his radio.

Maria sighed and ran a hand through her hair. "So we don't have the cylinder, but what *have* we got?"

Ryan shone his flashlight along the walls. "It's hard to know where to start, but considering the sarcophagus and shrine have been destroyed I think these pictograms on the wall are our best bet."

"What pictograms?" Scarlet said, staring hard at the wall now illuminated by Ryan's flashlight. "Are you sure they're not just scratches?"

Ryan sighed and shook his head. "It's me we're talking about. Of course I'm sure they're not scratches."

"I hope your knowledge of ancient symbols is as half as good as your sense of self-regard, kid," Camacho said.

"It is," Ryan replied seriously, and took a step closer to the wall. "This confirms it – I think the grand prize was definitely a key."

"You sure?"

He nodded. "This symbol here is for a key, without any doubt, and if my translation is correct it looks to me like Tanit was supposed to be guarding it. I guess that's why old Dirk had to use the idol to open her tomb."

"So the obvious question," Scarlet said, "besides why so many beautiful spies find you attractive, is a key to what?"

"I don't even know if there *is* an answer to that."

"None of us do."

"I meant an answer to the question of the key... but if there is an answer to it then the only place we're going to find it is in this inscription above the shrine." He paused a beat. "And what's intriguing about it is the similarity between these symbols and those on the idol, and the ones I saw back in Mictlan. There's a real connection here."

Camacho turned to him and passed a hand over the stubble on his jaw. "You mentioned something about that before."

"So *someone* listens to me," he said, turning to Scarlet.

"But what's the connection?" Maria asked.

"Hard to say, but Atlantis is lurking in the middle of all this somewhere."

Camacho let out a long frustrated sigh. "I don't know what the *hell* I know anymore. When I was a kid Atlantis was a mythical place, but apparently now I'm searching for it so I guess anything can happen from this point."

Ryan moved closer to the wall. "We're going to need pictures of all these and then send them over to Elysium. We need Alex and some computer power on the case. This one here of Tanit is bothering me." He started to snap pictures of everything in sight.

"You mean the figure in the skirt?" Maria said.

"It's deliberately ambiguous. Because it's a triangle with a circle on top of it and the two lines stretching out either side just beneath the circle, or head, it does indeed look like a woman in a skirt – so it could be a simple symbol representation of Tanit."

"But there's another way of interpreting it?" Camacho said.

"I don't know... I know I'm missing something. I'm going to email this stuff to Alex and see what she comes up with," Ryan said.

Camacho nodded. "With Kim and Alex working together they'll be all over this like a dog on a bone, I'll bet!"

"All we need now is for Joe to get that sodding stone key from Kruger and we're away," Ryan said.

"What do you think his chances are?" Maria said.

Scarlet smiled. "Better than average, darling."

CHAPTER TWENTY-FOUR

Hawke turned the key and fired up the jet boat. Seconds later he was pulling onto the Dadès River and racing north in pursuit of the fleeing men. The sun was higher now and reflected brightly off the water, dazzling him as he tried to steer the boat out into the deeper part of the river and increase speed to close the gap.

Korać was still in the lead and almost out of sight now, but Kruger's boat was closer. At its stern, Kamchatka now ordered the men to fire on the ECHO team and moments later they heard the familiar chatter of submachine guns.

The river was wide now, and starting to get dangerous. This was a favorite location for tourists to go white-water rafting and Hawke was beginning to see why as he struggled to navigate the boat between piles of lethal hull-smashing rocks and the gunfire of Kruger and the rest of his hired thugs. Ekel Kvashnin was particularly enjoying firing on Lexi, but the violence of the boats racing over the wild river disrupted his otherwise lethal aim.

"Damn Kamchatka! He wants to kill me," Lexi said as she ducked another shot.

"He wants to kill *all* of us," Hawke said.

"No… it's me he wants," she replied coolly. "It's the only way he can redeem himself in his own eyes after his failure to kill me in Berlin."

The engine roared and water sprayed up over the sides as Hawke spun the wheel hard to the right to dodge more bullets but then hung a hard left to correct the course before hitting the southern bank of the river.

"I see your river boatin' skills haven't improved since the day we met," Lea said.

"Shouldn't you be doing something useful?" he said, throttling down for a sharp bend coming up fast.

Her response was drowned out by the sound of Lexi Zhang's pistol as she fired off a series of rounds. Her aim was as true as ever and struck two of Kruger's men who were standing beside Luk. One crashed forward into the river while the other collapsed onto the deck of the jet boat, frantically trying to stop his throat wound from bleeding. Luk settled matters by kicking him out the back of the boat where he landed with a bloody splash in the rushing torrent.

Hawke had no time to swerve and ploughed right over the top of the injured man. A nasty growling sound and a drop in revs for a few seconds indicated the blades at the back of their boat had not done the man any favours, but there was no time to consider it as up ahead both the fleeing boats were turning another bend in the river.

"Is it wrong that I'm totally loving this?" Reaper said, reloading his gun and standing close to Lexi as he took aim. He loosed some rounds, the crackling of the shots echoing off the rocky canyon rising up either side of the river.

"You missed," Lexi said coolly.

"It's your perfume," the Frenchman said casually. "It put me off – what is it – Eau d'Assassin?"

"You know, you're very pretty for a legionnaire."

Reaper laughed. "Are you trying to put me off my game?"

"No, I just love tattoos," she said, circling his grenade tattoo with her fingernail. "How are things with Monique these days?"

Hawke rolled his eyes. "Christ almighty – now, really?"

"He has a point," Lea said. "And if neither o' you gowls can get a decent shot off then let me get past and have a go."

"Oh yeah," Hawke said, ducking to dodge a bullet and powering up out of the next bend. "Because your aim is even more legendary than Atlantis."

"Get stuffed, Josiah!"

She fired over the windshield, the ejector port spitting out the nine mil jackets into the water rushing past in a blur.

"You missed," Hawke said.

"Not my fault," Lea said, cursing. "Damned sights are totally bloody banjaxed."

"I do wish you'd speak in English," Lexi said.

"I was speaking in English, you silly cow!"

"Hey!"

"What the hell is that thing?" Lexi said, staring at a silver weapon in the hands of one of Korać's goons. It shone wildly in the bright sun, its reflection blinding them for a moment.

"Oh shit," Hawke said.

"What is it, Joe?" Lea said.

"I might be wrong, but I think it's a Raytheon Pike."

"A *what* now?"

"It's a hand-held laser-guided missile launcher."

"Sounds like trouble to me," Lexi said.

"He's right," Reaper said, swiping his monocular away from his eye and sliding it back inside his shirt pocket. "It's a Pike, all right. I read about it a few weeks ago, but I'm sure they're still in the testing phase so how they got their sweaty little hands on it – I don't know."

"What's it capable of?" Lexi said.

"It's a laser-guided munition that flies through the air without leaving a smoke trail so it's very hard to dodge after it's fired," Hawke said.

"But it's going to be a hard job for that asshat to get a fix on us with his laser in the middle of a bloody river chase, right?" Lea said.

Hawke frowned. "Sadly no. He fires it in our vague direction and then he can take his time fixing the laser on us and the missile comes home to daddy, so to speak."

"No need for further explanations," Lexi said. "He just fired it."

Hawke saw the tiny flash as Kamchatka launched the missile grenade and then aimed the laser on their jet boat.

"It's going to be one of those days," Hawke said.

"Where's the damned thing gone?" Lea said, shielding her eyes as she strained to see the incoming missile.

"Holy crap!" Lexi said. "It's right in front of us!"

Hawke saw it a second after Lexi – a small rocket-propelled grenade racing through the air to hit the laser beam Kamchatka was keeping firmly fixed on their boat. With half a second to spare Hawke spun the wheel to the right and the jet boat swerved violently to starboard.

Kamchatka raced to get the laser beam back on the jet boat's bow, but it happened too fast and the grenade slammed into the surface of the river beside them. A massive explosion detonated in the water a second later and sent a fireball shooting up into the air.

Hawke and the others were close enough to feel the shockwave but that was the worst of it except a heavy shower of river water that was blasted over their boat by the explosion. The former SBS man turned for a second to see if their stern was damaged by the blast.

"Joe – look out!"

He spun around to see the correction he had made to evade Kamchatka's Pike grenade had put them on course with the south side of the canyon – a flat wall of sandstone towering hundreds of feet above them.

"Oh, shit!"

He hurriedly spun the wheel back to port and the jet boat turned just in time to avoid a devastating impact. They heard a deep grinding sound as the starboard of the boat collided with the sandstone rock face but a small shower of sparks later they were pointing back to the middle of the river.

"It's better if the driver looks where he's going," Lea said.

"I was totally in control," he said, giving her a quick sideways glance to see if his outrageous lie had done the trick. The look on the former Irish Ranger's face told him it hadn't.

With the enemy slowing for another narrow bend, Hawke seized the moment to reduce the throttle and slow the boat for the narrow stretch ahead. He took the opportunity to check the mag in his weapon and slide a round into the chamber ready to take a shot.

He raised the gun to take a shot while steering the boat with his other hand when he saw the men in the boats ahead strapping strange circular cages to their backs.

"What the hell are they up to now?" Lea said.

Reaper shielded the sun from his eyes and absent-mindedly stroked his handlebar moustache "Exactement… what are they doing?"

"I know what they're doing," Lexi said.

"Me too," added Hawke. "Just when I thought this day couldn't get any more dangerous."

CHAPTER TWENTY-FIVE

The former Commando and SBS man had seen many insane things in his life, but this was new even to him, and now he watched with an overwhelming sense of rage and frustration as a red and white canopy burst into view and blossomed into fully formed airwings above Kruger's jet boat. "I don't believe it."

"What the hell is going on?" Lea asked again.

"I see Korać is a professional after all," Hawke said. "Our enemy is going airborne."

"Now I understand," Reaper said, nodding his head with admiration for the idea.

"That's a sodding paraglider wing," Hawke said.

"And that's another one," Lexi added, jutting her chin at Kruger's boat. "And those things on their backs are paramotors. They use them to provide power to take off and steer."

Hawke pushed the throttles forward but they were already at max and he knew he wasn't going to make it on time. Now he watched helplessly as first Korać took off from the back of the jet boat, with Kruger following a few seconds later. Van Zyl, Luk and Kamchatka soon joined them, flying up into the narrow canyon after the others. The last two remaining Serbian mercs on the team jumped off the boat and flew up behind the others.

Hawke shook his head in disbelief and began to scan the area for cover. A boat-to-boat fight was one thing but being attacked by an airborne force while they were stuck down on this river made them the proverbial sitting ducks. "Do we have any in the back of this thing?" he yelled.

Lexi looked in the rear of the boat. "Yes! But only one."

"If one of us can get airborne we stand a better chance of getting out of this," Hawke shouted over the roar of the engine. The enemy's boats were now out of control, and raced wildly toward the rocks at the canyon's southern wall. Korać's was first to hit, exploding in a savage fireball and spitting twisted shrapnel all over the surface of the river.

Hawke's jet boat was too far away to be damaged, but then Kruger's boat followed suit, ploughing into the cliff just west of the burning heap of junk that used to be Korać's jet boat. Accelerated by the burning fuel all over the surface of the Dadès River, the South African's jet boat exploded with even more fury than the first one and this time the ECHO team were closer.

They ducked as best they could as the flaming shrapnel rained down over them but the shockwave of the blast tipped their boat hard to port and threw them out into the river. "There goes the paraglider," Hawke thought as he flew through the air.

They landed in the burning hell of oil, gas and water and Hawke screamed at everyone to dive and swim away from the wreckage. He felt the burning heat of the boats as he dived under the surface and struggled to see Lea, but the water was too murky and disrupted with the disaster all around them.

He swam a few dozen yards before resurfacing and broke the surface of the water to see the others pop up all around him. He saw Lea was alive, swimming for the relative safety of their capsized jet boat. He breathed a sigh of relief, but it didn't last long. High in the sky, in the narrow slit at the top of the canyon, he saw the paragliders change direction and start flying toward them.

Then he saw the tiny red dots of their lasers dancing on the surface of the water like little devils.

"They're coming back!" he yelled, and pointed at the paragliders.

The others twisted around in the sloshing water and saw them, now much closer and just in time to see Kruger at the front, laughing as he prepared to fire another Pike at them.

Bobbing about in the rushing water like drowned rats, Hawke knew they stood zero chance against an airborne enemy armed with laser-guided missiles. All they had were a few waterlogged handguns and nowhere to hide.

Then his heart skipped a beat when he followed the path of one of the lasers. It crossed the river and ran up over the hull of their upturned jet boat – just as Lea was clambering and slipping up the other side of it.

"Lea! Get off the damned boat!"

She turned to see what he was shouting about. "What?"

"Get off the boat! Kruger's got a laser on it!"

High above their heads, Kruger, Van Zyl and Kamchatka circled them like hungry vultures, while Korać and Luk were rising on a therm behind them.

"I can't hear you, Joe."

"Get off the damned..." He gave up. He knew she would never hear him. He pointed up at the sky in the direction of Kruger and the others, only to see both Korać and Luk racing lower and loading their own Pikes. "Oh, Jesus..."

He wiped the water from his eyes and saw Reaper was closer to Lea. "Reaper – get her off the damned boat!"

But the Frenchman had already seen what was happening and had begun a hefty freestyle stroke across the rushing torrent in a bid to get to her. "Lea!" he yelled, but the sound of the paraglider motors and the white water crashing over the rocks drowned out his voice. He pointed to the sky. Lea finally noticed the red laser crawling up the hull of the boat. Then she looked up to see a puff of smoke as Kruger fired the Pike.

"Holy Mother of God!" she screamed, and dived into the water just as the missile ripped into the hull of the jet boat. A meaty explosion blasted the tourist boat into dozens of pieces and Hawke strained to raise himself out of the rushing river to see if Lea had made it.

Before he got the confirmation he needed, he saw a red light moving rapidly along the surface of the water toward him and followed its path to see Kruger now racing ever closer. They were nothing more than fish in the proverbial barrel, at the mercy of these men who were now hunting them for sport.

"What are we going to do?" Lea screamed.

Hawke's mind raced, but then he had an idea. "Over in the northern cliffs is a small cave – they can't follow us in there. Everyone dive and swim to the cave!"

Hawke pushed himself underwater and began to swim toward the small cave he'd seen in the base of the cliff. Its ceiling looked only a foot or so above the waterline from out on the river but when he emerged inside it he realized it was bigger than it looked and more than enough to give them cover while they figured out what their next play was.

"What now?" Lea said, wiping the water from her eyes and sweeping her long hair back. The others looked at him for a decision.

Hawke swam over to the entrance and looked up into the sky. "They're giving up and moving on. We wait till they're out of sight and then we go back to the tomb."

CHAPTER TWENTY-SIX

Alex Reeve had been staring at Ryan's email of the symbols for a long time when she finally blinked and rubbed her eyes. She needed a break, and now she was looking up at her father on the giant plasma screen in the Elysium briefing room. The sound was muted but she was reading the news ticker running along the bottom the picture. When he'd won the nomination to be the party's candidate she knew life was going to change for everyone, but only half as much as it would if he won the election.

Tonight was the first debate with Bill Peterson and the tension ran through the air like electricity. Peterson was a skilled orator and master-manipulator of public opinion who knew how to use rhetoric to get what he wanted. Not only that but tonight's debate was in New York, Peterson's home state – the state he had served as senator for longer than anyone could remember.

According to Team Brooke, they were expecting somewhere in the region of ninety million viewers and the general opinion was the first debate was the most critical – after that a good chunk of those millions would get the picture and not bother tuning in again. Everything was riding on it and she could see the tension on her dad's face as he stepped off the jet and made his way to his car among a throng of journalists and news crews. *I hope it's worth losing your family for, Daddy.*

She returned to her laptop where the symbols were still on the screen, along with a series of image attachments of various pictograms from inside the chamber in the Dadès Gorge mesa. Ryan had also included a terrible selfie of himself using perspective to make it look like he was squeezing Jack Camacho's head. The American was in the background talking to a Moroccan soldier and had no idea what Ryan had done.

She rolled her eyes, closed the selfie and turned her attention to the pictograms. Yes, Ryan was right when he said at least one of them was a symbol of Tanit, which was hardly surprising given it was her tomb, but like Ryan, something about it was bothering her.

Ryan's theory was pivoting around his Atlantis idea, and that was as good a place as any to start. She'd been with ECHO long enough to know that dismissing the impossible was usually a bad idea. After Poseidon, Lei Gong, Osiris, Medusa, Valhalla and Mictlan, she had no reason not to believe in Atlantis any more.

"I know what you're thinking."

Startled, she turned to see Richard Eden entering the room with two coffees.

"And what am I thinking?"

He pointed at the symbol of Tanit. "That Atlantis is a bridge too far?"

"Maybe, but if it was good enough for Plato then it's good enough for me."

Eden laughed and looked at the TV. "You think he'll win the debate?"

Alex shrugged. "Don't ask me. I never gave a damn about his career and I'm not going to start now."

"I thought you built some bridges during the Medusa mission?"

Alex sighed. "Maybe, but you never know with Jack Brooke." She said the name as if he were just another politician. "He's Dad one minute and then Mr Secretary the next."

"Or maybe Mr President the next?"

She looked at Eden, saddened that she probably had a healthier relationship with him than she did with her own father. "Like I said, don't ask me."

Eden smiled briefly and decided not to push it. Instead, he changed the subject and brought things back to business. "Any luck with the pictograms?"

"Yes and no. I don't know a whole lot about Phoenician culture, but this broken symbol here could be what we're looking for," Alex said, and let her hair down, shaking it loose and relaxing for the first time that day. She wheeled her chair across to another computer and opened another window. "Ryan found this one where the key was found so I think it's very important and connected to the key's meaning. I used some imaging software to clean it up and enlarge it."

Eden peered in closer at the pictogram Alex was indicating. Half of it had been blown away by a bullet in the fire fight, but what was left looked like a man's face and his raised hand. "You mean the raised hand?"

"I do."

"The raised hands of Ka?"

Alex shook her head. "A good guess, but I don't think so. The raised hands which made up the Egyptian symbol for Ka – their 'vital spark' or life essence – were never pictured with a face or head like this, but just two hands, usually forming a U shape."

"So what is it then?"

"Considering a bullet blew half of it away, it was tough, but at first I was thinking this is Atlas."

"Atlas?"

"Sure. If you look carefully you can see the hand is holding something up – indicated here by this very faint line – it has a convex curve, see? And here is a second arm. He's holding the world up."

Eden put his glasses on and leaned in close to the screen. "Well, bugger me! I think you might have something here. You said you thought it was Atlas *at first* – so you think something else now?"

She nodded. "I do. At first I got all excited because… you know – a symbol of Atlas in the Atlas Mountains, bla bla bla, but then I realized this wasn't Atlas at all but Hercules."

"Hercules?"

"Uh-huh?"

"What makes you say that?"

"The arms holding the world are straight like pillars."

"But we decided this was someone holding the world up. I might have been at school several hundred years ago but my recollection is that Atlas held up the world."

"Right," Alex nodded. "After the Titanomachy Atlas was ordered to hold the sky up above the world for eternity, and for whatever reason he was linked to the Atlas Mountains in Morocco. They were named after him, of course."

"So Hercules..?"

"According to legend Hercules also held the world up for a short time, so I think this symbol is a depiction of him performing that task. It's an allegory representing a great burden perhaps carrying ancient knowledge."

"I see."

"Not only that but this symbol of Tanit also points in the same direction. To the untrained eye it looks like a woman in a skirt who is holding her arms out either side of her body in an upright position."

"And to the trained eye?"

"The other way to interpret this symbol is two pillars either side of the sun, on top of a mountain. In fact the symbols of Tanit and the pillars are closely connected. Most depictions of the Pillars of Hercules show Hercules

178

struggling between two collapsing pillars in an attempt to hold them up, and for this reason they are leaning in toward him and make a triangle – just like the 'skirt' of Tanit. It all points to the same thing."

Eden squinted and cocked his head as he studied the image again. "Are you sure?"

"Pretty sure, yeah. These two symbols are both direct references either to Hercules or the Pillars of Hercules."

"Just tell me you know what you're doing."

"I do, but I can't take this any further now without specialist knowledge. I'm ninety percent certain that both these symbols are pointing to the far north of Morocco, but after that I'm out of ideas."

"Mr Bale?"

"A polymath genius, Rich, for sure... but not this stuff – his knowledge is broad but not always deep. We're going to need someone to help us decode these symbols. Any ideas?"

Eden frowned. "There are only two people in the world who have the knowledge to decode this stuff, and one of them is Dirk."

"And the other?"

"Dr Maati Khatibi. He's second only to Dirk when it comes to researching Phoenician and Punic semiotics. He's our best chance."

"Where does he work?"

"He doesn't – he retired last year. His last academic post was the Oxford Center for Phoenician and Punic Studies, but from what I can gather he's back in Morocco now."

"Do we have an address?"

"Only if you can find one," Eden said.

Alex turned around and begun furiously tapping into the computer. Eden took a moment to clear his mind and had a sip of the coffee. Five minutes later, Alex cleared her throat to get his attention and spun the monitor around for him. "I hacked the payroll in Oxford."

"Where?"

"The Blue Pearl."

"Ah," Eden said, his face lighting with pleasant recognition. "I know it well. You try and get in touch with him and I'll let Lea know where they're going."

"Sure," she said, and Eden left the room.

She pushed her chair back to the plasma screen and looked up at the towering figure of her father, only now he was barely recognizable because the news network were playing old videotape footage of him descending a military aircraft's airstair in his Delta Force dress uniform. Before she was born, she thought, and a smile broke out on her face without her even knowing it. He looked so young, she thought. He would be about her age right now with his whole life ahead of him.

She quietly wished him luck, not even knowing if she meant it or not, and switched off the plasma screen.

CHAPTER TWENTY-SEVEN

Ryan Bale received Alex's text with a mixture of happiness and frustration. She was replying to his earlier email and as usual she'd got right on it. She'd even come up with some stuff about the raised arms being a symbol of the Egyptian Ka – another reference to eternity. He was happy that they had a good lead but irritated that she had once again beaten him to it, but that was the way things went with Alex Reeve. She was sharper than a serpent's tooth, as someone once wrote, and he was proud to work with her.

Scarlet poked him in the ribs. "So what does HQ say?"

"Alex is of the view that the key Kruger stole is supposed to unlock something to do with the Pillars of Hercules... I just knew this had something to do with Hercules!"

"Hercules?"

"Or Heracles – same dude so take your pick."

With Chabat's men guarding the tomb and waiting for backup, they were making their way down the track toward the river in the hope of meeting up with Hawke and the others. Instead, they saw something altogether different – a number of men flying through the sky toward them at speed.

"What the hell are they" Maria asked.

"Paragliders," Camacho said, his tone indicating trouble ahead.

"Could just be tourists," Scarlet said.

Camacho shook his head and took a closer look. "Tourists aren't usually armed."

Maria took a step forward and shielded her eyes from the sun as she looked into the sky. "What?"

"They're carrying weapons of some kind," Camacho said.

"And if they're here on their way to us, then where the hell is Joe?" Ryan said.

"Just what I was thinking," Maria said. "Maybe something happened to them."

Scarlet slid the bolt-action on her gun and rolled her eyes. "All right, no need to turn into a bunch of big girls' blouses," she said sharply. "We have an enemy engaging with us so get into defensive positions."

"You're not the boss of me, lady," Camacho said with a grin.

"You can't possibly believe *that*, can you Camo?"

Now the enemy was close enough for them to hear the buzzing hum of the paramotors and then they saw the red dots of the laser sights.

"I'm getting a bad feeling about this," Ryan said as he watched the crimson-colored dot racing along the track toward them.

"Whatever they've got is laser-guided," Camacho said.

"Which means our day just got really shit," said Scarlet.

"And that little red dot is getting closer," Maria said. "Only twenty meters."

A puff of smoke from one of the paragliders and a cracking sound a second later was the opening shot of the attack.

"Run for cover!" Scarlet screamed, and they scattered over the side of the mesa as the laser-guided missile raced toward them at seven hundred miles per hour.

They took cover in the sagebrush as the paragliders deftly swung the airborne fighting machines away from the river and toward their enemy. The out-of-synch buzzing of the motors was now much louder as Kruger and his men approached rapidly from the east.

Ryan watched with unconcealed terror as the laser dots danced around on the ravine floor, snaking and hopping over the sandstone boulders as they closed in on them. "This is not good," he mumbled, but no one else heard.

The red dots were closer now, flicking like fire through the canopies of the jujube trees and canary grass a few yards from their defensive position.

Ten meters to his right, he watched Scarlet Sloane take a calm, measured aim with her gun, and then there was a puff of smoke and a cracking sound. A second later one of the airborne goons was dead, slumped forward in his harness and his Pike tumbling out of his hands. It landed on the rocky slope with a metallic smack, followed a moment later by a handful of the small missiles.

"I've got to get that bastard weapon," he heard Scarlet say.

"Why?" he called out to her. "Is it more effective or something?"

"Without a doubt," she called back. "But I just want to play with it."

And with that she was gone, kicking up dust as she scrambled through the juniper and esparto grass on her way to the weapon. Above her, the dead man in the paraglider was spinning around out of control as he lost altitude.

He raced toward the slope, his corpse still slumped in the harness, and rammed into the side of the canyon at speed. A terrible crunching sound echoed down the canyon as the paraglider dropped from the sky and smashed into the river's rocky shore a hundred feet below.

Not fifty yards west, Scarlet was snatching up the weapon and turning to get back to cover. Camacho was firing with his pistol to keep the paragliders busy, but it wasn't enough, and now Scarlet was running with all her might as several little red dots chased her along the rocky shore.

Another goon fired, and a Pike rocket raced toward the former SAS woman faster than the speed of sound.

"Hurry up!" screamed Maria.

"Show us what you're made of!" Camacho yelled.

"She's made of vodka and bullets," Ryan called back, shaking his in disbelief at the indescribable act of courage he was witnessing as Scarlet leaped into the air. She dived for the cover of a juniper pine just as the rocket slammed into the ground at her feet and exploded.

The force of the explosion propelled her through the hot, desert air and she crashed into a clump of acacia before cursing loudly and rolling into the cover of an almond tree a few yards away. A cloud of gritty dust blasted up into the hot Moroccan air and the desert breeze whirled it all around her. "Is that all you've got?" she screamed as she loaded the Pike and aimed it at the man who had shot at her. "Pathetic!"

She fired the laser-guided missile at the man and grinned as he struggled to manoeuvre the paraglider out of the way. Below in her defensive position, Scarlet Sloane casually kept the laser dot on his body as he twisted and turned in the harness in a desperate attempt to shake it off.

"What's the matter?" she screamed up at him. "Want to cancel our date already?"

The man fumbled to unstrap himself from the harness, the idea presumably being to drop into the river which he could use for some kind of cover, but he couldn't extricate himself from the harness anywhere quick enough, and a split second later the rocket blasted through him and detonated. The man, the paramotor and the rig above him were consumed by an enormous white-hot fireball and plummeted down through the blue sky into the river like a dead bird.

When the others saw Scarlet had secured one of the Pikes, they knew their advantage was gone, and quickly turned in the sky. They gained altitude and seconds later disappeared over the ridge line of the canyon high above. Scarlet and everyone else knew it would take half an hour to hike to the ridge, and accepted the enemy had gotten away.

She didn't have much time to think about it because as soon as she got up from her cover and began dusting herself down Camacho noticed a beleaguered Joe Hawke and the others from the team marching in their direction along the south bank of the Dadès River.

"What the hell happened to you?" Ryan asked.

"You'll never guess," Lea said.

Ryan smiled. "Um – you were shot at by a bunch of psychopaths in paragliders holding laser-guided missiles?"

"Don't tell me..." Hawke began.

"All right, we won't," Scarlet replied curtly. "We need to get out of here anyway, so there's no time."

"You mean you don't want to brag about how you saved all our asses just now?" Camacho said, giving Scarlet a tight shoulder-squeeze.

"Perhaps later," the Englishwoman said coolly. "When you're all paying attention."

Hawke rolled his eyes. He didn't need to be told what had happened – he already knew just by knowing Cairo Sloane. They had obviously come under attack by the same men who had fired at them in the river, and Cairo had gone above and beyond to fight them off and save the day. It was a habit of hers and he was glad she was on his side.

"So if we need to get out of here in a hurry," Lea said. "Where are we going?"

"No idea, darling," Scarlet said. "The *boy* here and Alex are nerding their way through various ancient clues and think it might be something to do with the Pillars of Hercules. I think not letting Kruger slip the net might have been a better..." without warning she stopped talking and pulled her gun, firing a shot into the gravel between Ryan's legs. A cloud of rock dust flew into the air and Ryan nearly jumped out of his skin.

"What the fuck was that for, you nutter?" he yelled.

"Cobra, *boy* – about to crawl up your trousers and bite your nuts."

He spun around and searched for the offending creature. "You're kidding?"

"No, I'm not kidding. I shot him to spare him the disappointment of what he might find."

"Oh, *very* drole," Ryan replied.

"I have a sneaking admiration for snakes you see, and I think letting him endure the inside of your trousers only to discover the contents of your Y-fronts would constitute animal cruelty."

They all fell about laughing, including after a few seconds even Ryan, and turned to march back up the track on their way to the chopper. Back on board the mood soon sobered when they realized they were once again well behind Dirk Kruger and had only the vaguest reference to the Pillars of Hercules to point them on their way. Alex had contacted them again to explain there was no runway where they were headed so they decided to take the chopper north. As they flew away from the canyon, Hawke's mind began to focus on how he was going to end Kruger's quest for Atlantis if their luck didn't change.

*

It looked like some early snow was more than likely judging by the look of that sky, and the wind had already started to strip a lot of the leaves off the ash trees outside Davis Faulkner's office in Langley, Virginia. Such was life, he considered mildly. A circle, from birth to death to rebirth. It went around and around treating some a lot better than others. But idle metaphysical speculation would have to wait because he had his orders.

He had thought carefully about the Oracle's words since their last conversation, and he knew his loyalty was being weighed for quality like gold with an unknown provenance. He couldn't let the Oracle down. It simply wasn't done, but then he had sworn loyalty to something else – what was it called now? Ah yes, he remembered – the United States of America.

It was impossible to divide loyalty. That was obvious and the truth was any indecision he felt was his conscience playing tricks on him. He knew where his heart belonged and it was with the greater force. His work as Director of the CIA was child's play compared with the Oracle's divine vocation. In his mind there was no question about who he served.

He snatched the cell phone off his desk and spun around in his leather swivel chair as he waited for the other end to pick up.

"Yes, sir?"

Faulkner smiled. This particular number was only ever called by him so there was no need to waste time with introductions and how-d'ya-dos. He lit his cigar and blew a vast cloud of silvery smoke into the confines of his plush corner office. "Agent Kelly I have some wetwork to put your way."

"Yes, sir."

"I need a small package put together in the Caribbean."

"Yes, sir."

"We're looking at maybe a couple of Apaches and a small ground force of, say, a dozen specialists. It's a covert invasion of a small private island down there. Called Elysium. Leave the infrastructure if possible but kill anyone and everyone you see. I'll send more details later but start putting it together right now."

"Yes, sir."

Davis Faulkner hung up and recalled one of Aesop's fables that his mother used to read to him when he was a child. The Fisherman used to play his pipes by the water to catch the fish, but none appeared. One day he threw his net into the water and hauled it to shore full of fish, and then he played his pipes again. This time they danced and hopped in the net. Faulkner knew that he was dancing to the Oracle's tune, but the promise he held in his hand was irresistible.

He glanced outside as he slipped his phone in his pocket. Yes, certainly snow was a possibility.

CHAPTER TWENTY-EIGHT

They crossed the High Atlas Range and flew over the sunflower and tobacco crops in the agricultural lands in the north of the country. The Eurocopter approached the town of Chefchaouen form the south and Lea almost gasped when she saw the setting sun lighting up the dazzling azure walls of the town below them. She saw at once why the world called this bewitching place the Blue Pearl.

"I've never seen anything like it in my life," she said to herself.

Hawke turned to her. "What was that?"

"I said I've never seen anything like this. It's incredible."

No one disagreed as they watched the late sunlight illuminating the walls, houses and shops of Chefchaouen – all painted in bright, neon blue, and nestling in the safety of the breathtaking Rif Mountains.

They touched down and made their way north into the town. Khatibi's house was in the Souika District, and it was only thanks to Ryan's basic grasp of Arabic that they were able to follow the road signs pointing to their destination.

As they cruised through streets still busy with traders and tourists, Lea noticed handfuls of locals standing here and there, chatting and smoking and the occasional man walking along in a djellaba – a long robe with a pointed hood.

"Look like they're out of Star Wars," she said.

"Eh?" Hawke said.

"Those guys."

"Or maybe," Ryan said, "Star Wars looks like it's out of here?"

As they made their way deeper into the town and cruised past the Medina, Hawke cursed. Heavy rains in the last few days had caused some subsidence on many of the local roads and he struggled here and there when the sealed top crumbled under the weight of their vehicle.

Lexi sighed and ran her hands through her hair. She wasn't sure where home was any more, but she knew she was far away from it.

"Problem?" Scarlet asked.

"Blue is all they have…"

"It's bloody amazing!"

Lexi sighed a second time. "On the way here I was reading about El Badi Palace in Marrakech."

"And that is..?"

Ryan interrupted. "A highly impressive ruined palace ordered by the Sultan Ahmad al-Mansur in the late 1570s. Today it's one of the country's most popular tourist attractions, drawing thousands of visitors each year, all coming to see what was once a luxurious palace, built of gold, onyx, cedar wood and ivory."

"I can answer for myself, Ryan," Lexi said with a scowl.

"And your point is?" Lea asked.

"All we get is blue."

"Well why don't you ask Mr Khatibi why he doesn't live in Marrakech?"

"I might."

"This place is supposed to be amazing for *kif*," Ryan said, peering inquisitively through the car windows as if in search of something.

"What's that?" Camacho asked.

"A very finely chopped local cannabis. This place is pretty much the cannabis production capital of the entire country."

"So what?"

"So, if you see anyone selling the stuff, give me a bell."

An eye roll from Lea. "Ryan – over there by the crossroads."

"What?"

"There's a big shop with DOPE written over it. I think you should go in there."

"Very drole," he said as they reached their destination. Khatibi's house was on a steep road which approached the eastern limits of the town and gave an impressive view of the mountains beyond.

"Right," Hawke said, switching off the ignition and checking the mirrors. "We're here, and from the looks of things we're the only ones as well. Let's go."

"Oh God – he's not going to be wearing a fez, is he?" Scarlet said.

"Why the hell would he be wearing a fez?" Ryan said, aghast.

"I just had an image of him wearing a fez."

"Isn't that Turkey?" Lea said.

"No, it's Egypt, isn't it?" Camacho said.

"Your ignorance is actually frightening," Ryan said. "Tell me, Cairo. When you used your tiny mind to conjure that image of Khatibi wearing a fez, did it include a camel and a box of dates?"

"Now don't be *silly*, boy."

"And it's called a tarboosh in Morocco," Ryan said wearily.

"Well, I'm definitely not going up if he's got a tarbrush on his head," Scarlet said.

Ryan rolled his eyes. "Tar*boosh*, I said, and it was an Ottoman idea that never got this far west."

"I'll go," Lea said. "I'm the only one here who is vaguely sensible."

"Hey!" Hawke said. "What's that supposed to mean?"

She shrugged her shoulders and kissed him on the cheek.

They walked up the steps and knocked on the door. A few moments later it swung to reveal an old man in a badly-fitting linen jacket and dishevelled shirt. He had thin black hair scraped back and set in place with some kind of product that smelled vaguely antiseptic. Lea was dimly aware of Scarlet suppressing a giggle and turning away to face the street. She rolled her eyes and turned to the elderly man. "Dr Khatibi?"

"No, I am his brother."

"Can we speak to him?"

"Who are you and what do you want?" The man's English was excellent, with only the vaguest hint of an accent.

"We need his help with a confidential matter."

"Well you're not going to get it. My brother was arrested last night for fighting over a game of tric trac."

"Backgammon," Ryan told the others.

"Arrested?" Hawke said. "Where is he being held?"

"In the local spa, where do you think? He's in the jail, of course."

Hawke glanced at the others and knew they were already thinking the same thing that he was. "And where is the jail?"

"The Comissariat Police on the Avenue Allal El Fassi... over in El Hafa."

He turned and spoke in Arabic and a moment later a young man appeared in the door. "You're in luck – my son Joumari is going there to visit him. He's not being released until the morning."

The drive through the city to Comissariat Police in the El Hafa District took less than ten minutes, and now the sun had sunk lower and the city was cooling down. Hawke weaved their hired Pajero through the still-busy streets of Chefchaouen, passing various souks and tourists gathering outside restaurants for their evening meal.

They parked up at the south end of the avenue and Hawke studied the perimeter wall of the building from the driver's seat. It wasn't exactly fortified like Fort Knox, but there were several police officers and even a few soldiers milling about the place.

"Right," Hawke said, turning to Joumari. "Whereabouts is Khatibi being held?"

"It was a minor offense, so he's in the cells on the north side of the jail."

"And what's the best way to get there once we're past the main reception?"

Joumari looked shocked. "Wait… *what?*"

"We're breaking him out," Scarlet said. "Do make an effort to keep up."

"But you cannot break him out!"

"Of course we can, and you're going to help."

"I will not."

Lexi sighed and reached into her bag. After a few seconds of mumbling and cursing she pulled out a small bundle of American bills. "Five thousand dollars."

"Five thousand dollars?" he said. "You have to be joking!"

Lexi shook her head and pulled a second bundle of Wolff's money out. "All right, ten thousand but not a penny more."

"No one gets hurt?" Joumari said.

The ECHO team exchanged a quick glance but Scarlet was next to speak. "Of course not."

Joumari's eyes widened as he stuffed the money into his pockets. "The best way is along the western edge of the inner yard, and then up to the second floor. But you will still have to deal with the guards stationed on the corner of his cell block."

"Just leave that to us," Hawke said taking one last look at the building.

"What about guns?" Lea asked.

Hawke shook his head. "We won't get past all those soldiers and police with guns. They'll have the place on a lockdown in seconds. We go in unarmed and tool up on the other side. All right, let's party."

Hawke, Reaper and Joumari left the Pajero and stepped out into the street. The Englishman waved a fly off his lip as he made his way across the narrow side road, flanked by Reaper on one side and Joumari on the other.

Joumari spoke next. "When we get inside, the reception will be to our left through a door. Let me do the talking and I should be able to get all of us through without any trouble. I think that Mansouri and Tazi are on shift. They should be no problem."

They crossed the road and stepped into the main entrance. A moment later Joumari sighed.

"What's the problem?" Hawke asked.

"The good news there seems to be only one man on reception."

"And the bad news?"

"The bad news is that it's neither Mansouri or Tazi. It's Hajji."

"And that's a problem why?"

"We don't get on and he never breaks the rules."

"Then we'll have to make some new rules," Hawke said. "Let's go."

Hajji turned out to be everything Joumari promised and ten percent more. He was the kind of annoying little box ticker Hawke couldn't stand, and as Joumari bartered and pleaded with him to let the two foreigners into the jail, Hawke and Reaper shared a glance of concern as what little time they had slipped away.

Reaper moved first, nudging Joumari out the way and speaking to Hajji in French, the old colonial language of the country.

Hawke watched as his friend pretended not to hear something and ask him to come closer. Hajji leaned toward the screen and raised his voice, but it was too late.

CHAPTER TWENTY-NINE

Reaper thrust his arm though the aperture at the bottom of the screen where documentation normally changed hands, and grabbed Hajji by his necktie, pulling him forward hard until his face smashed into the acrylic screen giving them a terrible technicolour view as his lips split open and his nose broke. Reaper repeated the exercise a second time and knocked the man out, then he released him and he slumped back into his soft chair.

"Eh bien, what now?"

Joumari looked at the unconscious body of his colleague and winced. "He had that coming," he said, darting around the other side of the reception and taking Hajji's keys. "And the armoury is this way, follow me."

They followed their Moroccan guide along a grimy corridor before turning a corner and finding themselves standing before a chunky iron door. Joumari pulled the keychain from his pocket and opened the door to reveal a small room which smelled vaguely of gun oil and tobacco. The armoury was where the prison secured rifles in the event of a major riot in the prison.

They moved into the room and Reaper kept watch as Joumari unlocked one of the gun cabinets. By the time the Moroccan was unlocking the ammunition container Hawke had already selected three rifles and checked them over but when they stepped back out into the corridor two large guards were waiting for them.

Hawke moved first, pushing Joumari back into the armoury and powering a meaty punch into the first guard's face. He felt the nose give way under the force of the strike and a squelchy crunching noise confirmed it a split second later. The guard staggered backwards and gasped for air as the blood from his broken nose poured down over his top lip and into his mouth.

A few yards to his left, the former French legionnaire was bringing a heavy steel toecap boot up into the second guard's groin. He howled and doubled over, just in time for his face to meet with Reaper's right hand, now tightened into a heavy and dangerous fist.

Hawke's man had gathered his thoughts and after regaining his balance he padded over to the Englishman with one thing on his mind, and this time drew his service pistol to underline the matter.

Hawke saw it coming and charged into the fray, disarming the man with a savagely fast and violent twist of his wrist. The man screamed as his wrist broke and dropped the gun to the floor, but Hawke wasn't dropping down a gear until his opponent was out for the count. With no chance for the man to fight properly with a broken wrist, Hawke knew his opponent was a wounded bird, and decided to be merciful. He smashed a high-velocity hook punch into his right jaw and cracked his head back against his neck, knocking him out instantly.

Reaper was now heavily engaged with his own battle, powering a vicious salvo of punches into the smaller man's stomach and winding him harshly. The man gasped and panicked as he strained to get air into his lungs but Reaper was relentless with the punches.

Hawke made a big show of leaning against the wall and checking his watch. "Going to be much long, Vincent?"

Reaper ignored it, spitting some blood on the floor and then smashing a brutal shovel hook into the nerves behind the man's right ear. He dropped unconscious to the floor a heartbeat later.

"You finally took him out," Hawke said with a grin.

"I like to fight with a flourish," Reaper said, dusting off his hands and wiping the blood from his mouth. "I spar with finesse... you belt things."

Hawke clapped him on the shoulder and laughed as they went back inside the armoury.

"What happened?" Joumari said, poking a nervous face outside the door and seeing the two unconscious guards.

"We had a small disagreement about visiting times," Hawke said.

Freshly armed, they moved through the shadows until they reached the custody area. When the three men approached Khatibi's cell and pulled the keys out the other prisoners began to roar and whoop and bang on their cell doors. Despite the location Hawke was surprised by the strong smell of hash in the cell block, and moved fast to unlock Khatibi's door.

Hawke peered inside and saw a short man with perfectly combed hair and an expensive jacket. A pair of tortoiseshell glasses perched on an aquiline nose and concealed two dark brown eyes. "Who are..."

Before the sentence had left his lips, Hawke and Reaper burst in and grabbed Khatibi giving him no chance to respond or even talk. Both men had trained for extractions like this and both of them had done it more than once for real so it took seconds to drag him down the corridor and through the reception area.

As they burst into the street a number of soldiers had positioned themselves on the roof of the police station and were putting some heavy assault rifle fire on the Pajero.

Hawke was surprised by the speed of their reaction and knew there was no way they could cross the street and get to the Pajero without getting turned to Swiss cheese by those rifles. He made a split-second decision and yelled at Lexi to get away and a second later the Pajero was skidding along the avenue. He breathed a sigh of relief as it turned a heavy left and got out of range of the snipers.

But he was still exposed and so was Reaper and Khatibi.

"What now?" Reaper said.

"This way!"

Hawke and the Frenchman grabbed Khatibi's arms and hauled him up a flight of steps which led into a small garden area to the south of the police station. "This place is like a rabbit warren," he said. "We'll lose them in here and coordinate with Lea to rendezvous with the car."

"Who *are* you?" said the old man, in a panic. "What do you want?"

"Relax, Professor Khatibi," Hawke said, grunting as he pounded up the steep, blue steps. "We want to talk to you about Atlantis."

"About Atlantis?" Khatibi said. "Are you crazy?"

Hawke was considering how to answer this when a chunk of wall twelve inches from his head exploded in a blast of bright blue plaster and sprayed all over him. He turned to see the soldiers were closing fast, able to move much quicker without the extra weight of a hostage.

Reaper pulled the PAMAS from his holster and opened fire on the soldiers. They hit the deck and rolled to the sides of the stone alleyway. "I can't keep them back forever, Joe…"

"What do you mean… *Atlantis?*" Khatibi asked again. "This is nonsense."

"We haven't got time to explain," Hawke said, fixing his eyes on Khatibi. "Will you come with us?"

A second gunshot exploded into the stone steps at their feet and kicked up another cloud of the blue paint and fragments of rock chips.

"We have no time. Do you want to help us find it or not?"

"I..."

Hawke rolled his eyes and pulled his phone from his pocket. A second later the professor gasped when he saw the photos they had taken of the carvings back in the Tomb of Tanit. "Ya Allah! Where did you get this?"

A third shot nicked Khatibi's shoulder and tore his jacket. His eyes widened with horror as he realized he was now a fugitive. "I have little choice."

"In that case run for it!"

The three men sprinted up the stone steps and rounded a corner. To the east a crescent moon was rising above the ghostly blue town.

"So what now?" Reaper asked,

Hawke pulled out his phone again and started to make a call.

"What are you doing?" Khatibi asked nervously.

"Nil desperandum, Dr Khatibi," Hawke said. "Just calling a cab and then we're out of here."

"But we need to get to my house. I need my papers."

Hawke gave him a look and sighed. *What is it with professors and papers?* "Fine," he said. "We'll take the cab to your place."

CHAPTER THIRTY

They coordinated with Lea as they sprinted through the twists, turns and winding steps of the Blue Pearl, always one step ahead of the local police and soldiers. Turning a corner in the moonlight, they found themselves at the top of a fight of stone steps, and waiting at the bottom for them was their ride.

"There!" Hawke yelled.

They sprinted down the steps, dodging the bullets from their pursuers who were now barking orders into radios.

"Get in!" Hawke said to Khatibi.

"But can I really trust…"

Before he could finish his sentence they were bundling him into the back of the Pajero. It was a tight squeeze inside but Scarlet had improvised by ordering Ryan into the trunk space at the back. Now Lexi hit the gas leaving the local police with nothing but a shower of grit in their faces and a cloud of diesel fumes drifting slowly up into the twilight sky.

"I enjoyed that!" Hawke said. "Last time I did anything like that was when we got a journalist away from the Taliban."

"Enjoyed it?" Scarlet said. "It was a total pig's breakfast."

"All right," he conceded with a mischievous grin. "It wasn't the best exfiltration."

"You can say that again," Lexi said, glancing in her mirror. "Where are we going?"

"To hell in a handbasket," Scarlet said.

Hawke gave her a look. "To Professor Khatibi's place. He needs his notes."

"Ah… *notes*," Ryan said, tapping his temple with his forefinger. "All my notes are up here."

"Like all your friends, you mean?"

"I do not have imaginary friends!"

Khatibi huffed. "Who *are* you people?"

Lea showed him her ID, issued by Eden.

"You know Richard Eden?" he said.

"Yes," Lea said. "We're all on the same side here."

"All right," Khatibi said, beginning to relax. "Where did you get the pictures I saw on this man's phone?" He gestured to Hawke.

"In Tanit's tomb," Ryan said nonchalantly.

"Tanit's *tomb*?" Khatibi replied. "Is this some kind of joke?"

"No joke," Scarlet said, fishing a crumpled packet from her pocket and jamming a bent cigarette in her lip. "True story."

Khatibi looked at them like they were insane. "Tanit was a goddess…a mythological figure! You are clearly deranged."

Lea held up her phone and showed him more photos of the symbols Ryan had taken in the Atlas Mountains. Khatibi leaned in closer, a look of interest growing on his face. "Where did you take this photograph?"

"Same place as the others, Doc," Hawke said. "The Dadès Gorge."

"You mean the Dadès Gorge in the Atlas Mountains here in Morocco?"

"Yes," Lea said. "We found the tomb of Tanit there but it was looted by a man named Dirk Kruger."

Khatibi's face fell. "Dirk Kruger? I hate that man!"

"Join the club. We think he stole some kind of key, and there was an inscription in the tomb that referred to the Pillars of Hercules, but beyond that we need your help."

"Are you with us?" Hawke asked.

"Yes but I still need my notes!"

As he spoke, Lexi skidded to a halt outside his house and seconds later they were filing inside his home.

Khatibi called out for his brother but there was no reply. "We don't have long," he said. "This is the first place they will look for me."

Hawke watched as the professor began fumbling about through piles of disordered papers stacked up all over his front room. Clutter filled every corner – cups of cold mint tea, a damaged backgammon board, two broken television sets, at least half a dozen ashtrays and even an old oud being used as a bookend. Above the desk was a fine-looking scimitar, which Khatibi proudly described as an original Ottoman antique.

"Hurry up, professor!" Lea said, glancing nervously out the window.

"I have them!" he said proudly. "My filing system looks messy I know, but I can find everything when I need to – ah wait."

"What is it?" Hawke said, glancing at his watch.

"These are not the papers we need." He put them back down and resumed his search through the endless piles of junk.

"Bloody hell, you could lose a corpse in here," Scarlet said.

"Aha! At last, I have them." Khatibi waved a thin sheaf of papers in the air victoriously. "We can go."

"Great, let's get out of here," Hawke said.

The professor took a closer look at the papers and shook his head. "No...no – wrong ones. Sorry!"

He crouched down his knees and started going through more stacks under the desk, throwing any unwanted papers out behind him where they drifted back to the floor like giant snowflakes.

"This is ridiculous!" Reaper said.

"This is why you should keep your notes in your head," Ryan said smugly.

"We're not all fucking polymorphs, dweeb," Scarlet said.

"Polymaths, *darling*," Ryan replied. "A polymorph is…"

Scarlet pointed a black fingernail in his face. "Shut up!"

"Got it."

Khatibi finally spoke from beneath the desk. "Now I have them!"

"Are you *very sure*, professor?" Lea said gently.

"Yes, absolutely… yes!" He crawled out backwards, smacking his head on the bottom of the desk as he emerged back into the light. He cursed in Arabic and then stood and faced them. "Here they are. We may go!"

"Too late," Reaper said. "Our friends are here."

The door smashed in and soldiers rushed into the house.

Khatibi looked like he needed to change his trousers and then surrender, but Hawke knew there was no talking your way out of a situation like this. From the authorities' point of view they had broken into a public building, snatched a citizen currently being held in custody and then fired on both policemen and soldiers. It would take months to sort out and those months would be spent split up from each other and in prisons all over the country.

So he exploded into action, and the rest of the team needed no orders to join him, with only Khatibi scuttling away. He hid back under his desk and covered his head with the sheaf of research papers in his shaking hands.

Camacho grabbed the first man, immediately disarming him and punching him in the face, but he was tougher than he looked and fought back hard, improvising by snatching Khatibi's scimitar off the wall and whirling around with the vicious blade to get the feel of it.

Camacho took a step back and searched for a defensive weapon while the man grinned and pushed forward. He slashed the blade through the dusty air of Khatibi's apartment with a metallic *whoosh* sound and almost took off his head, but the American ducked just in time and staggered backwards away from the sword.

The man pounded closer, but Camacho reacted like lightning and smacked the sword out of his hand. He brought his fist up hard into the man's temple and knocked him out cold.

Hawke looked up to see Scarlet struggling with another soldier.

"Any help, Cairo?"

"No, I've got it thanks."

She ducked and spun around striking him off balance with the heel of her boot.

"He's got a hookah pipe, Cairo."

"I know!" she said excitedly. "That's even better than a fez."

"Cairo, correct me if I'm wrong, but aren't you called Cairo because you were born in Cairo?"

She spun around again and knocked the man out with a second axe kick. "True story, Josiah."

"So why the mindless amusement about hookah pipes and fez hats?"

"Just trying to lighten the load and put a smile on your face."

Another soldier burst into the room, and Scarlet snatched up Khatibi's hookah pipe from the unconscious man's grip and rammed into her new opponent's face. The pipe's windguard tore into his cheek and he howled in agony in response to the wound before knocking the pipe to the floor.

Scarlet snatched the pipe back up. "Don't you ever break my hookah pipe," she said, and gripped the pipe by the water jar as she swung it at the man's head. The hose flicked out like a whip and lashed his eyes, causing him to stumble backward and grunt in pain as he reached up and rubbed his eyes with his hands.

She struck again. It came to a sudden stop when the pipe's plate smashed the bridge of his nose. With the bone and septal cartilage now crushed down into his nasal cavity, the man's instinct was to take a step back and reach up to his face with his hands.

As he desperately tried to measure the damage done, Camacho stormed forward, grabbed a heavy marquetry chair and brought it down on the soldier's head, wincing as the back of the chair smashed to pieces. The man dropped down to the floor, almost out for the count and covered in a shower of mother-of-pearl inlay that had popped out of the teak panel with the force of the blow.

He groaned and tried to get up, but Scarlet seized the day and brought the pipe down on his head. The heavy glass water jar at the base of the hookah shattered on contact with the man's skull and he went down like a bag of lead weights.

"Turns out all he needed was a good hookah," Scarlet said.

"I like your style," Camacho said, and winked at her. "*Babe.*"

Hawke was wrestling with another soldier now who was approaching fast with his gun raised. A yard from Hawke he suddenly toppled over to reveal the winking face of Lexi Zhang standing behind him. She was holding Khatibi's lampshade, and had used the chrome tube like a kendo shinai sword to belt the soldier around the back of his head and knock him unconscious.

"Thanks, I owe you."

"Yes… you do," she said and fled into the hall to take down another of the men. A second later she was making short work of the last man in the hall, essentially using his face to practice some Kung Fu hook kicks she had been learning. The man looked like he'd rather fight a starving lion, but there was no escaping the wrath of Agent Dragonfly tonight as she knocked him out of the hall and through the kitchen. Another kick sent him tumbling out into the rear courtyard. He tried to get up but the blows were relentless.

The final strike sent him stumbling backwards until he tripped over the small wall running around Khatibi's fountain and he went arse-over-backwards into the water, cracking the back of his head on the flow control cap. He collapsed and the blood from his wound spilled into the bubbling water, turning the zellige tilework from terracotta to crimson. Outside, the local muezzin was reciting the *adhan*, and the Islamic call to prayer now mixed with the noise of the chaotic scene inside Khatibi's apartment.

"I hate that these guys can't last *longer*," Lexi whined to Ryan.

"Said the actress to the bench of bishops," he replied.

"Don't overdo it," Scarlet called out from across the room.

"Sorry."

A quiet voice squeaked from under the desk. "Is it over?" It was Khatibi.

"Yes, and thanks for the help," Scarlet said. During the fight the overhead light had gotten knocked and was now swinging back and forth creating crazy moving shadows over the cluttered room.

"Ah, you're welcome!" he said. "Because while you were brawling like thugs I found what we'll need when we get to the Pillars of Hercules." He pushed his head out from behind the safety of the desk and looked up at them, blinking at the swaying light bulb. "Shall we?"

CHAPTER THIRTY-ONE

The Eurocopter's powerful Turboméca Arriel's turboshaft powerplant was cruising them high above the Moroccan clouds. They reflected the bright light of the crescent moon back up to the chopper, almost as bright as day. Everyone was tired, and most were sleeping, but Hawke, Lea, Ryan and Maria were awake and counting the minutes down until their arrival at Jebel Musa, the Mount of Moses.

The Pillars of Hercules was the ancient name given to the two elevations either side of the Straits of Gibraltar – the Rock of Gibraltar to the north and Jebel Musa to the south. Some had argued that the southern pillar was Monte Hacho in Ceuta, a Spanish city in Africa which bordered Morocco. Khatibi had spent his life studying the region and was certain the southern pillar was Jebel Musa.

On the flight, Khatibi and Ryan and used the professor's research to work out the inscription was also indicating some kind of temple, and given Jebel Musa was on the tourist trail, that meant it had to be underground.

"So we're definitely looking for an entrance inside the mountain," Khatibi repeated.

Scarlet cupped her hands on the glass so she could see below and peered dismissively out the chopper's window. "So that pointy little mountain is the southern Pillar of Hercules?"

Khatibi nodded. "Yes."

"Not more bloody potholing," was all she said, and then she leaned back in her seat and closed her eyes again.

Lea looked at the twin peaks far below them. "So what's the skinny on old Heracles, Ry. Why did het get these named after him?"

"During his Twelve Labours, this was the furthest west he got... simple. Back in those days, if you were Greek, then this was pretty much the end of the world. It was the tenth challenge, when he had to collect the Cattle of Geryon."

"Now he's talking about cows," Scarlet said. "Heaven help us."

"Let him finish, Cairo," Maria snapped.

Camacho stepped in. "Just everyone calm down. Ryan – please."

"I'm not talking about cows *per se*, but Hercules's mission to cross the Libyan desert to fetch them. It was one of his twelve labours. There are several references made by writers such as Pindar or Strabo that refer to the limits of his journey in the far west as being marked by the Pillars of Hercules, and Plato even goes so far to state that it is beyond these pillars that Atlantis is to be found."

"People think of these legends as all taking place in ancient Greece but this is not always the case," Khatibi said from nowhere. "We have the Pillars of Hercules and part of the Atlas Mountains right here in Morocco, for example."

Ryan nodded in agreement. "According to the myths, there's a famous legend detailing a meeting between Atlas and Heracles, so we know they met at least once. As you know, Heracles was made to perform twelve labours as a punishment for killing his family."

"Which on reflection seems fair enough," Lexi said.

"Oh, sorry," Scarlet said. "Is that you being funny or were you making a serious point?"

"Drop dead."

"Kapow!" Ryan said, giggling.

Scarlet looked at him. "Really?"

"Sorry. Anyway, so off he goes on his twelve labours and one of them just happens to be getting hold of some golden apples."

"As in the golden apples of Valhalla fame?" Lea said. He nodded.

"All this shit is coming together," Scarlet said, lighting a cigarette. "I just wish I cared."

Ryan shook his head at her and continued. "So these particular golden apples belonged to Hera, Zeus's wife and sister."

"The plot thickens," Lexi said. "Wait – what? His wife *and* sister?"

"I'm afraid so, yes, and if that's not scary enough, the garden was also guarded by Ladon, a sort of cross between a serpent and a dragon. Definitely not fuckaroundable with, if you get my drift. The constellation Draco is supposed to be Ladon."

"We finally reach your millionth factoid," Scarlet said.

"Anyway," Ryan said, ignoring her, "old Ladon was guarding the Garden of the Hesperides, and…"

Lea looked at Ryan, confused. "Wait – who?"

"The Hesperides – the famous evening nymphs."

"Oh, *I* remember."

"Great. So the thing is Heracles was reluctant to go and fight Ladon for the golden apples so he went and asked Atlas if he would do it for him."

"As you would."

"Except Atlas was busy holding the entire world on his shoulders."

"Sorry to interrupt," Scarlet said, "but are we still working on the premise that all of this shit really happened, or not? It's just that the whole planet being held up by one chap is pushing even my broad mind."

"It *might* be metaphorical," he said bluntly. "So Heracles made a deal with Atlas that involved him holding up the world while Atlas got the apples, the only problem being that when Atlas returned with the apples, he offered to finish the task himself, and Heracles got the impression he was trying to fool him into carrying the world forever."

"So what happened?"

"Heracles got sneaky and told Atlas he accepted the offer, but that first he wanted to rearrange his cloak, so he asked Atlas to hold the world for just a second."

"And then what?"

"Then Heracles took the apples and ran away, of course."

"This is riveting – it really is, *boy* – but is it going anywhere?"

"Maybe – some of these symbols seem to refer to the golden apples."

"So we're looking for more golden apples?"

"Not at all," Khatibi said. "Golden apples are a metaphor for immortality throughout European folklore."

"So we're searching for more sodding eternity?" Scarlet said.

"We're searching for Atlantis, Cairo," Lea said. "I thought we were all on that page by now."

"And this mysterious temple is down there somewhere?" Maria said.

"Heads up," Hawke said. "We're here and we're not the first ones."

Peering down on the mountain's amazing twin peaks with their night vision they were able to see Dirk Kruger's expedition already set up and a dozen men milling around some pickup trucks.

"Bastard worked it out first," Hawke said.

"He had more to go on," Lea said, trying to soften his frustration and disappointment.

"Not fun being late to the party, though," Camacho said.

Scarlet looked at him, lingering a second too long at his biceps. "You're very good at stating the obvious, darling."

"That's not all I'm good at, babe."

Ryan rolled his eyes. "I'd say get a room but first, I'm not sure there's a hotel room big enough to accommodate your two egos and second, we are somewhat busy at the moment."

Scarlet tickled Ryan's chin with her finger. "Aww – is Baby Ryan jealous?"

"Jealous?" Ryan and Camacho said in unison.

"Oh *please*," Scarlet said, leaning forward to kiss the American.

"Guys," Lea said. "Ry's right. Can we leave the mating ritual till later?"

Scarlet agreed with Lea, but squeezed Camacho's bicep and gave him a wink before pulling her gun out and sliding a round into the chamber. The chopper was descending now.

Camacho smiled back. "This really could be the start of a beautiful relationship."

"Don't count on it," Ryan mumbled. "Scarlet doesn't do beautiful relationships, but she *does* have a good line in rough shags. Just ask the Royal Navy."

"Hey, you little nerdgasm," Scarlet said. "I'll give you a good line in rough shags, all right."

"No thanks, I'm in love with Maria and I couldn't afford the pharmacy bills anyway."

Before Scarlet could respond, Lea pointed to a column of smoke that was now pouring out of a crack in the mountain's southern slope. "Looks like they might have found what they're looking for, guys."

"At least it saves us fucking about in the dark," Scarlet said.

Hawke raised the night vision binoculars to his eyes again and leaned forward. "Hang on a second – what the hell's he got down there?"

"What is it?" Lea asked.

He took a second look and shook his head in disbelief. "He's got a sodding Kaman down there."

Ryan looked over at him in the darkness of the Eurocopter. "Sorry, Dirk Kruger has an alligatorid crocodilian down there?"

Scarlet rolled her eyes. "A *what?*"

"Caiman," Lea said. "That's how Ryan says caiman."

"Why the hell would Kruger have a caiman down there?" Camacho asked.

"Kaman," Hawke said, spelling it out. "Not sodding *caiman.*"

"I thought that was odd," Ryan said.

"What the hell is a Kaman?" Lea asked.

"The Kaman K-MAX is a synchropter. Lockheed Martin's finest autonomous flying technology, right here, right now for your pleasure."

"Sorry – so it's a helicopter?" Ryan said, taking the binoculars and having a look.

"Yes and no," Hawke said. "It's a synchropter, like I just said. It has two intermeshing rotors that give it tremendous lift. It can carry things heavier than itself."

"Why the hell has Kruger got one of these out here?"

Ryan answered. "My guess is he was one step ahead and knew about those rocks blocking the entrance to the vault."

"Eh?"

Ryan passed the binoculars back to Hawke and he saw the Kaman rising into the air down on the side of the mountain. Attached to the four-hook carousel beneath it was an enormous boulder which the Kaman was now lifting away from the rocky slope to reveal an entrance.

"Let's get down there," Hawke said. "By the looks of things we've no time to waste."

They landed and hiked along a goat track until they reached Kruger's camp where they took cover behind some boulders. From here they watched the last of the South African archaeologist's crew disappear inside the mountain.

"Looks like we're on," Hawke said.

They reached the entrance and saw Kruger had rigged up a small generator for light and drills and was already long gone inside the depths of Jebel Musa. They followed the path, reassured by how much they had reduced Kruger's forces but still aware they would be dangerous.

The tunnel took a sharp dive down and they held on to the roughly hewn sides to stop themselves sliding, but then they reached their destination.

The Temple of Hercules.

It was smaller than any of them had expected, and they could easily see Dirk Kruger, Van Zyl, Luk, Kamchatka and Korać at the far end. It looked like the Serbian warlord had replenished his force of goons as well.

"Take a look here," Ryan said, indicating the sides of the tunnel. Either side of them they saw thick stone walls that had retracted back into the sides of the rock and on the floor at their feet they saw the stone column Kruger had taken from the Tomb of Tanit. "This is what he needed the stone key for – to pull back these massive stone walls."

They moved closer to the temple and saw the walls in here were roughly carved out of the mountain's granite, but the floor had been worn smooth over countless centuries of use. Piles of treasure were stacked here and there. Looking closer, Hawke saw that the walls were lined with alcoves each one blocked with a door, and whatever Kruger wanted with them he'd done it, because now he was preparing move out and he had a large smile on his face.

"All right" Kruger barked. "Prepare to move everyone out!"

Across the room Luk and Kamchatka were hauling a trunk out of one of the alcoves and moving it toward the entrance. The South African's eyes glazed with rage when he saw them.

"What are you fools doing?" As he asked, Van Zyl swung his gun over his shoulder and moved out of sight.

"What do you think they're doing?" Korać said, his voice dripping with contempt. "They want to get paid for their trouble. We all do... and maybe there is no Atlantis!"

Kruger was staggered. "No Atlantis? Don't you see it? This temple is where people would stop and pray before travelling across the sea to Atlantis. These symbols are coordinates to Atlantis, you fool! This place proves there was an Atlantis. What do you think I've been doing for the last ten minutes?"

Khatibi and Ryan shared a glance.

"Now!' Kruger said sharply. "Get the bomb rigged and then destroy this whole place!"

"What about the bags of treasure?" Korać said.

"Yes what about that?" said Luk. "Like we said, we still want to get paid for our trouble."

Kruger got up in his face and grabbed him by the collar. "Don't give me any of that crap, domkop! I'm not frightened of you and your little knife. You'll get paid when the job is done."

Kruger released him and pushed him back against the rocky wall and then turned to the others. "Forget the fucking treasure. It's *nothing* compared with what we'll find at Atlantis."

As he spoke, Korać placed a bomb the size of a football inside the furthest alcove and activated it. "We have ten minutes to get well away from here and then it's all nothing but dust."

"Shit," Camacho said. "That looks nasty."

"What do you mean?" Lea asked.

"Not liking the look of that bomb at all," he repeated. "Looks like it might have a motion sensor on it."

"And you look like dead men walking."

They turned to see Van Zyl bearing down on them with a submachine gun. Without alerting Kruger or Korać to their presence, he moved his finger off the guard and swung the gun into Hawke's face.

"Get up, you pigs."

Hawke and the others slowly got to their feet and raised their hands in the air.

"Look what I found!" Van Zyl called out.

Kruger looked over and sneered at them. "Got you bastards at last... wait – is that you, Maati?"

Khatibi looked at his boots for a moment before raising his head. "Yes, Dirk."

"What are you doing with these people?"

"Richard and I are trying to stop you from desecrating this temple!"

"Richard – you don't mean Richard Eden?"

Khatibi nodded and Lea stepped forward. "We work for Richard Eden, and he's told us all about you. We're not going to let you destroy this place and we're certainly not going to let you plunder Atlantis."

Kruger laughed. "I've heard everything now. You bastards work for Dickie Eden! Jesus Christ." He turned back to the alcoves and then spoke over his shoulder. "Willem – take Mr Khatibi out to the trucks and make sure he's secured. Mr Korać – keep the rest of these bastards under guard while I finish up."

Van Zyl removed Khatibi while Korać approached Hawke.

But he got too close, and the Englishman reacted in an explosion of defensive moves, throwing a handful of grit into Korać's face and grabbing the muzzle of the weapon simultaneously. The gun went off, firing the rounds into the floor of the temple and spitting up clouds of dust and rock chips.

Lea screamed and Ryan brought his hands up to cover his ears as Van Zyl slipped away and took cover.

Kruger spun around and his eyes darted over to the fracas at the entrance to the temple. He pointed at them haughtily. "Kill them!"

Then a fire fight exploded all around them with both sides taking cover as they fired on each other for control of the temple.

"I need another clip!" Ryan shouted.

"Here," Camacho said and threw one over. "And it's a magazine, son. No one's used clips for about seventy years."

With limited rounds the gunfight was over in minutes, and that meant only one thing. A number of Korać's men rushed them and things broke down into a hand-to-hand combat situation. Judging by the tattoo on his

218

shoulder which read СПЕЦНАЗ, Hawke's opponent was a former Spetsnaz soldier. Russian Special Forces were trained well and fiercely aggressive, but Hawke was former SBS and that meant he had the edge and he knew it.

The man kicked things off by pulling a ballistic knife from his belt and lunging forward at Hawke's face. The Englishman pulled his head back and simultaneously brought up his left arm to block the knife from coming any further. He disarmed the man with one hand and thrust a punch upwards into his jaw. The man fell backwards and struck his head on the wall.

All across the cavern the fighting was intense. Maria Kurikova blocked her opponent's onslaught and immediately brought up a counter-strike into the base of his jaw. The man moved back to dodge her attack, so her punch landed in his windpipe. His eyes widened in shock as he realized he couldn't breath and it gave the Russian spy the only chance she needed. She brought her right boot up hard and fast into his balls and his instinct sent him doubling over, just as she knew it would. She brought her left knee up into his face and knocked him out cold.

Scarlet was fighting hard closer to the entrance, bringing her knee-length boot up to her opponent's groin and showing less mercy than Vlad the Impaler. He collapsed to the floor in a howling mess, dropping his guard long enough for the former SAS woman to send him off to sleep with a speedy palm strike.

"I *cannot* believe you crushed his giggleberries like that," Ryan said. "It's just not right."

"Anything goes when you're over a barrel," she said.

"Said the archdeacon to the understudy," Ryan replied.

"Reasonably amusing for you, but don't think it makes you funny. You're not."

"Gotcha."

A second man stormed over to Hawke and drew back a knife ready to attack. Hawke stumbled over an unconscious man and fell on his back. The man seized the advantage and jumped on him, raising the knife. Hawke strained against the man's arm as he plunged the knife down and inched the tip of the blade closer to his eye. He grunted with the effort of stopping the knife from plunging into his eye, and he felt the blood pound in his ears as he pushed himself to the max to fight off the heavier man.

With the blade now less than an inch from his eye, and above it the grinning, sweating face of the Serbian merc as he mocked him, Hawke was starting to think he was in trouble, when suddenly a startled, frozen look of surprise flashed on the Serb's face and he released the knife before collapsing in a heap on the floor beside the Englishman.

The man rolled off him to reveal Lexi standing behind him, this time holding not a lampshade but a fist-sized rock.

"Thanks. I owe you."

"You know how you can pay me back."

Hawke gave her a look, rolled over and leapt to his feet. "Give it a rest, Lexi."

"You can't blame a girl for trying."

Hawke looked up to see Kruger and Korać fleeing from the cave. They had what they wanted and were evacuating as fast as they could.

"He's getting away!" he yelled, his mind racing. He ran over to the alcove and saw the bomb now had less than seven minutes. "Jack – try and get this bomb defused and save this place if you can. Ryan – work out what Kruger was up to if possible and then everyone get the hell out of here. I'm going after that son of a bitch."

"And I'm right there wit' ya!" Lea said.

CHAPTER THIRTY-TWO

Alex Reeve was taking a break in the Elysium headquarters building. With Hawke and the others damn near getting themselves killed like a bunch of amateurs on the Dadès River, Kruger slipping the net once again with his hired thugs and her father's first televised presidential debate coming up in just a few hours she could feel the pressure rising. One glance down at her wheelchair sealed the deal and she pulled a Coke from the fridge and rolled herself out into the tropical breeze for some important Time Out.

The Coke was bad which is why it tasted good, and she took a long drink before setting the can down on the low wall which separated the compound's north lawn from the beach. To say she had fallen in love with this place was an understatement but she could already feel the long, cold shadow of Washington DC approaching her.

She could be accused of many things but naivety wasn't one of them. She knew what fate awaited the immediate family of a President of the United States and it wasn't good. The United States Secret Service was charged with protecting the First Family and there was a persistent fear among them of something happening to a member of the President's family.

The Constitution was amazingly prescient in its content, and there was provision built into it in case of a crisis. That provision was the Twenty-Fifth Amendment, used several times in the past, including the succession of Gerald Ford to the Presidency after Nixon's resignation and the appointment of Nelson Rockefeller to the Vice Presidency, both in 1974. Most recently, and dramatically it was invoked after President Grant was kidnapped by the madman Klaus Kiefel on his rampage across America during the Medusa attacks. That had put the traitor Teddy Kimble in the Oval Office.

The concern was if any of the President's close family were kidnapped they could be used as leverage to blackmail the Commander-in-Chief, and that was why the Twenty-Fifth was necessary. But the fear of an attack against the President's family never went away, and that meant a big change was coming in her life if her father won the race to the White House.

She knew they would demand her return to the United States and when there put her under the protection of a USSS detail and she dreaded it. Sure, she could refuse – but what if something happened to her. She didn't exactly lead the life of a shrinking violet, wheelchair or not. She didn't want to be responsible for annihilating her father's entire career and endangering the vital national security of her country to make a point and settle an old grudge against her dad.

But it would be hell. When Chelsea Clinton was at Stanford she was trailed around everywhere by a Secret Service detail dressed casually but always carrying handguns under their shirts, and always within sight of her. They wouldn't be much use anywhere else, she thought glumly. They also had her dorm windows replaced with bulletproof glass and had her carry a panic alarm. Imagine that, she thought – having two or three strangers following you from room to room for eight years.

Despite her doubts, part of her wondered if she had spent long enough with the ECHO team, hidden away on Elysium. Not that she had ever told anyone this, but her presence on the island base wasn't entirely altruistic. The truth was she had felt something for Joe Hawke since the day she had saved his life back in Serbia, and when he had walked back into her life during the Poseidon adventure, she had begun to harbor secret thoughts about the two of them getting together. It was innocent enough, she told herself, but she knew it was unlikely. First, she was back in the wheelchair after the elixir had given her a newfound freedom, and while she had no idea what Hawke felt about that, she knew his lifestyle was as fast and hard as they came. Would he give that up for her now? The other problem was Lea.

She like Lea a lot and counted her as one of her closest friends. They had been through so much together that she could hardly bring herself even to think about betraying her so badly. It was here where the conflict between her head and her heart raged like a wildfire. Could she sacrifice her friendship with Lea for a relationship with Joe Hawke? She wasn't even sure if the Englishman had ever had any feelings about her. During the only time they had spent together in her father's mountain cabin she had been too nervous to bring the subject up, and then the Medusa disaster kicked off and she had missed her chance.

She thought no, in which case, maybe being here on the island was just causing her too much pain. Maybe she could use a fresh start, and just maybe... renewing the relationship with her father might be the answer. It felt like the hand of fate was intervening in her life once again, and who was she to fight it? It was all so confusing, and the time to make a decision was racing upon her. The presidential election was almost here, and her father was the favorite to win. She sighed and closed her eyes for a few moments. Somewhere deep inside her, a voice from her younger days told her life wasn't supposed to be this complicated.

She opened her eyes and raised the can to her lips, taking another sip of the Coke. She winced as she swallowed it and set the can back down. The Caribbean sun had worked its magic on the drink and it was already too warm to enjoy.

And that was when she saw them

In the sky were several black smudges. Obviously aircraft, she thought. She focussed on them and saw the sun flash on their bodies as they began vectoring toward Elysium.

What the hell? she thought.

She had never seen anything like this before in all her time on the island. The occasional tourist plane that went off course, sure, but Eden had various arrangements with local ATC that Elysium was a no-fly zone except for his small fleet of Gulfstreams and that was respected.

Worse than that, she now saw they were helicopters. Black Helicopters. That meant military – she counted three of them now closing fast on the private island. As they approached she saw they were Boeing AH-64s, and behind them at a safe distance what looked like a Sikorsky Black Hawk.

"Why the hell are three Apaches making a low pass over this island?"

She felt her stomach turn and spun around in the wheelchair.

She began pushing the wheels forward as fast as she could, the hot rubber burning her hands with the sunlight and friction and she powered herself forward as fast as she could go.

Now the sound of their dual GE T700 Turboshaft engines was reverberating ominously around the area, bouncing off the surface of the sea and the mountains rising grandly above the compound.

She wanted to warn Eden, but her phone was inside and there was nothing she could do but push the wheels hard and fast.

And then the monstrous killing machines swooped even lower and the shooting started. She nearly jumped out of her skin when the grim, heavy clunking of the 30 mil chain gun started up, firing the lethal bullets along the shore and up the beach directly behind her at a terrifying six hundred rounds per minute.

They tore through the warm, turquoise water in seconds and were quickly shredding their way up the sand and racing up behind her. *My God,* she thought – *they're actually aiming at me!*

She thought she was dead when Richard Eden burst out of the compound and ran toward her with all his might. Behind him she saw the figure of Kim Taylor making a panicked call on her cell phone.

Eden grabbed the handles on the back of the chair and pushed her ahead of him as he sprinted back to the headquarters buildings only seconds ahead of the savage gunfire.

They both knew their only hope was to get inside and go to the bunker. It was an original feature of the compound back when it was built and operated by the French Navy, and Eden had kept it up just in case of an emergency just like this. In all the years he'd worked here they'd never needed it until now.

And now they needed it almost as much as they needed oxygen.

CHAPTER THIRTY-THREE

When they reached the entrance to the cave, Kruger was already long gone. His pickup was racing off down the slope. Korać, Luk and Van Zyl were climbing into the Kaman, with the Serb at the controls, and Kamchatka was clambering into a 4Runner but stopped to swing around with a machine pistol.

Scarlet raised her gun. "Drop it like it's hot, motherfucker!"

Kamchatka laughed. "The only thing's I'm dropping is you, bitch!" He fired a burst from the gun and forced them to the deck. They fired back and kept Kamchatka pinned down around the front of the 4Runner to stop him getting to the door.

"Where's Khatibi?" Lea yelled.

"Tied up in that Silverado!" Hawke said.

"Take the Silverado and go after Kruger!" Scarlet yelled, aiming at the 4Runner. "I'll keep this twat tied up."

Hawke swung open the door of the Silverado and started the engine. "Quick – he's not getting away this time."

Hawke and Lea piled in and they started down the hill. With Hawke at the wheel, the Silverado skidded along the gravel path and down the slope after Kruger. As Lea untied Khatibi, the Englishman checked the mirror and immediately saw Scarlet firing on Kamchatka. Somehow he had gotten into the 4Runner and was now skidding down the hill. They were getting smashed again.

"He's getting away!" Lea said.

Hawke stamped on the throttle to kick the automatic transmission down into third. The extra torque made the revs roar and the pickup surged forward but just as they were gaining they heard something that changed everything.

The sound of the intermeshing rotors of the Kaman K-MAX thundered above them but before anyone could react they all felt the heavy blow of the carousel smashing down on the roof of the Silverado.

"Shit!"

"What is it?"

A metallic crunching sound gave the answer first and then they saw the claws of the four-hook carousel as they tightened around the cab's roof.

"Cover your faces!"

The hydraulics whined as the hooks tightened on the roof and then punctured through the windshield and side windows, spraying a lethal shower of shattered glass all over them at high velocity.

"They're not going to try and lift us up?" Lea said.

"Surely impossible!" Khatibi replied.

Hawke shook his head and grimaced. "The good news is that this Chevy probably weighs about five thousand pounds, and the K-MAX can lift six thousand as I recall, and probably around five thousand at this altitude, so absolutely no problem."

Lea looked at him. "Okay, right. Hang on – if that's the good news, what's the *bad* news?"

"The bad news is because it has twin-intermeshing rotors, that means there's no need for a tail rotor… and destroying tail rotors is my patented method to bring down a chopper."

*

A grim silence filled the tomb as their eyes fixed on the time bomb Korać had left in the sarcophagus. Scarlet returned from her failure to stop Kamchatka, and saw the American CIA man studying the bomb. He turned to face his friends, shaking his head as he did so. "No way."

"And what does that mean, darling?"

"It means I was right. It has a motion sensor on it, right there," he leaned in and pointed at what looked like a small battery neatly attached to the side of the bomb. "Touch that or any other part of this thing and it's going up in half a heartbeat."

"Shit."

"Exactly."

He turned to Ryan. "This means you have precisely four minutes to get what you need out of this place before we're running for our lives."

"Oh joy."

"Hurry up, Ryan," Camacho said. "Three minutes, forty seconds."

Ryan looked more closely at the temple layout and saw at once what Kruger had seen – there were twelve alcoves, and in front of each one was a constellation carved into a flagstone.

"These must correspond to the twelve labours of Hercules," he said with confidence. "And these constellations are the clue. To open the alcoves and find what Kruger saw, we have to stand on the stones bearing the relevant constellation."

Scarlet stood on one and nothing happened. "Idiot."

"No – it has to be in the right order! We have to stand on the stones in the order of the twelve labours!"

Camacho looked at the bomb timer. "So let's get on with it then, shall we? Three minutes."

*

The Silverado lurched up nose first and at high speed as the Kaman began to lift the pickup into the air. They grabbed on to anything they could to steady themselves but they were trapped and had nowhere to run. Ahead of them they watched the taillights of Kruger's pickup disappearing into the distance.

Lea sighed. "Whatever happens, he's long gone."

"Yeah, I got that," Hawke said.

"This is a very precarious situation!" Khatibi said, peering out the shattered window as the Rif Mountains flashed by in a blur.

"No shit," Lea said.

"And they're taking us higher," Hawke said. "Something tells me this is a one-way journey."

"So what are we going to do?" Lea said.

"Only one thing we can do," Hawke said, craning his neck to look up at the chopper. "Someone has to climb up that load chain and take out the crew of the Kaman." He pulled his head back into the cab a paused a beat. "Professor?"

"What!?"

"He's just kidding," Lea said, turning to Hawke. "Right?"

"Right. You two stay here. I'll be back in a sec."

*

Ryan turned to Scarlet. "So what was the first labour of Hercules?"

"You're asking me?"

"No, of course not! I'm just talking to myself out loud. The first labour was to slay the Nemean Lion – Leo!" Ryan ran over to the alcove with the Leo constellation in front of it and stood on the stone. Slowly the rock partition slid down to reveal the first symbol. It was similar in style to the ones that had led them here from Tanit's tomb. Ryan nodded his head and snapped a picture of it. "That's the first coordinate. Sweet."

"Two minutes and thirty seconds," Camacho said.

"What was the second labour?" Maria asked.

"The Lernaean Hydra," Ryan said without hesitation. "Everyone search for the Hydra Constellation!"

Scarlet looked from Reaper to Lexi and then to Camacho. "Who does he think we are?"

"You must have learned them for your camping or whatever it is you do in the SAS," Ryan said.

"Camping?"

"You know."

"Well, sure… but that was a long time ago," Scarlet said defensively. "Besides, I'm not a fucking sailor."

"No, that's your hobby not your vocation," Lexi said with a wink.

"Ah! Here it is," Ryan said. He repeated the process, standing on the correct stone and revealing the next symbol. "That's the second coordinate."

"Two minutes," Camacho said.

"Third labour was the Ceryneian Hind. Look for the… oh, forget it." Ryan searched and found Scorpio. "The Constellation of Hercules was a stag in the Greeks' eyes."

He repeated the process again, activating the alcove partition and taking the picture.

"One minute and forty seconds, Ryan."

"Fine… fine… I can do this!" He worked his way speedily through the other Twelve Labours – the

Erymanthian Boar, the Augean Stables, the Stymphalian Birds and the Cretan Bull.

"Sixty seconds, *boy*."

"Mares of Diomedes next then… that just has to be Equuleus, Latin for little horse…" he mumbled and chuckled to himself. "Who knew they had such a good sense of humor?"

Scarlet peered over Camacho's shoulder and saw the clock down to seconds. "Ryan, just to let you know that I'm going to start edging towards the entrance now, and I think it's a safe bet Camo, Reap and Lexi will be joining me although perhaps Maria might stay."

He looked up. "Eh?"

Maria grabbed his shoulders. "For fuck's sake hurry up!"

"I'm done now – Hippolyta next…" he snapped the image and moved around to the tenth labour. "Cattle of Geryon, as I was explaining earlier…"

"Thirty seconds," Camacho said. "We're out of here. That means you too, Ryan."

"Wait!" He activated the Hesperides alcove and then turned to do the last one – the twelfth labour: Cerberus.

"Twenty seconds… run!"

Ryan snapped the picture and they made a break for it, just reaching the entrance when the bomb detonated. A savage fireball blasted out the entrance of the cave and illuminated the side of the mountain for a few seconds until it burned out. Seconds later a shower of dust and rock splinters rained down on them.

"Talk about close…" Lexi said.

"That was *too* close," Reaper said.

Maria coughed some of the dust up and stretched out on her back, looking up at the stars. "Real constellations!" she said.

Ryan groaned, moved over and stretched out beside her. "Oh, *shit!*"

They all turned to look at him. "What?"

"I dropped my phone in there…"

Scarlet stared at him. "You *what?*"

Ryan let the awkward silence stretch another couple of seconds before grinning and producing his phone from his pocket. "Just kidding. Ha!"

"I'll stick that phone up your fu…"

"Easy, babe," Camacho said, and took Scarlet by the shoulders to kiss her.

"If you put it like that," she said. "I'll let it go."

"So what now?" Reaper asked Ryan.

"Now we work out how these symbols convert into coordinates and then we sail to Atlantis."

CHAPTER THIRTY-FOUR

At the top of the load chain now and a thousand feet above the mountain, Hawke's presence was noted and one of the side doors opened to reveal a grinning Willem Van Zyl. He tried to kick the former Commando but Hawke was ready for him and grabbed his shirt, pulling him from the chopper. The two men fell back away from the helicopter and landed with a heavy smack on the flatbed of the swaying Silverado. Van Zyl landed on top of the Englishman and wasted no time in pulling his arm back and aiming a solid punch right in the center of Hawke's face.

The movement of the shoulder muscles through the South Africans torn shirt had telegraphed the punch half a second in advance and Hawke took evasive action, flicking his head hard to the right to dodge the strike. It worked, and Van Zyl screamed in agony as he ploughed his own fist into the corrugated stainless steel base of the flatbed.

Distracted by the pain for a heartbeat, Hawke was able to raise his arm and grab the side of his opponent's face, pushing his thumb deep into Van Zyl's left eye socket. The South African howled like a baby and the instinct to save his sight made him leap off the Englishman and take a step back.

He collided with the side of the pickup and nearly toppled over the side, but the Silverado now swung like a five ton pendulum in the other direction and made him fall forward again.

Hawke was getting dizzy but knew he had to stay focussed. If Van Zyl got a serious strike in then he was flying over the side and the only thing down there was a thousand foot drop to the bottom of the ravine.

Van Zyl approached, pulling a hunting knife from his belt and flipped it over in his hands before slashing the blade in the air. Hawke heard someone screaming and glanced up to see Luk peering out of the chopper. He roared with laughter and then went back inside the cabin. A moment later the Kaman began to swerve violently to the left and right, and the motion was soon transferred down the load chain to the Silverado which responded by swinging more and more dangerously back and forth beneath the speeding chopper.

Hawke tumbled backwards and grabbed the side of the truck to stop himself going over and falling to his death. At the end point of the arc now, the truck was now almost on its side and both men fell off the truck, holding on to the side now while their bodies dangled over the edge. The hunting knife went bye-bye over the edge and tumbled out of sight in the rocky valley far below them.

Above their heads the chopper's powerful engine roared in pain as it struggled to keep level while holding the swaying truck on its carousel. Inside the cab Hawke saw the terrified faces of Lea and Khatibi as they were thrown about all over the place.

Van Zyl edged away from him and began to pull himself back in but Hawke knew the best play was to wait for the truck to swing the other way. When it did, he used gravity to help himself get back inside the flatbed, and then the fighting got real.

Van Zyl took a swipe at Hawke but he dodged it and fired another back, striking him on the jaw and sending him flying back onto the cab's rear window. Hawke saw

Lea was holding something out the cab window. It looked like a tire iron, and he wanted it badly but the truck was now starting its swing toward the other end of the arc and Van Zyl was padding back over for a second round.

Swipe. Punch, crack and stagger back. Hawke felt the pain as Van Zyl's ring-encrusted knuckles ripped into his jaw, but at least the South African hadn't noticed the tire iron. Hawke flicked out his right boot and tripped the man over. His flight was aided and abetted by the sick-making swing of the truck now approaching the end point of its arc once again. With the Silverado now almost on its other side, Hawke clawed and strained his way forward to the cab while Van Zyl struggled to hang on to the tailgate.

He grabbed the tire iron. Its chunky weight felt good in his hands, and now the truck was approaching the base of the arc again and they were flat for another few seconds. He had no time to waste.

He raised the iron to a fighting position and gripped it tightly as he swung it hard and fast at the South African's arm. He felt the smash and crack as the arm broke clean in the center of the radius bone. Van Zyl reacted predictably, reaching for the wounded arm and grunting in agony. Expecting the reaction, Hawke's next move was baked into the first one and now he brought the tire iron up once again from the other side and smashed it into Van Zyl's jaw, knocking him clean off his feet and tumbling out the back of the Silverado.

He flipped over and over on his way down to the bottom of the ravine, but moved out of Hawke's sight when the truck began its next swing. The Englishman knew he had only one play – he had to get into the cab of the Kaman and end this before they decided to release the truck. He only had to look at Lea's terrified face to know there was no alternative.

He climbed up the load chain once again, his hands slipping on the grease as he went, desperately trying to cling on as the chain swung back and forth. He heard Luk's roar of laughter once again and presumed he thought he was dead. Good. The element of surprise was his only ally in a situation like this, and he couldn't let these men get away.

At the top of the chain now, he had to let go with one hand so he could grab hold of the Kaman's starboard skid. It was a risky move even without the violent pendulum effect, but he had no choice. The rushing wind whipped his hair as he grabbed hold of it and then brought his other hand up to solidify his grasp on the chopper. His legs hung out below him, bashed about in the downdraft but at least they were away from the swinging pendulum effect. Looking below he now saw the true terror the Silverado had been put through as it swung back and forth beneath the chopper.

He pulled himself up on the skid but Luk leaned out and caught him in the act.

"I don't think so, Mr Hawke," he said.

Hawke wondered what new hell was winging its way toward him but found out soon enough when the certified nutcase from Hong Kong swung his legs out and, grasping hold of his seatbelt, began smashing his boots down on his fingers.

The pain was agonizing and keeping hold of the skid was all but impossible as his instinct drove him to let go of it. He swung back and down, now holding on with only one hand. Knowing what was coming next he swung his hand back up in preparation for when Luk smashed his other hand and just managed to switch grips before falling from the skid.

Luk frowned but had an answer in the bank. Gripping hold of the belt for his life, his old enemy from Kowloon brought both boots up at the same time and smashed them own on both of Hawke's hands, and this time he had no chance but to let go. He fell away from the chopper but the truck wasn't there – it was at the endpoint of its arc and all Hawke saw beneath him was the same rocky ravine that had claimed Van Zyl's life. The chopper had moved over higher ground now and the drop was down to less than one hundred feet but he still didn't fancy his chances.

He reached out and grabbed the load chain, now at forty-five degrees as it began to pull the beleaguered Silverado and its desperate passengers back into yet another violent, wild swing the other way. Hawke pulled himself along the chain and waited until the truck was beneath him before jumping back down onto the flatbed.

"Well," he said to himself. "That went well."

CHAPTER THIRTY-FIVE

Hawke, Lea and Khatibi watched in horror as Korać turned hard to port and piloted the Kaman out over the cliff edge. They all knew what was coming next, and then the Serbian commander went ahead and released the four-hook carousel gripping the roof of the Silverado.

The heavy pickup dropped away from the K-MAX and plummeted toward the mountain slope beneath them. Still outside on the flatbed, Hawke knew he had only one chance to stay alive and made his way through the buffeting crosswind toward the cab.

Lea was there to meet him, and hurriedly moved away from the door so he could climb inside.

"Room for one more?" he said, and clambered in on top of her. He righted himself behind the steering wheel and put on his seatbelt.

"Are you kidding?" Lea said.

"I think he's not kidding," said Khatibi.

"Belts on please, ladies and gentlemen," Hawke said, mimicking the voice of a seasoned airline pilot. "We will shortly be touching down in Morocco and I'm sorry to say we may experience a little turbulence."

He leaned forward in his seat just in time to see the K-MAX disappearing off to the west but there was no time to worry about the enemy now. The boulders and scree of the Rif Mountains were rushing up to meet them and they would be making contact in five... four...

Three... two...

One! The Silverado smashed into the rocky mountain and immediately bounced back up another ten feet into the air while simultaneously moving forward down the slope. It smashed back down a second time and this time stayed down. The engine revved wildly and Hawke struggled to keep the steering wheel under control as the pickup raced down the thirty degree slope toward the ravine.

"Don't worry," he yelled at Lea and Khatibi. "This isn't my first time."

Lea and the Moroccan exchanged uncertain glances as the Englishman wrestled to heave the wheel to avoid smashing into a large boulder and the cab filled with the smell of burning brake pads.

He pumped the brakes in bursts but the pads were long gone. Passing one hundred miles per hour, he dropped into third gear but even engine braking was beyond this situation and the Silverado continued to tear down the desert slope toward the ravine.

Hawke's mind raced and he considered trying to steer out of it, but he knew turning wasn't an option. To turn the car at this speed meant an instant roll and then the next time the vehicle would be stationary was when it was on fire at the bottom of the ravine.

Not an option.

Lea gripped the dashboard. "Ravine racing towards us, Joe!"

The roar of the engine and the sound of gravel and scree spraying up the sides of the pickup added to the sense of chaos and lack of control as he continued to pump the brakes and change down again into second. The 4.3 litre V6 responded with a wild growl of anger and the revs shot up into the red, but this time the engine braking slowed the doomed Silverado to forty miles per hour.

"We're almost over the sodding edge of the cliff, Joe!"

But this time Hawke made no reply. The situation was getting grimmer by the second. He glanced over his shoulder at the back seat. "Grab those magazines!"

"What the fuck?" Lea said. "This is hardly the time!"

"Get them, tear them apart and stuff them down your jacket sleeves and jeans, right now! You too Professor!"

Lea's eyes widened, "Ah – gotcha!"

When they had done as he'd asked, he did the same while Lea took the wheel. Then he changed the Silverado down into first and this time the engine screeched like it was going to explode.

He jammed his foot down on the brakes hard one last time and between that and the first gear engine braking he reduced the pickup's speed to twenty miles per hour. *Not too shabby under the circumstances*, he thought.

"All right ladies and gents – time to depart the stricken vessel!"

He opened his door and kept it in place with his leg as he manoeuvred to leave the speeding Silverado.

Khatibi peered outside the truck. "You cannot be serious?"

"It's this or you go over the ravine," Hawke said flatly. "The magazine you just stuffed down your pants should help cushion some of the impact. Do *not* stretch your arms or legs out to defend yourself. Your instinct will tell you to do this, but I'm telling you not to because if you do you'll break every bone in your arms and legs. In other words, listen to me and not your instinct."

"This is not very reassuring."

"Where's your spirit of adventure?" Hawke said as Lea climbed over his lap toward the door. "Hello..." he said. "What's all this then?"

She kissed him on the lips. "Not now you mad bastard."

He laughed as she leaped from the car and disappeared behind in a blur of dusty twists and tumbles. "Think of it as something to tell the grandchildren, Professor."

Khatibi looked like he was going to be sick, but one look at the rapidly approaching ravine helped the decision-making process and he reluctantly opened his door and turned to leave.

But stayed put.

So Hawke leaned over and gave him a friendly nudge, pushing him out of the cab and leaving himself the sole passenger on RMS Silverado. The ravine was now less than a hundred yards ahead and they'd be over the edge in seconds. He got as close to the ground as possible, bringing his hands up under his chin and tucking his elbows in tight to his sides.

And then he leaped from the pickup.

He smashed into the ground hard, and immediately began tumbling wildly as the Silverado raced away in a cloud of diesel fumes. Seconds later it vanished over the edge of the ravine and was gone.

But Hawke was still tumbling over and over. Every rock felt like it was tearing a hole in him as he skidded and smashed over them, slowly coming to a halt in a haze of scree dust and blazing Moroccan sunshine.

Pulling himself onto all-fours, he started to pull the magazine padding out of his jacket and coughed up some of the dust. Aware of a shadow he looked up to see the silhouette of Lea Donovan standing between him and the sun.

"Thanks to your brilliant plan," she said quietly. "We now have to walk about a million miles to get back to the others."

"I'm fine thanks," he said.

"Stop being such a big baby," she said. "And aren't you glad I came up with that magazine idea?"

He rubbed the dust out of his eyes and staggered to his feet.

"Where's the professor?"

"Just over there. I think he tore his jacket."

"You think he tore his jacket?"

"Uh-huh."

"He can fix it on the sodding boat then, can't he?"

*

The flight to Rabat on the Eurocopter took longer than any of them could bare, but things were still moving fast because thanks to the coordinates from the Temple of Hercules and a 4G wifi connection, Ryan and Khatibi were able to determine the exact location of Atlantis. They all felt they had a chance finally to overtake Kruger.

They touched down in the commuter town of Salé to the north of the built-up city and after hiring an SUV they raced into Mellah on their way to the Marina Bouregreg.

"All looks pretty tame to me," Scarlet said with a sneer as she looked around her new surroundings.

"Tame?" Ryan asked. "This city's past is even longer and dodgier than yours."

"Oh, now that's very funny," she said, glancing at his grinning face.

Ryan winked at her. "Just saying. This place is where the Barbary corsairs used to come into port to restock."

Lea sighed and pulled her sunglasses down from her forehead and over her eyes. "Ryan, say pirates if you mean pirates."

"You're lucky he didn't say buccaneers," Scarlet added with a laugh.

"If you've *quite* finished," Ryan continued, "I'm simply making the point it's not *tame*, even if it wasn't always the capital."

"How's that then?"

"A French general switched it from Fez to Rabat after the invasion in 1912."

"Please don't say that word," Scarlet said.

Khatibi looked at her. "What word?"

"Sober," Lexi said. "Scarlet has a fear of the word sober."

Lea rolled her eyes and turned to watch the city flash past as they headed west through the Quartier Bettana and closed in on their destination. If she asked him, she knew Ryan would be able to tell her about the French colonial architecture, or the influence of Moorish culture, but she just didn't want to hear it. The truth was she was starting to feel lost. She was rarely on the same continent long enough to see two sunrises in row, and it she felt like it was beginning to get to her.

And yet she was still running. Still running toward the truth of what had happened to her father, still running hand in hand with Joe Hawke... but was she running towards something or away from something? However she felt about it all, ECHO was her only family. There was her brother Finn, working for the police in Dublin, but they hadn't spoken in years, so if she had any family at all, then it was the people around her now, and those back on Elysium.

Any thoughts she had of leaving the team seemed almost ridiculous. No matter how tired of this she got, it was her fate now, and there was nothing she could do about it.

Her thoughts were interrupted rudely by the sound of a loud horn and a grotesque string of abuse flowing from the mouth of Scarlet Sloane. Startled, she looked up from her daydream to see the former SAS woman giving a mouthful of loud abuse to a cab driver who was dangerously tailgating her. "Why don't you get off my arse?"

"Said the bishop to the rugby team," said Ryan, giggling at his own joke.

"Urghh," Lea said.

"Will you please just *stop* that?" said Scarlet.

"Sorry."

Scarlet slowed now as she pulled up into the marina area and cursed as she brought the vehicle to a stop and slammed the automatic transmission into park. With the former SAS woman at the wheel the journey through Rabat had been more hair-raising than strictly necessary and they were all very grateful to arrive and get ready to sail out to sea. Eden had spoken with the Moroccan Government who had agreed to the use of a French-built VCSM coastguard vessel, and as they approached the docks they all sensed the spectre of Atlantis rising on the horizon.

CHAPTER THIRTY-SIX

The VCSM inshore patrol vessel was one of just two operated by the Royal Moroccan Navy, and was used primarily for ocean surveillance off the country's coast. It wasn't usually armed but a light machine gun had been installed on the boat's foredeck for the purposes of the mission.

Now, they were cutting though the North Atlantic Ocean at twenty-five knots and following the course heading to the Dacia Seamount that Khatibi had worked out. Looking at the map he was sending them to precisely the middle of nowhere, but they had no other play and decided to take the chance.

Lea's thoughts were largely restricted to how incredibly long it took to get anywhere by sea, accustomed as she was to flying around from country to country on board extremely fast private jets. The VCSM wasn't exactly sluggish compared to many sea-going vessels, but it still felt like they were crawling along at a snail's pace as the ship ploughed through the choppy ocean yard by yard.

Standing at the bow she had resisted Hawke's pathetic attempt to recreate the Titanic scene with Jack and Rose, and turned to watch him as he made his way back inside the ship. Looking down the starboard side of the deck, she saw Reaper speaking in French with some of the crew. They were sharing tobacco and laughing crudely at a joke that thanks to the Frenchman's hand gestures she had not the slightest inclination ever to know.

Down the portside, Maria and Lexi were leaning on the rails either side of a very green Ryan Bale, trying to comfort him as he emptied the contents of his stomach into the heaving North Atlantic. She smiled when she saw it and recalled the time they had taken the ferry from Dublin to Holyhead and the exact same thing had happened. That was a long time ago, and now he had Maria Kurikova to take care of him.

Like Hawke, Lea had hoped the Moroccans might have been able to provide more of a force to help them, but she knew she should be grateful enough for the ship. There was no other way to get out to the Dacia Seamount and then dive down to the ocean floor, and the officials in Rabat could easily have denied them the vessel.

None of this was new and the ECHO team were more than used to making do with depleted forces and whatever equipment they could lay their hands on. While they usually left Elysium with all the kit they needed things moved so fast that most times they had to improvise and this was one yet another of those times, what with Wolff's weapons long since lost in Serbia and Morocco.

She wandered back to the bridge and joined Hawke. He was speaking quietly with Jack Camacho and Scarlet while Captain Bekri and his first officer were studying a nautical chart of the area. For now at least, it was a scene of organized calm, but she knew how fast scenes like this fell apart. She sighed. Silvio Mendoza and Aurora Soto were dead – their mangled bodies stretched out on a mortuary slab in Munich – but somewhere out here in all this nothingness was that bastard Dirk Kruger and his hired gorilla Dragan Korać.

Not to mention Luk and Kamchatka.

"Coffee?" Hawke said.

She shook her head. "I can barely stand up in this bloody boat, never mind drink a sodding coffee."

Hawke smiled and nodded. "It can take some practice, I admit."

"So how we doing?" she asked, keen to get back to dry land as soon as possible.

"We're getting there," Bekri said with a broad smile. "Although I have to tell you I've sailed these waters many times before and I can guarantee you there's nothing at the Dacia Seamount except saltwater and seasickness."

"But we're diving there, don't forget," Reaper said.

Bekri gave a sceptical nod of his head and raised his palms in the air. "That's why we'll do the sonar scanning of the ocean floor. If there really is something out there then we'll find it – I promise."

"Let's hope so," Hawke said with more confidence. "We're not the only ones searching for it and let's face it – Atlantis is a pretty big prize... not to mention the other half of the ten million bucks for getting the idol back from Kruger."

"As long as your coordinates are right then we have as a good a chance as anyone," Bekri said with a warm smile.

"The coordinates are right," Hawke said, glancing out the rain-lashed porthole at Ryan Bale as he was dry-heaving over the rail with Maria's hand on his back. "Ryan hasn't let us down yet."

The hours went by, tedious and frustrating. Being a former Marine Commando and SBS operative, Hawke had spent more than his fair share on board boats and submarines, but since joining ECHO he had moved around the world much faster thanks to Sir Richard

Eden's fleet of Gulfstreams. Going back to life on the ocean wave might have been relaxing as a pastime but it just felt like a hindrance when he was in pursuit of Dirk Kruger. From the look on her face, it seemed Lea felt the same way.

She sighed. "I can't believe how long this is taking."

"That's sea travel," Hawke said. "The fastest corvettes in the world struggle to go faster than sixty knots, besides, Kruger's on a ship as well, so he's not going any faster than us. He just had a bit of head start, that's all."

"Must you see the silver lining in every cloud, Joe Hawke?"

"Sorry – is it annoying?"

"A little."

"When life gives you lemons..."

"Yeah, yeah – make lemonade, I know."

"I was going to say throw them back and get some apples."

She laughed. "All right, you and your damned optimism win again."

"All I'm saying is look for the advantage to every situation."

"In every disaster, there is opportunity," Lexi said. She walked over to them in the cabin and leaned against the wall. "Old Chinese proverb."

"So what's the opportunity for us being stuck out here for so long?"

"Simple," Hawke said. "We have longer to plan our attack."

"You always have an answer..."

"Plus, we have other things we could do to pass the time." He moved to her and put his arms around her waist.

"Oh *God*," Lexi said, and walked back outside the boat.

Lea smiled. "I like where this is going."

Another long hour passed until then they reached their destination – two hundred and thirty miles off the coast of southern Morocco – and then Bekri began a systematic sonar survey of the ocean floor, following Khatibi's coordinates precisely. For a long time, it was just two men speaking in Arabic as the sea slowly grew less peaceful with the gathering storm.

"There's nothing here!" Bekri said. "Just as I told you."

"But the coordinates must be right!" Lea said. "They have to be."

"They are right," Ryan said. "I've just been a total idiot."

"Hallelujah!" Scarlet said.

"So why can't we see anything?" Lea asked.

"Plate tectonics," Ryan said. "The Mid-Atlantic ridge moves at around two and half centimetres a year and the coordinates are derived from the constellations!"

"But the entrance is hundreds of metres out of place," Lea said.

"Which means it sank to the ocean floor a very long time ago indeed," Hawke said, nodding with satisfaction at yet more proof of their theories.

They moved the ship in line with Ryan's theory and a few moments later things changed fast.

"My God…" Bekri said. "This can't be real. There must be a problem with the survey instruments."

Hawke took a step forward and frowned. "What's the matter?"

"This part of the seabed here," Bekri said, pointing at the screen. "It's registering as less than seventy feet deep in some places."

"So what's the problem?" Maria said.

"The ocean floor has been mapped here many times and the Dacia Seamount is at least two hundred feet below the surface of the sea according to all previous oceanographic surveys."

"So what's going on then?" Scarlet said.

"There are three options," Hawke said. "First, the Dacia Seamount has got a hundred and thirty feet higher since the last survey, second, there has been some kind of cover-up concerning the true depth of this part of the ocean floor, or third, the instruments are wrong."

Bekri shook his head vehemently. "They're not wrong. They're properly calibrated – I checked them before we left, before we started and I'm doing it a third time now."

"And something tells me the Dacia Seamount hasn't grown by a hundred feet since the last survey," Lea said.

"Which leaves the Nixon Option," said Ryan.

"We can't get caught up in who's covering this up, or why," Hawke said. "That's strategic stuff for later. Right now the mission is to locate Atlantis, and I think this means we're getting closer."

"There!" Khatibi said. "Those look like concentric circles."

"It can't be," Ryan said, peering into the screen at the survey information. "My God – you're right! There is no way they are natural formations."

"So what are they then?" Hawke asked.

Ryan and Khatibi shrugged simultaneously. "Could be anything," Ryan said. "The remnants of some kind of temple or public space… anything. And this here looks like a wall – and is that some stairs?"

"So this means we found Atlantis?" Lea said, looking at the others. They all heard the excitement in her voice.

"I guess we made it," Scarlet said, turning to hug Camacho. She looked up into his eyes.

"I guess we did," he said.

Without saying another word, Scarlet laced her arms around Camacho's waist and kissed him hard on the mouth. The American didn't resist, but moved his hands up to the small of her back and squeezed.

"Oh *God*," Ryan said, and lowered his voice to an Attenborough whisper. "And here we see the female Mantis as she cannibalizes her mate..."

Without breaking from the kiss, Scarlet reached out and slapped the back of Ryan's head.

"I can't believe we discovered Atlantis!" Maria said.

"And about time too," said Lexi, and the two women high-fived each other.

Khatibi tutted and shook his head. "It's far too soon to tell. We must launch an exploration of the ocean floor. That is the only way we can be sure."

Hawke sighed. "We don't need a full sub at this depth, just regular wetsuits and then dive down."

"We have some scooters," Bekri said.

Hawke faced him. "Scooters?"

Bekri nodded. "Yes – underwater scooters. They are used for scientific purposes along the coast. They go a little over three miles per hour so will be much faster than diving."

"It's not just Dirk Kruger who has all the luck," Hawke said. "How many have you got?"

"Three."

"Fine, I only want two or three of us going down at first anyway. We can't be sure what we're going to find down there and if there are any booby-traps we don't want the whole team getting wiped out. I'll take Lea and Ryan, unless you're desperate to go, Cairo?"

"Me?" Scarlet shrugged her shoulders. "Absolutely no fucks given over here, darling. If I'd wanted to piss about underwater I'd have joined you and the other girls with the white polo-necks back at SBS HQ."

"That's good then."

"Very good," Ryan said. "Much better if just the three of us get wiped out."

"Exactly," Hawke said, getting the sarcasm but not taking the bait. "We need to make sure we keep a good force on deck for when our friends show up. We know they have the coordinates and they left before us so they must be around here somewhere."

"Too late," Reaper said, lowering his binoculars. "Kruger's already here – looks like an old tuna boat but fishermen don't usually walk around the deck with submachine guns... and it looks like Kruger's already dived – no sign of any minisub."

Hawke looked through the binoculars and immediately saw what he was talking about. Somewhere approaching the horizon around three miles away was a stationary tuna boat. "He must have deployed a drift anchor," Hawke said. "Or that thing would be all over the place in this weather."

"How deep is it here again? Lexi asked.

Bekri answered. "According to the radar, the ocean floor beneath that tuna boat is around five hundred meters down."

"Anchor chains are that long?" Lexi looked amazed.

Hawke suppressed a laugh and hid his smile. "No they're not. A drift anchor doesn't attach the ship to the seabed with a chain like a regular anchor. It's designed to stabilize boats in rough weather like this by creating a lot of drag. It works a bit like a brake and slows the boat down."

"Are you sure you're not making that up?" Lexi asked with a sideways glance.

"Absolutely positive," he said.

"Sounds plausible," she said.

"I don't suppose we have any APS rifles on board?" Hawke asked.

Bekri shook his head. "What are they?"

"They're Russian rifles designed for underwater penetration."

Ryan raised his head. "Did someone say something about Scarlet in a bath with a Russian sailor?"

"Drop dead, *boy*."

Ryan laughed. "Is it true you think about sex every five seconds?"

"Yes," she replied coolly. "But never with you."

A howl of laughter went up and Lea high-fived Scarlet.

"We should have left you in that Serbian fort," Ryan said grumpily.

"All right," Hawke said, suddenly all business. "This is serious. Kruger's here and now his crew know we're here, so we need to get on. They will have radioed down to Kruger and alerted him of our position."

"Then to the Batscooters!" Ryan said.

CHAPTER THIRTY-SEVEN

Hawke peered over the edge of the VCSM and stared down into the dark gray sea as it heaved up and down in the building storm. SBS frogman training was the most extensive in the world and even though it had been a while, a raging, black ocean didn't unnerve him in the least.

"If you think you're going down there without me you can forget it, boyo."

He turned to see Lea standing by his side. She had wandered down from the bridge and was zipping up a heavy duty waterproof jacket.

"I wouldn't dream of it," he said.

The ship rose with a violent swell and tipped several degrees to port as a new wave of rain lashed over the deck. They grabbed on to the rail and waited for the vessel to stabilize for a few seconds before making their way back inside.

Hawke, Lea and Ryan put on foamed neoprene wetsuits and prepared to make the journey to Atlantis. The bubbles in the neoprene helped its wearer float but at lower depths the increased pressure squashed them, allowing a neutral buoyancy for underwater swimming. Hawke didn't know what to expect down there, but he didn't want to waste time coming all the way back up to the surface for wetsuits, weapons or explosives if he didn't have to.

"What if we have to go deeper?" Ryan asked as he zipped up his suit.

"The scooters are only designed for the depth we're going to, and you're designed that way too," Hawke replied. "So unless you want collapsed lungs, nitrogen narcosis and to be suffocated while simultaneously getting crushed to death, then no, I wouldn't recommend going any deeper, however..."

"There's just no way a sentence like you just said can end in the word however," Lea said.

"*However*," he repeated slower, "if we find an actual complex down there – a citadel, or whatever – we can always come back up and use the minisub to investigate further."

"Christ almighty," Lea said, shaking her head as she watched Ryan complete the task of putting on the suit. "You had to ask, didn't you?"

"There's no such thing as a stupid question," Ryan said. "Only stupid..."

"Wankers," Lea replied instantly. "I know, yeah – thanks, Ry."

Once in their wetsuits the crew lowered the scooters into the water off the back of the ship and the three ECHO members climbed aboard.

"So what do we do now?" Ryan asked.

"Pretty much the same as any expedition to an underwater site," Hawke said. "We dive down, check it out, and then come back again."

They sank beneath the violent waves and seconds later the calmness under the storm-lashed surface fell upon them.

"What's it like down there?" Scarlet asked over the comms. "Has Ryan's personality reached crush depth yet?"

"What does that even *mean*?" Ryan asked. "It makes no sense."

"Much like you, *boy*."

"It's just fine, Cairo," Hawke replied over the comms. "We're passing twenty feet."

Hawke checked the depth gauge as he steered his scooter toward Khatibi's coordinates. "You still have us on radar?" he muttered.

"Why? You're not thinking of running out on us, are you *darling?*"

"As a matter of fact," Hawke said, enjoying the banter, "there's a great little bar down here I wanted to try."

The three of them continued to push down into the depths, turning on their headlights. Now, a trio of white arcs shone into the darkness of the ocean and lit their way as they cruised down to the sea floor.

Hawke took a few moments to search around for Kruger and his men but saw no one. According to the latest report from Bekri, Kruger's ship was now half a kilometre to the north but they had clearly not found the place with their sonar yet or they would already be here. Peering into the gloomy water from behind the safety of his scooter's windshield, he thought he saw an arc of light that might indicate a headlamp belonging to Kruger's crew, but it was nothing, so he returned his attention to their mission and pushed onwards.

Unrestrained by his lack of fitness thanks to the scooter, and motivated by sheer enthusiasm, Ryan was now in the lead and so far ahead he was almost out of sight. If it weren't for his headlight Hawke would never have been able to make out in the gloom.

"Slow down, mate," He said over the comms.

"Yeah, take it easy, Ry," Lea added. She was in between the two men and slightly higher in elevation.

"I'm fine," the young man replied. "But I can't see a thing yet – not even those sodding circles. There's nothing here!"

Lea shook her head with frustration. "What a waste of frigging time!"

"No, wait," Hawke said, steering his scooter to the right and heading toward a ridgeline running north-south. "I see something over there!"

They made their way north for a few seconds, and he got the feeling they were being watched and turned to check over his shoulder once again. Kruger and the rest of his monkeys hadn't come all the way out here for the swimming, and it was only a matter of time before their survey led them to this exact spot.

But for now, they were still alone.

"Holy crap in a bucket," Lea said. "Check that out!"

Another hundred yards ahead of them was a long fissure in the seabed. At first it looked like one of the countless splits and cracks in the ocean floor, but as they got closer they recognized the same oddly shaped features the sonar had picked up earlier back on the ship.

"That's it!" Ryan said, increasing the power to his scooter and speeding up in a bid to get there first.

"You're not trying to be the first man to set foot on Atlantis, are you, mate?"

"Of course I bloody am!" came the reply.

Hawke and Lea accepted the challenge and also increased their revs. Both scooters shot forward, their headlamps shining three pale white arcs onto the ocean floor ahead of them. As they headed for what was looking more and more like the steps the sonar had revealed, Hawke thought he saw a flash of light in his peripheral vision but dismissed it so he could focus on the more important task ahead of him.

He was no archaeologist, and neither were Lea or Ryan, but he thought there had to be some kind of rules about maintaining the integrity of a newly discovered site, especially one as incredible as Atlantis. This had to be the greatest discovery of all time, after all.

"It's the steps all right," Ryan said. "And I'm going in!"

"Just take it easy, mate," Hawke said, now a hundred yards behind and closing. "We don't know what's down there, or where it goes."

Up ahead, Ryan Bale was buzzing like a swarm of wasps. All those years he'd spent drinking in front of a computer and getting keyed on dope all day and night seemed like an eon ago now, as he raced on an underwater scooter down a smashed-up stairwell beneath the surface of the Atlantic Ocean. If it hadn't been for Lea calling him that day none of this would be happening.

And what had he been doing when she called? Truth was, when he'd picked up the phone he had a king-size reefer hanging off his lip and a hangover the size of Manhattan behind the eyes. He'd been up all night hacking the Ministry of Defence in a bid to uncover evidence of UFOs. Even at the time he thought it was a threadbare life, but now with all this, just thinking about it almost made him want to break down.

Not that he would ever tell them, but these people had become the best friends he'd ever known, and for the first time in his life he'd stopped hating himself and realized he could do whatever he wanted with his life and not just want others decided for him. Hawke had taught him never to give in and not be afraid of adventure, and he would never forget that.

"Looks like it's opening out a bit," he radioed back to the others. He turned to look over his shoulder and saw two headlamps turning into the stairwell above him and close the gap.

"Just slow down, ya tool," Lea said. "It's been there for bugger knows how many millennia – it's not going anywhere!"

"No can do," he replied cockily. "I've got an ancient civilization to discover. This time next year people will talk about me in the same hushed tones of reverence currently reserved for the crew of Apollo 11."

Inside his diving mask, Hawke rolled his eyes. "Not if you drive into a bloody wall they won't, so just watch where you're going."

"I'm Armstrong though, right?" came the half-humorous reply.

Hawke heard Lea sigh. "Yes, mate. You can be Armstrong if you really want."

"In that case, let me say – Houston, the Eagle has landed!"

Hawke pulled up beside him and Lea a moment later. They looked at each other through their masks and then followed to where Ryan was pointing.

Lea gasped. "What is it?"

"Atlantis!"

CHAPTER THIRTY-EIGHT

Shifting off their scooters, they finally stepped onto the surface of Atlantis and were met with another cloud of silty dust. An underwater current caught it and whipped it up around their faces before the area cleared again. From within the confines of his mask, Hawke looked around and took in the ancient site.

He was staring at what looked like a modern-day disaster zone and all around was the kind of devastation left behind by an earthquake or tsunami. Broken buildings jutted up out of banks of sand and silt and pieces of smashed pottery and twisted jewellery were scattered all across the site. It looked like pictures of the debris field he had seen around the wreck of the Titanic, and for the first time he was struck by the thought that this was not only an amazing archaeological site, but also a mass grave.

He called up to the ship and made his report while Ryan and Lea poked around in the detritus and shone their underwater flashlights into various nooks and crannies.

"It's just ruins," he said. "Clearly there was something here a very long time ago but it looks like it was totally destroyed."

"Yes," Ryan said. "But by what?"

"Maybe the same thing that sank Valhalla," Lea said.

"It's just amazing down here though," added Ryan. "And talking of Valhalla – call me crazy but this place is a lot like there... some kind of holy site maybe. Outstanding!"

"I'm very pleased for you darling but we have a little problem up here." Through the underwater comms Scarlet's voice sounded like it was coming from the dark side of the moon.

Hawke instinctively looked up to the surface and immediately knew what she was talking about when he saw the shadow of another hull moving toward their ship. Kruger's crew must have seen them and sailed over. "I see your problem," he said. "How far away are they?"

"Four or five hundred metres," Scarlet said.

Lea looked up. "You've drifted quite far away from the site," she said. "That might be a good thing because we don't want anything damaged down here."

Scarlet responded, but her tone had changed. "Listen, we're coming under fire and..."

Hawke frowned. "Scarlet?"

"Radio's down," Ryan said.

Lea sighed. "Isn't that just plain... arsing... fantastic."

"Forget it," Hawke said. "There's nothing we can do to help them and we've got our own mission down here. Focus on the job and trust them to do theirs, and then if..." he was interrupted by Ryan's voice over the comms.

"This is more than weird," he said, riding his scooter a few more yards and then coming to a stop again on the seabed. He climbed off and awkwardly hopped a few yards to the ruins. "Call me crazy but this looks almost identical to the Ishtar Gate."

"Ishtar Gate for Dummies, please mate."

"The Ishtar Gate was one of gates that led into inner Babylon."

"Babylon being in Iraq?" Lea said.

"Yes – right in the center on the plain between the Euphrates and Tigris, just about fifty miles south of what today we call Baghdad."

"But we're not exactly fifty miles south of Baghdad, are we?" Hawke said, his voice crackling through the underwater comms.

"It's definitely the same as the Ishtar Gate though," Ryan repeated as he continued to shift sand and detritus off the ocean floor to reveal more of the ruins. "This is without a doubt a depiction of an aurochs, and this…"

"A what?"

"An aurochs – it's a type of wild cattle that we used back then. Extinct now though – died out around three or four hundred years ago… but they were a key feature of the decoration on the Ishtar Gate, and that's what his little fellow is right here – not to mention this band of flowers here – and here's a lion too!"

"It's too big and heavy for us to take back to the surface with the equipment we've got," Hawke said.

"But we have to come back and get this thing!" Ryan said.

"I agree," Lea said. "I'm more than a little curious to know how a bloody gate from Iraq wound up in Atlantis."

"But I don't think it's from Iraq," Ryan replied. "I'm saying it's *similar* to the one we know from Bablyon – but there are differences. The Babylonians made heavy use of a semi-precious stone called lapis lazuli. It's hard to tell because of the decay but it seems to me that this one is more like a simple indigo… like some kind of reproduction of the original Ishtar Gate. Call me crazy, but this whole place looks like it was destroyed on purpose."

"Hold up," Hawke said, peering ahead of them. "Looks like the tosspots have arrived." Up ahead, emerging from the darkness of the ruins were three headlamps. "And it looks like they got here first, mate. Their boat must have been off course because of drift, not inaccuracy – they'd already found the place by the time we'd arrived."

"And now they're coming up from the center of the ruins," Ryan said, crestfallen. "So Dirk Bloody Kruger gets to be Armstrong,"

"They've got scooters as well," Lea said.

"And by the looks of that canvas bag around his neck I'd say he's not letting the idol out of his sight," Hawke said. "And it looks like they're armed, too."

His sentence was cut short when a metal bolt narrowly missed his head and flashed past into the gloom over his shoulder.

The fight was on.

*

Up on the surface, Reaper swung the GPMG around and fired at the tuna boat, punching holes in the wheelhouse cabin and smashing out the acrylic windows. Korać's men dived for cover before firing back. By the looks of things, they were restricted to submachine guns. Reaper knew the Browning had a range of around half a mile or eight hundred meters, but the range of their Uzis was more like two hundred meters, so he told the captain to move the VCSM to a quarter of a mile and maintain that distance. This meant he could fire on them with impunity and they had no chance of striking back.

"You were saying?" Scarlet said.

He watched with growing anxiety as the men on the foredeck wheeled a large mortar into view and began to lock it into place. "And that's what, exactly?" she said.

"It's a Sani," Maria said. "A Russian heavy mortar."

"Range?" Lexi asked, looking through the binoculars. "Depends on the model," Maria replied. "Maybe five hundred meters, or maybe seven kilometers."

"And we have the Browning," Scarlet said. "Talk about bringing a bowl of custard to a knife fight."

"No, we can take them, just make sure we..." Reaper suddenly looked off the ship's starboard bow. "What the *hell* is that?"

Everyone followed his eyes to the horizon just in time to see the Hellfire air-to-surface missile tearing through the sky toward their ship.

"Jump!" Camacho yelled.

Bekri hit the alarm and it sounded through the klaxons all over the vessel. "Abandon ship!"

And then a second later there was no ship.

*

The merc approached fast through the gloom, and Hawke quickly saw he was holding a weapon of some kind. "Christ on a bike!" he yelled at the others. "They're armed with APS rifles!"

"That's just arsing fantastic!" Lea said, twisting her head to try and see the threat. She turned and looked over her other shoulder.

Hawke watched as the goon got closer and raised the APS to fire. He knew that because standard rounds had both poor accuracy and velocity underwater, the Russians had come up with the brainwave of redesigning the bullet into a much longer shape, almost like a miniature harpoon. The genius of the Soviet Union, he thought with a shake of his head.

The merc fired and the four inch-long steel bolt tore past him, leaving a trail of bubbles in its wake. The bolts were sharpened to a lethal point and had it hit him it would made just as much damage as a regular bullet, but thankfully it missed and raced off into the gloom of the ocean.

To his far left a second merc came into view, and then a third thundered down from above him. The man on the third scooter tried to hit him with the stock of his APS rifle but narrowly missed before pulling up sharply and turning around for a second attack. Before he could gather his thoughts, a familiar face joined the fray.

"It's Kruger!" he told the others. "He's firing!" He pulled the handlebars hard to the right to avoid the bolt, and was instantly reminded of how slow underwater movement really was. The sea scooter chugged painfully slow to the right and he leaned over just as the bolt raced past him leaving another trail of bubbles in its wake.

He spun around one-eighty degrees just in time to see the harpoon-bullet disappear into the gloom of the ocean, and then pulled up hard to gain more elevation. He thought he was getting the better of him, but then he heard a deep, bass roar from the surface a few hundred feet to the north that changed everything.

The former SBS man looked into the distance to where the VCSM had drifted only to see it disappear before his eyes – one minute it was there and then the next it was gone, and all that was left were chunks of burning wreckage and gnarled, bent steel from its carcass.

*

Reaper was first to emerge from the water. When he came to the surface he thought he'd arrived in hell and the spray dome was still hundreds of feet in the air above his head. Where the VCSM had once been was a wide field of broken, twisted detritus, slowly sinking through the burning oil all over the ocean. The sky above was gray from the storm and black from the fires, and everywhere was the smell of oil and grease and then the storm blew another layer of saltwater and dead fish into his face.

He took a deep breath and slowed his breathing before starting to search for his friends. He trod water while turning three-sixty to scan the horizon but there was nothing but carnage everywhere. The dead body of Maati Khatibi bobbed to the surface a few yards to his right and he offered the kindly professor a quick prayer, but the holy words were broken by the noise of helicopter rotors, and by the sound of it they belonged to a substantial machine.

Then Lexi broke the surface and screamed as she gasped for air. He yelled at her and swam over, and then Camacho appeared though the burning wreckage to the south and also began pushing his way through the water to join them. Maria called out in the smoky gloom, and he turned to see her rising high above him on the swell as the storm stirred the sea again and made things even worse.

"Are you okay?" he called out, spitting more seawater from his mouth.

"Yes."

"Lexi?"

"I've been better, but I'll live long enough to kill whoever fired that missile."

"Me too," Scarlet said, swimming toward them from the south.

"The Professor is dead," Reaper said.

"That makes at least two then," Maria called back. "I just saw Bekri's body over there."

"How the hell did Kruger get a chopper out here?" Camacho asked.

Maria pointed to the north. "Well, I don't know but there goes his boat..."

They turned to see the old tuna boat moving away through the smoke.

"It doesn't make sense," Reaper said. "Why blow us up and then run away?"

And then it made sense.

Before anyone could think about the question, a second Hellfire scorched through the leaden sky and ripped into the tuna boat's hull, tearing it to pieces. The detonation was colossal, and Reaper yelled at the others to dive before the shockwave reached them.

CHAPTER THIRTY-NINE

Alex Reeve was still in shock as Richard Eden pushed her along the carpeted corridor at the heart of Elysium and tapped in the keycode to get into the bunker. Kim was beside them and as he calmly tapped in the secret numbers, they all heard the sound of the Apaches as they continued their attack on the island.

An enormous, deep explosion from somewhere above rocked the whole building, and they all knew they had started shelling the ECHO GHQ with their compliment of Hellfire missiles. Eden shook his head and cursed. The AGM-114 Hellfire was a savage anti-armor air-to-surface missile that would wreak devastating damage on their compound.

"Jesus!" Alex said, as Eden moved them inside the bunker and sealed the door. "How many of those things have they got?"

"Up to sixteen on each chopper, and you said you saw three so we could be looking at nearly fifty of the things."

"What about the anti-aircraft defenses?" Kim asked.

"We can operate them from in here."

"We can?" Alex asked, surprised. She had never seen the bunker before, and was shocked when Eden flicked on the lights to reveal what looked to her more like Cape Canaveral's Mercury Control Center. A waist-high panel full of switches and controls ran around the room and above them several plasma screens began to flicker to life.

"Yes, we can. Don't forget this facility was built and operated by the French Navy as a listening post during the Cold War." He turned to face her and smiled. "As a consequence it has all of the trimmings."

He flicked more switches without hesitation and a few moments later the whole room was buzzing like an industrial quantum computer. Alex stared up at the plasma screens and saw various views of the island in the hot sunshine.

"You'll recognize most of these views," Eden said as he started to punch in some codes on one of the keyboards. "Screen One is the north beach, Screen Two the east and so on, plus over here are more immediate images of the compound.

As he spoke, Alex and Kim watched the Apaches buzzing from screen to screen like black wasps as they circled the compound and swooped for another attack. A thick column of smoke was now rising from the hangar where they housed the Gulfstreams, and with only one out on a mission, currently in Marrakech's Menara Airport, that meant the other two had almost certainly been destroyed.

"Only natural," Eden said, noting her expression. "Knocking out aircraft is always the first phase of any attack – and air defenses, of course – so we need to get a wriggle on."

With that said, he fired up the island's anti-aircraft missile system, a series of Rapier installations positioned in strategic locations on the island. The Rapier was a British surface-to-air system which was designed to defend against low-altitude strikes and was a serious bit of kit.

On Screen Four, one of the Apaches was now making a low-level approach just above the ocean on the island's western side.

"Looks like they're going for the Briefing Room," Eden said.

"Who the hell are they, Rich?"

He shrugged his shoulders and shook his head. "That's for us to find out but the first order of business is protecting Elysium."

She knew he was right. Like the others, what she knew about the island was limited. The details of the Consortium were sketchy, including even Eden's place within it, but they all knew how central Elysium was to their missions. It was just another member of the team, and now it was under attack.

The Apache fired one of its Hellfires and they watched in tense silence as it streaked toward the fourth plasma screen in the bunker. A second later there was a tremendous explosion which they not only saw on the screen but felt through the floor. Alex stared in horror and when the smoke cleared it revealed the devastation to the western end of the compound. It was total. All that remained of their Briefing Room was a burning ruin of twisted concrete support pillars and bent steel.

"I can't believe they're doing this," she said, almost unaware of her words. The attacking chopper had turned to its portside and was now travelling north.

"Whoever *they* are," added Eden as he engaged one of the Rapiers and tracked it onto the enemy Apache before firing.

They watched the plasma screens as the Rapier tore away from its installation at Mach 2.0 and screeched into the sky.

"Maybe we'll be okay," Alex said, as she watched the screens.

"I'm not sharing your optimism. Each one of the installations is equipped with four missiles already fixed into the launcher, but after that it's a two-man lift job to

271

get more missiles into the firing position because they weigh nearly a hundred pounds each. There's no way we can leave the bunker so when the launchers are empty they're empty."

"How many chances does that give us?"

"We have six, so that means twenty-four. We're going to need more to fight off three Apaches, plus there's still the Black Hawk you saw as well. That's a utility chopper designed to carry a squad of soldiers. The fact it's lurking behind the Apaches waiting until our defenses are taken out can mean only one thing – whoever they are they're planning on landing some boots on the island."

They saw the Apache try and take evasive action, pulling hard to port and gaining altitude in a staggeringly sharp climb, but it wasn't enough to outrun the Rapier, and seconds later the missile struck its target and a ferocious fireball exploded in the sky above the ocean.

'One down, two to go," Alex said.

Eden frowned as he activated the second Rapier. They were largely automatic but he had taken manual control to be sure of getting the result he desired. "Two plus whatever they've got in the Black Hawk."

The end of his sentence was punctuated by a terrific, fierce explosion so deep in its intensity that Alex thought it had landed right on top of them.

"What the hell?" she gasped.

Eden replied coolly. "Must be the Ammo bunker, so now we're out of missiles even if we could reload the launchers."

Kim Taylor watched the plasma screen in silent disbelief for a few seconds before alerting the others to what was happening. "Er, guys – looks like we have company."

Eden and Alex turned in their seats to face her. "What is it?" Eden asked.

"The Black Hawk just touched down on the north beach – check it out."

They all watched in grim silence as a dozen armed men in full black Special Forces gear jumped out the chopper, fanned out in a professional formation and began making their way up the beach toward the compound.

Eden slammed his hand down on the control panel. "Who the hell *are* they?"

"I don't know, Rich," Alex said. "But whoever they are, I don't think they're here to deliver a kiss-o-gram."

Kim tried to raise a smile but the situation's uncertainty just didn't let it happen. The formation the men were using was a classic fire and movement tactic used by Special Forces and other highly trained forces all over the world, but something told her these were not from just anywhere, but her own country.

"I think they're Americans," she said.

"Americans?" Eden said with surprise. He shook his head, a confused expression crossing his face. "What makes you say that – the Black Hawk?"

"Yeah, but not just that. What they're wearing, the weapons they're using, how they're moving. I've trained among these people and my money's on them being Americans."

"But why would Americans attack Elysium?"

Kim shrugged her shoulders. "I have no idea." She watched more closely as the last of the men slipped out of sight of the CCTV camera, and then a second later the signal was cut and the image of the north beach was reduced to fuzzy static. "And now they've cut the CCTV feed."

For a moment Alex felt like she couldn't breathe. The island was the safest place on earth because of its isolation, but that also made anyone on it vulnerable if there was ever an invasion – like right now. She knew they couldn't stay in the bunker forever, and she also know it wouldn't take the soldiers too long to find its location, either.

"What are we going to do?" she asked.

Eden sighed low and long and rubbed his temples as he contemplated the unthinkable.

"Rich?" Alex said.

"We need to leave the island. We have no choice – not with most of the team in the middle of the Atlantic thousands of miles away. The Apaches give them total air superiority and now we know at least a dozen enemy soldiers have their boots on the ground. I can't believe I'm saying it, but I'm giving the order to evacuate."

"And just give up?"

"There's nothing we can do."

"The hell there isn't," Alex said. "Can we call out of here?"

"Of course."

"Then we still have a chance."

CHAPTER FORTY

Hawke, Lea and Ryan heard the second explosion on the surface but they felt none of the shockwave because it was too far away. When he scanned the sea to the north he saw the tuna boat was now also missing, turned into a similar quantity of burning wreckage and debris as the VCSM.

Kruger and the rest of his goons also saw it and immediately broke off their attack before retreating to the remains of their boat, leaving Hawke, Lea and Ryan alone among the ruins of Atlantis.

"What the hell was that?" Ryan called out.

"We're under attack," Hawke said. "They've hit the ship... and she's drifted a lot more than I thought she would as well – I can barely see what's left of her."

"My God!" Lea said through the comms. "The whole team is on that ship!" As she spoke, pieces of the destroyed ship began to rain down a few hundred feet in the distance, leaving twisting trails of bubbles in their wake.

"But who's attacking us?" Ryan said. "Can't be Kruger – he wouldn't have destroyed his own boat!"

"We have to get back!" Hawke yelled. "There might be survivors!"

"But what about Kruger?" Ryan yelled. "He still has the idol."

"Forget him," Hawke said. "The team needs us – besides, by the look of his boat he's not going anywhere."

They spun their scooters around and weaved in and out of the broken ruins on their way out of the destroyed metropolis.

"I don't like this, guys." Ryan said. "Maybe they're all dead, and now we're in the middle of the ocean without a ship."

"At least Atlantis was unharmed," Lea said.

Leaving the ghostly ruins of Atlantis far behind, Hawke looked over his shoulder at the ancient site and agreed with her. "We're coming back here," he said. "Wait a minute..."

"What is it?" Lea asked.

"Am I going insane or is Atlantis *glowing?*"

"Eh?" Lea and Ryan twisted around on the scooters. "Turns out you're not going insane," Lea said.

"It really is glowing!" Ryan said.

And then it happened.

The ruins of Atlantis began to rupture and then exploded in a massive fireball.

The blast was enormous, spewing an enormous cloud of silt and dirt into the water all around the ruins in a gargantuan sphere. It reminded Hawke of the old nuclear tests the French did in the South Pacific when they used to detonate twenty kiloton bombs in lagoons. Exactly like those tests, the water behind them was now illuminated with the brightest light he had ever seen. "Close your eyes!" he yelled.

He knew what was coming next. Behind them, whatever had detonated in the ruins had created a rapidly expanding bubble of gas that was about to generate the mother of all underwater shock waves. "Hold on to the scooters if you can!"

But as the shock wave overtook them, they were soon blasted off their scooters and sent tumbling over in the water in all directions. Hawke felt like he'd been hit by a concrete wall.

Dazed by the explosion, they swam upwards through the filthy water toward the final location of their ship and their friends. The VCSM had drifted in the storm further than Hawke thought and the massive underwater detonation of Atlantis has pushed the wreckage even further away. It felt like he'd never get there, but then the light broke through. "I can see people swimming in the water. There are survivors!"

"We have to help them!" Lea said.

The sea got murkier again, and for a long time they swam through more silt-laden gloom as they struggled to reach their friends. "Keep going!" Hawke shouted. "We have to help the survivors."

"But where are they?" Ryan said as they emerged into the light once more. "They've gone!"

"Eh?" Hawke looked up and saw he was right. Where once had been the kicking legs of several survivors, now there was no movement at all. Then he broke the surface and got the answer.

There, rising and falling with the ocean wave was a Mil Mi-14.

When Ryan reached the surface he joined Hawke. "What the hell is that?"

Before Hawke could reply Lea arrived and gasped. "What the hell..?"

"It's a Russian anti-submarine chopper," Hawke said. "And as you can see from the nifty way it's parked on the sea, it's amphibious."

The side door was open and inside he could see Reaper and the others on their knees with their hands behind their heads. Beside them were Dirk Kruger, Dragan Korać, Luk and Kamchatka in the same position.

A man in a black flying suit pointed a megaphone in their direction. "Welcome aboard."

Hawke and the others exchanged a glance and Lea shrugged her shoulders. "I'm not staying around here that's for freaking sure."

*

Their hosts said nothing as they climbed into the chopper, struggling against the powerful downdraft of the Mil's five mighty rotors. Inside the atmosphere was calm but oppressive and Hawke counted at least three submachine guns pointed at the prisoners.

"Please," said the man in the flying suit. "Feel free to get on your knees and put your hands behind your head. We will be at our final destination shortly."

Hawke had no choice but to comply, and before he had even followed the man's instructions the door was closed and the chopper rose up out of the water, banking hard to starboard and gaining altitude sharply.

The flight seemed anything but short, and Hawke had to wait a long time until the guards began talking among themselves before he could turn to Scarlet. "What the hell's going on?"

"They blew up our ship with a Hellfire and then repeated the courtesy for Kruger's tuna boat. Now we're all going on an adventure weekend together."

"Where?"

She shrugged. "Check out the tattoos on their wrists."

Hawke glanced at the men again and saw the strange markings: ΆΘ.

He turned to Ryan. "What the hell are they?"

"Oh sodding hell," Ryan said.

"What?"

"It's Greek," he whispered. "I can't be sure but my money's on it symbolizing the word *Athanatoi*."

"The Immortals!" Hawke said, but was interrupted by Lexi.

"Oh my *God*," she said genuinely shocked. "What the hell is that?"

Hawke peered through the chopper's tiny window and whistled with surprised admiration. "Looks like some kind of oil rig, only much bigger."

"It's a Seastead," Ryan said, looking through the next porthole a few feet to their right.

"A what?" Lea asked.

"It's like a floating city," he replied, grinning and nodding with respect. "The mother of all tax havens."

"It must be at least a kilometre long," Reaper said shaking his gently with shock.

"They're being talked about as the answer to overpopulation problems," Ryan said casually. "But there are some issues to do with sovereignty and what laws would be in effect there. To be honest I thought they were only theoretical until about twenty seconds ago."

"It's pretty bloody amazing, I know that," Lea said. "They must be residential buildings on the south side, and tennis courts? This is crazy."

"Who the hell would build an entire floating city in the middle of the Atlantic Ocean?" Scarlet asked. "It's not even like it's anywhere near Atlantis – we must be hundreds of miles away from there by now."

"Nearly a thousand miles away by my calculations," Ryan said. "So not quite in the middle of the Atlantic, but almost."

"It's impressive," Hawke said. "I'll give them that."

"There are three basic designs for a Seastead," Ryan continued. "A small structure that floats on pontoons, a structure that is basically designed like a ship only immobile, and then a larger platform design which is supported by massive columns submerged into the ocean below to stabilize it in the way a keel does on a ship. It's hard to tell from up here but my money's on the latter because of its sheer size."

"But why here?" Lea asked. "Why not closer to Atlantis?"

"Judging by how long we've been in the air we must be in the middle of the Atlantic Ocean by now, over the Mid-Atlantic ridge," Ryan said.

"But why a thousand miles from the ruins?" Lea said.

"There must be a reason, and I think I have an idea." Maria said, biting her lower lip with excitement.

"What is it?" Hawke asked.

"I'm thinking this could be another source of the elixir."

Ryan nodded. "I think that's a pretty good guess. A floating city like that would cost hundreds of billions of dollars to construct. It must be here for a very specific reason, and considering we know that Atlantis is over a thousand miles away and totally destroyed, the logical conclusion is that whoever built it must have had a very good reason to do so. A source of eternal life would fit the bill, and a Seastead would be the perfect way for anyone who wants either to guard it or access it with the minimum of effort."

"By building a whole city over it?" Scarlet said, her tone heavy with scepticism.

"Easier than sailing a ship all the way out here every time you want to get to it, and if you have the money then why not?"

Hawke stared at the vast rig on the horizon, trying to steady himself as the chopper turned to land above the increasingly choppy waves far below. He'd read about

Seasteads a long time ago but all he could recall was they could be towed around by a tugboat. This thing was far too big for that and must have been constructed on the site somehow, presumably with the assistance of a couple of large container ships.

It was literally like a small city on the horizon, but in the middle of the ocean. As they got closer he saw the residential buildings Lea had seen but in greater detail now, and there was even a marina and palm trees dotted along its perimeter. More interesting that that was what looked like some kind of refinery on the north edge, which he pointed out to the others.

"When I read about Seasteads I always visualised something a little more industrial, like an oil rig," he said.

"Maybe in the early days," Ryan replied. "But the architects' imaginations soon ran wild and it wasn't long before these things were being cooked up. It's a classic start-up city but instead of being for normal people, apparently it's full of psychopathic maniacs guarding sources of eternal life."

"When you put it like that, I wish this bloody chopper would hurry up so we can get there!" Scarlet said, peering down at a large white yacht moored at a marina jutting out of the platform's support structure. Beside it was a small container ship.

"We can't be more than a few seconds away," Hawke said, but then the chopper turned suddenly to port and their view of the Seastead was gone, replaced with nothing but an unbroken horizon and a dark gray sky.

"I'm not digging the look of that storm," Lea said.

"Could be to our advantage," Hawke said.

"Here we go again…"

"Just saying."

He felt the chopper descend and then it landed on the platform's Helipad. A few minutes later, the door opened and one of the men opened the door. He was holding a submachine gun in his hands, pointing it menacingly in their direction. "Get out."

The storm had risen in power by the time they stepped out of the chopper, and they had to hold on to rails at the edge of the Helipad to stop getting blown over. The guards kept well back in case any of them tried anything funny, and moments later they were standing on the platform in the blasting rain and wind at least a hundred feet above the ocean.

Close up, the construction looked even more incredible. Hawke took the opportunity to study its design, and recalling Ryan's words about the three main kinds of Seastead he could see by the gargantuan substructure that this was a platform based on semi-submersible columns.

Ships always had the choice of avoiding storms by setting a new course and using their radar to sail into calmer weather, but a Seastead had to be designed to withstand the most savage of storms. Looking at the sheer size of the semi-submersible columns at work in the rising storm, Hawke could see up close how they worked to stabilize the immense construction they supported.

The man with the C8 carbine was joined by several others and they gathered around the chopper in the blasting wind. He stepped up to them and raised his weapon. Behind him, two men dragged another man from the complex. He had been badly beaten and was barely conscious. He was dressed the same as the other men and had the same tattoo on his wrist.

"You're just in time to see Lazarus here meet his maker," yelled the man.

He raised the gun and aimed it at Lazarus, who said nothing, and merely closed his eyes.

"All traitors die for their crimes in the end," the man said, raising the carbine.

A bolt of lightning burst from the sky and struck the conductor at the top of the Seastead. The armed guards looked up for a second and Hawke knew if he ever had one second to save his life and those of his friends, then this was it. Without hesitation, he burst into action.

CHAPTER FORTY-ONE

Hawke seized the muzzle of the carbine and forced it down so it was pointing at the platform. The man's reaction was fast, squeezing the trigger and loosing a savage burst of rapid fire into the deck where the bullets pinged off the riveted steel sheeting in all directions. The Englishman heaved the weapon up into the air and directed an arc of bullets at the welcoming committee and made everyone run for cover. The noise of the gunfire was deafening but the magazine was empty in seconds and left only smoke and the smell of gunpowder, soon whipped away by the howling wind.

Hawke wrenched the carbine from the man's hands and whirled around in an arc to bring the stock of the heavy weapon smashing down on the back of his head. His collapse onto the platform ignited a chain reaction and within seconds chaos had spread around the Helipad. The ECHO team darted behind the chopper for cover while the men in black retreated to the relative safety of what looked like some kind of heating installation unit. The man they had called Lazarus was gone, into the shadows like a frightened lizard with one chance to save its life and Kruger, Korać, Luk and Kamchatka slipped down a ladder leading to the substructure.

The men returned with an M2 machine gun, a serious piece of kit requiring a two-man crew, just as they had faced in their assault on the Temple of Huitzilipochtli. It started firing at them and seconds later its crew was backed up by another man holding an M203 grenade launcher. The breech-loaded, single-shot launcher was a lightweight piece of kit attached to an M4 carbine and fired standard low velocity forty mil grenades from the handheld weapon.

Its operator was solemnly loading and firing the grenades on them and one of the rounds landed inside the Mil which the ECHO team were using for cover.

"Run!" Hawke yelled, and they scattered away from the helicopter before the round detonated. It exploded inside the chopper causing an enormous fireball to engulf the area. The fuel tank ignited and then the whole machine was blasted into dozens of pieces and black smoke belched up into the sky above the platform.

Hawke was now using a hangar behind the helipad for cover, and everyone was with him except for Lea and Camacho. He scanned the helipad zone but there was no sign of them. The thought of the explosion getting them and blasting them off the Seastead into the ocean crossed his mind for a bleak second but then he saw them.

In the chaos, Lea and Camacho were trying to get up after a grenade blast on the far side of the helipad. Athanatoi swarmed like ants and soon overwhelmed them. One man grabbed Lea roughly and yanked her down to her knees. In a heartbeat he had the muzzle of a Browning pushed into her throat and was dragging her back into the shadows.

Hawke's eyes flicked from the terrible image of her getting snatched to the scene a few yards away where Camacho was struggling to his feet after the blast, but the Athanatoi man got to him first, planting a heavy boot in his ribs. The kick was so hard it propelled the heavy American into a half roll, forcing him onto his back and leaving him stranded like a turtle on its back.

Camacho was fast, but the Athanatoi was faster, pulling his gun and bringing it into the aim right in the CIA man's face. "Up."

A crestfallen Camacho wiped the grease and soot from his face and moved slowly to his feet, raising his arms above his hands. "Take it easy with that thing, would ya? I got kids."

The man waved the pistol toward the door and Camacho heaved a sigh of disappointment as he knew he was out of the fight. Then they were both gone, in the same direction as the man who had dragged Lea out of sight.

Hawke's attention was brought back to his own struggle when the crew on the M2 and their grenade-launching support amped things up another notch, working the weapons with terrific efficiency, and seconds later grenades were exploding all around them. Hawke knew this was one fight they had no chance of winning. They were outmanned, outgunned and playing on the enemy's home turf. There was only one play, and he had to give the order.

"Jump!"

And with that, the ECHO team leaped from the platform and tumbled through the howling storm toward the icy, black ocean a hundred feet below.

Smashing through the surface from this distance was almost like hitting concrete and the experience was made ten times worse by the freezing temperature of the water which enveloped him as he plunged deep into the sea. Every time he did this he got the memory of basic Commando training in Devon when they seemed to spend a lot of their time in freezing cold water and mud. The SBS selection process was even less merciful when it came to sorting the wheat from the chaff, and he knew many of his team had no such training or experience.

The storm meant almost zero visibility so he gave up any notions of looking for the others and made his way to the surface as fast as possible. He broke through moments later and was greeted by a sharp smack of sea spray on his face. He gasped for air as he struggled to find his buoyancy and after sweeping his hair out of his face he scanned the horizon for the others.

It was a vision of hell – a dark, freezing cold sea heaving up and down in response to the storm swirling around the Seastead – and for a few seconds he was totally alone. He couldn't see or hear any of his friends. The storm had scattered them like dead leaves across the raging ocean and staring up at the Seastead's grim, industrial substructure so high above him he wondered how the hell they would ever get back up there.

He refocussed his attention on the surface of the sea. Somewhere out here his friends needed his help, and in conditions like this time was of the essence. Not only was the icy temperature a serious consideration, but the prospect of getting sucked out to sea by the powerful currents was all too real. It would be a lonely, painful and terrifying death.

He saw Maria first, trying to orientate herself in the storm while the waves sucked her up and down like a toy boat. Behind her, Ryan emerged from the water and gasped for air. He turned to see Lexi Zhang clambering up the first few rungs of a scaffolding ladder running up the eastern edge of one of the stabilizer columns, but a second later a wave swept her away as if she weighed nothing and pushed her further under the immense substructure.

As he desperately searched for the others, Hawke now realized they were coming under fire. All around him he saw the telltale splashed of bullets as they ripped through the surface of the water and drilled into the black ocean.

CHAPTER FORTY-TWO

"Dive!" he yelled, his voice almost inaudible in the howling storm. "Incoming!"

His training kicked in and he dived, pushing through the water with a powerful breaststroke until he was beneath the substructure and he resurfaced to see that this time Lexi was halfway up the northeast scaffolding with Scarlet and Ryan a few rungs beneath her, but then another wave blasted them all off once again. Reaper was making his way to one of the support columns.

It was chaos, but they worked hard and pulled together. They knew now was the time to take the fight to the Oracle, who he knew in his heart was on the Seastead, high above him now like a god. He gripped the rungs on the southeast column a few hundred yards away from where Scarlet was now helping Ryan out of the water and trying to move up the scaffolding to safety yet again.

Lexi broke the surface a few yards from him and immediately swam over to the scaffolding. Hawke reached out his hand and pulled her up out of the stormy sea and told her to go up the ladder while he searched for Maria. It was getting dangerous but they had come so far in this hunt they could never give up now, no matter how hard it got, and the vision of Lea and Camacho as hostages added more fuel to the fire burning inside him to make things right again.

"And be careful!" he shouted. "It won't be long before those bastards realize where we've gone and come after us."

She nodded, swept her wet hair out of her face and began to scramble up the slippery scaffold toward the bottom of the Seastead. That was when Hawke saw Maria out in the sea. She had drifted further out in the swell and was now nothing more than target practice for the goons above. They shot at her as if she was a cork bobbing about in a barrel. The rage rose inside him when he heard a roar of laughter from the platform above. This wasn't just a matter of Seastead security to them – they were enjoying it.

He leaped from the scaffolding and crashed back into the white, foamy sea as it lashed against the column. After the initial dive he came back to the surface for a few moments where he made a judgement about Maria's location and after calculating wind direction and drift he took the deepest breath of his life and went back under.

It seemed to last forever but he knew he was getting close when he saw the familiar white streaks of the underwater bullet trails. She must be close, he thought, and then he saw her legs kicking a few feet above him. She was back on the surface again, and risking a direct shot to the head or upper body. He knew he had to act fast and reached up to her legs.

A bullet trail slashed through the water in between the two of them but he never flinched. This wasn't a mission he could give up. Grabbing her left ankle he pulled her hard under the water.

She didn't know what had happened and lashed out but he was ready, and then a moment later they were face to face in the dark, violent sea, surrounded by bullet trails. He reached his arm around her upper body and began powering the two of them through the water with one arm. Maria was strong but she was light, and that meant he was able to get her back to safety.

Pulling her up the scaffolding was a tough job. His fingers slipped on the wet rungs and the waves were almost irresistible, but when she was above the surface she was able to help herself and soon they were both climbing up out of the sea to join the others.

Hawke gripped hold of the ladder and started to make his way toward the first platform of the Seastead. The storm was high now and whipped up a tremendous sheet of sea spray, soaking him. A second later it was followed by an immense wave that smashed into the rigging beneath the platform and nearly wiped him off the ladder.

He clung on for his life, spitting seawater out of his mouth and trying to get his breath back. Looking down, he saw the storm throwing the large yacht around as if it were a rubber dingy in a wave machine. Down there, below him on the ladder, he saw the desperate faces of his friends as they willed him on up the ladder.

He made another seven rungs before another massive wave smashed into him once again. This one was heavier and faster, and the violence of the blow almost tore him and everyone else off the ladder yet again. This time he held his breath as the freezing water crashed into him, but he knew he couldn't withstand many of these waves. He craned his neck up and saw he was only a few yards from the top. If he could just get to the top of the scaffolding and through the hole in the substructure, he could rescue Lea and Camacho.

Glancing to his left he saw another colossal wave fast approaching. By the look of it they were all in a lot of trouble. It would give the boat a damn good beating, and if it struck while he was on the scaffolding he would be flung into the ocean like a rag doll.

Careful not to slip on the soaking ladder he made his way through the icy cold sea spray and finally reached the manhole in the base of the substructure. He clambered up inside and found himself in the base of the Seastead and could hardly believe what he was seeing. The section he was standing in was a vast space of support struts surrounding what looked and sounded like some kind of engine room, and from this perspective he could see that the sea directly below the structure was sealed off from the ocean by enormous steel walls creating a separate area for larger ships to dock.

Hawke fixed his eyes on his friends as they joined him. They were tired after fighting the sea. "Me and Scarlet are going topside to get Lea and Camacho."

"Ooh – a double date!"

He gave her a look but said nothing. "Reaper's going to lead Lexi, Maria and Ryan and go after Korać and Kruger. We don't want those two loose cannons on deck. We know they came down here somewhere."

Hawke and Scarlet jogged along a narrow section of the scaffolding along the western edge of the platform and made their way up a flight of service stars to where they thought the entrance would be located. When they reached the top of the stairs they saw that their sense of direction was right, but there were two men blocking their path.

"I'll take the one on the right," Scarlet said.

"But he's the biggest."

"Your point?"

"Fine," he said with a shake of his head.

They approached through the shadows and struck like lightning. Scarlet took the heavier of the two men and Hawke now knew why she wanted to fight him – she wanted to use his weight against him, and it was working as she rolled out a series of martial arts moves against him and essentially turned him into a human punch bag.

Hawke struck the second man but despite his smaller size he was more seasoned than his colleague and knew how to hold himself. He struck back hard and made Hawke sing for his supper, dodging, ducking and weaving to avoid a ferocious salvo of punches.

The man moved fast and used some kind of martial arts Hawke had never seen before. In a flash he had Hawke in a headlock. Hawke struggled but the man had a good grip on his head and was now pushing his face into the steel mesh behind him as hard as possible. Freezing seawater sluiced up over the scaffolding and hundreds of feet below he watched the slate-gray Atlantic heave and swirl in the turmoil of the storm.

"I would kill you fast," the man said in a heavy Baltic accent, "but I like to make my victims suffer."

"Are you single? If so I know a woman you might really get on with."

"What?"

"Shut it, Joe," Scarlet said. She ploughed the heel of her boot across her opponent's cheek, delivered by an eye-watering roundhouse kick that was rapidly becoming her signature move. The man howled and staggered back and gave Scarlet the chance she needed. She leaped forward and raised her leg above his head, smashing it down on his skull with a ferocious axe kick. He crumpled over and fell back over the rail, tumbling down into the sea.

Hawke threaded his arm up into the space between the goon's arm and his own squashed face and used the force he was pressing down with against him. Instantly tumbling over with the sudden loss of the support his arm was providing, Hawke leaped to his feet and kicked him in the face.

The man screamed, but Hawke's luck was out already. At the other end of the platform several armed men were pouring out of a stairwell and taking cover behind the engine room housing in the center of the substructure.

The goon was now on his feet and ready for revenge, but Hawke blocked his first strike and powered a hard fist into his lower right jaw. The man spun around like a top and then tumbled off the edge of the platform, screaming like a baby all the way down until he hit the surface of the raging sea below.

Scarlet glanced at her watch. "We're really going to have to do something about that gut of yours. That was over two minutes."

"I do not have a gut."

"You tell yourself that."

The banter was broken by more gunfire, and they dived for cover behind one of the four main support struts. They knew their time was running out. On the far wall Hawke saw the control mechanism for the main entrance to the platform's topside and knew there was only one play.

"There it is," he said. "That's our way to the platform – this must be how people arriving by ship get up top."

He leaped from the cover of the strut and sprinted as fast as he could toward the control panel. Anticipating a savage volley of defensive fire he wasn't disappointed when they let rip with their weapons, and he immediately launched himself into a full-speed parkour roll. As he tumbled over on his shoulder against the cold, slippery steel rivets and plates of the platform floor, he heard the bullets from their automatic rifles tracing over his head and pinging off the scaffolding on the east side of the platform.

He came out of the roll running and then dived behind the main strut on the south side. Wasting no time he pulled the lever down and a bright green light on the control panel flickered to life followed by an ear-piercing klaxon as the Seastead's entrance began to slide slowly open. He noticed that beneath them a bidirectional tidal gate was also opening allowing the sea into the area below the structure.

Still under heavy fire, he returned the same way he had come with a second parkour roll, only this time they were ready and their aim was better. He felt one bullet rip into the sole of his boot halfway through the roll. But then he was back where he started beside Scarlet.

"And that was forty seconds," Scarlet said with a sigh. "I could have done it in half that time. You really do want me to start calling you Joe Pork, don't you?"

"Try it," he said. "If you think Cairo's the worst I can come up with, think again."

"Point taken."

The entrance was now almost fully open and the men began to retreat up the ramp leading to the topside. They were fleeing the incoming danger now racing toward them thanks to Hawke opening the gates. Below, the storm outside powered the yacht into the heart of the Seastead's docking area on the beat of the raging ocean below its hull. Boats didn't have brakes, and Hawke knew it was coming in too fast. He winced as the savage pulse of the raging storm powered the boat's bow into the steel wall at the end of the docking bay.

He guessed the yacht belonged to whoever owned this place, and after Ryan's tattoo observation on the chopper there was only one intelligent guess as to who that was – the Oracle. The fact he had just trashed his yacht brought a quick smile to his face, but the mission had only just started.

"Come on," he said. "We have work to do."

CHAPTER FORTY-THREE

Deep in the substructure on the far side of the platform, Reaper, Lexi, Maria and Ryan were in hot pursuit of Dirk Kruger, Korać, Luk and Kamchatka. The former legionnaire's eyes were peeled as they moved stealthily through the forest of support struts and pipes. Somewhere down here in this industrial jungle were four of the most dangerous men he had ever met, and now they were cornered animals, trapped on a maniac's secret ocean base with no chance of escape except a violent and bloody shootout.

"It's four on four," Reaper said. "They're ours for the taking."

And then he saw them – quick as a flash and then gone again. They had broken into two groups. The South African and the Serb had gone to the north while Mr Luk and Kamchatka had made tracks to the south.

"We need to split up," he said. "I'll take Ryan and go after Kruger and Korać. Maria – you go after Luk and Kamchatka." He turned to Lexi. "I need you to get ready to blow up that refinery."

"Got it," Lexi said with a cold smile.

"Move out!" Reaper said,

The Frenchman led Ryan through a cloud of steam emanating from a cooling duct and noticed the young man was sticking close by. To their right he heard one of the men they were hunting slip on something and curse as he stopped himself from falling over.

Reaper yelled at Ryan to get down and the next second he was unloading his mag at the targets. Korać was faster than Kruger, but they were soon tucked down behind one of the support struts and returning fire.

"They're looking for a way out of here," Reaper said, dodging a bullet. "And they're putting their money on a boat moored down in the docking bay."

More bullets traced around them and Reaper saw Korać was now covering for Kruger as he was trying to descend the scaffold toward the marina below them. "It's now or never, Ryan!"

*

Maria Kurikova moved stealthily along the perimeter gangway running around the western edge of the Seastead as she moved south in her pursuit of Luk and Kamchatka. Her face was as cold steel as she moved through the sea spray, gun in her hand. The Russian hitman Kamchatka had tried to kill Lexi in Berlin and by the look on her face this was payback time.

Then she saw something and turned.

Without aiming, Kamchatka fired on her from the hip. The muzzle flash produced a cloud of gunsmoke, and then Maria took cover behind the scaffolding.

Luk and Kamchatka now retreated further into the shadows, keeping up a barrage of fire to hold the ECHO member back, but Maria Kurikova was having none of it.

She powered forward with her gun in her hand, keeping low to avoid the bullets tracing overhead, and took cover behind a stack of crates covered in some plastic tarp. More bullets raced overhead, and she knew she had only one magazine to take both of them out. She made a silent prayer and resumed the pursuit.

*

Korać was now crouch-walking backwards using the cowling of an elevator motor for cover. Kruger was further down and on the marina now, making his way to a boat moored on one of the jetties. Thanks to Hawke opening the bidirectional tidal gate all of the boats were now getting smashed about by the sea and the South African was having a hard time finding one that was still seaworthy, never mind trying to get on board one of them.

Reaper fired on Korać, but missed. The Serbian commander was as hard-nosed and battle-worn as they came, and barely flinched as the bullet ricocheted off a steel girder a few inches from his head. With a Heckler & Koch MP7 gripped firmly in his hands he spat fire right back at Reaper and Ryan, keeping the bursts short and professional.

"Reap!" Ryan yelled. "Head's up on Kruger in the marina – he's getting on a boat!"

Reaper looked through a gap in the platform and saw the South African clambering up onto the bow of a large powerboat rocking violently back and forth on the furthest jetty. The plan was obviously to drive the thing right out of the tidal gate and worry about its range later when he was free of the danger on the Seastead.

Korać had also heard Ryan's scream, and turned to see his benefactor deserting him. Reaper didn't need an invitation to take advantage of a mistake like that and took the shot.

He was wide, striking the Serbian in the shoulder and knocking him back to his left. He grunted in pain but there was no scream. He began to move back and flipped over on his stomach to belly crawl his way to the powerboat. "Dirk! Wait for me!"

Kruger ignored him, and began to steer the boat along the marina in the direction of the gates.

Korać cursed him and fired a burst of shots at the boat, but realising he had limited rounds and that killing the enemy was more important than taking Kruger out, he turned the gun back on Reaper and Ryan.

Reaper returned fire and sent the Serb scuttling back into the shadows again, and then glanced at Kruger below. "Bon sang! He's getting away!"

"No he damn well isn't!" Ryan said, and leaped from the platform.

Reaper was in shock as he watched the young man plummeting through the air toward the water below, but he had timed it perfectly and landed with a heavy smack on the bow of the powerboat.

"Ryan!" Reaper yelled. "What the hell are you doing?"

But Ryan couldn't hear, and all the Frenchman could do was watch as the young man made his way from the bow to the bridge. A moment later he was fighting with Dirk Kruger, hand to hand on the starboard bow while the boat moved through the water with no one at the controls.

Reaper's focus was brought back by a bullet whistling an inch past his nose. He threw himself down to avoid the next bullet and give himself time to reload his gun. As he smacked the magazine into the grip he heard more rapid firing and pulled himself up to look through a crack to see Korać having one last shot at the man who had betrayed him and left him for dead.

Below, Dirk Kruger and Ryan Bale were now fighting on the stern of the boat, but their struggle was interrupted by the sound of the gunfire aimed at them. They both looked up and saw the Serb pouring fire down on them. Ryan moved first, and went to dive off the boat. Kruger hesitated for a second before following him in an attempt to escape the savage fire of the submachine gun, but then it happened.

And Reaper saw it first.

Korać wasn't aiming for the fighting men but for the gas tank.

And he hit it before either man had abandoned the powerboat.

Reaper yelled. "Non!" but it was too late. The bullets tore into the gas tank and ignited the fuel and a split second later the entire boat was a vicious fireball engulfing both men. Reaper could hardly believe what he had just seen and screamed with rage as the acrid black smoke of the burning wreckage reached his nostrils.

His eyes hurriedly scanned the surface of the water for survivors but there was nothing except fire and smoke. He yelled and spun around, bringing his gun into the aim with Dragan Korać's stubble-covered face bang-smack in the center of his sights.

The Serb smirked and raised the HK at him, squeezing the trigger, barely able to conceal his delight at the thought of filling the Frenchman full of lead, but instead he got nothing more than the hollow click of dry-firing and realized he had used his ammo destroying the powerboat.

"Please!" he pleaded, dropping the submachine gun and raising his hands.

"A mercenary never begs for his life," Reaper said. "Only for a quick death."

And with that he emptied his magazine into the Serbian's chest, blasting him back into a dead heap that tumbled down the steel steps behind him and landed with a bloody crunch on the marina.

Reaper looked down with disgust as a wave reached up and heaved Korać 's corpse back into the freezing brine of the sea.

But there was no satisfaction, only the terrible empty feeling of irretrievable loss as he thought about Ryan.

CHAPTER FORTY-FOUR

Kim Taylor unleashed a ruthless salvo of bullets from the submachine gun as she fought with everything she had to safeguard the island's last line of defense. She pushed them back and Eden shut the electric door again. The men who landed in the Black Hawk had made their way to the bunker with terrifying speed.

"We can't keep them out of here forever," Kim said. "Any chance your Dad never got your phone call, Alex?"

"He got it... I hope."

Eden checked the CCTV and frowned. "And now our friends are coming back with explosives. They're going to blow the door open."

"Let's see them try," Kim said, bringing the submachine gun to her hip once again. "Open the door!"

Eden hit the button and Kim fired more rounds into the corridor, taking out one of the men and causing the others to retreat once again.

"Keep it up, Kim!" Alex shouted. "The cavalry's here."

Kim turned and looked on the one remaining plasma screen to see several fighter jets screeching across the sky. On their tails were the instantly recognizable skull-and-crossbones of the VFA-103 Strike Fighter Squadron, better known to the world as the Jolly Rogers, assigned to Carrier Air Wing Seven. "When most people ask their Dads for help, Alex, they don't usually get an aircraft carrier strike group."

Alex shrugged her shoulders. "What can I say? The USS Harry Truman is two hundred miles north so Dad sent these guys down to help, I guess."

"We owe him," Eden said, the relief obvious on his face as he closed the door one more time. "Let's hope they're not too late."

*

Captain Jonathan "Poker" White pulled on the stick and raised the nose of his F/A-18F Super Hornet. Instantly he was pulling three Gs as the fighter jet tipped on her starboard side and turned around the small island below. From up here it looked barely inhabitable except for the small complex set in between the two mountains either side of it.

Behind him, Lieutenant Commander Ben "Sleuth" Holmes, the crew commander, was scanning above his head for the Apache. One was still down at sea level but one had climbed higher to evade them.

"Bandit at three o'clock," Sleuth said. "Angels Two."

Poker pulled harder and brought the Super Hornet around another forty-five degrees, ascending to two thousand feet. The rogue Apache was in visual range now and Sleuth went to launch one of the missiles.

"Wait a minute," said Poker. "They got US markings! They're friendly."

"Orders are to take them out, Captain," Commander Holmes said coolly.

"They're American choppers!"

"We don't know who's in 'em or why they're doing what they're doing. Our orders are to take them out so they're out."

"All right – we're on the bug," Poker replied.

In his capacity as the Weapon Systems Officer, or Wizzo, Holmes activated a Skyflash air-to-air missile and fired. It ripped away from the Super Hornet and closed in on the Apache at a terrifying velocity.

The chopper executed an evasive manoeuvre and the missile tore past it with a foot to spare. The helicopter exploited the F18's faster speed and slowed to a hover forcing the jet to pass over it. Then they fired.

"We have a spike at six o'clock," Sleuth said, watching the radar.

Poker banked hard to port and the missile missed.

"We're vaping like a freight train, Sleuth. They'll be able to see us for miles."

"Go around."

Poker flew the F18 in a circuit and the other Apache came into view. It was hovering over the island preparing to fire another missile at the main compound.

Sleuth fired another Skyflash and this time they were luckier. A second later the chopper was a fireball.

They went around once more and now the last surviving Apache was trying to retreat. One Skyflash later it was a shower of burning metal.

"What about the Black Hawk on the beach?"

"Take her out."

This time the Wizzo selected an AGM-65 Maverick air-to-ground missile and three seconds later the Black Hawk on the ground was blasted to pieces. Stinking black smoke bloomed up from the paradise below.

"We're all done here," Sleuth said. "That's an RTB. I repeat an RTB."

"That was no USAF flying that Apache," Poker said. "He was a total grape."

"All right, let's firewall this baby and go home."

*

Kim Taylor and Richard Eden fought the last of the men back along the corridor and pursued them out of the complex, using their order to retreat to their advantage. On the beach, the men scrambled desperately to get into the Black Hawk, but Eden pushed forward with his machine pistol.

Driven by the instinct to protect the island and everyone on it, he fought fiercer than ever. Using the palms along the backshore for cover, he poured fire on the men as they climbed into the chopper. His bullets struck one man in the back and he tumbled out of the chopper and crashed dead into the sand, but the others were on board and the rotors were powering up to raise the helicopter off the beach and get to safety.

"They're pretty damn desperate to get out of here!" Kim said.

"Something tells me they don't want us to know who they are," Eden replied, firing again and striking the side of the chopper. He ran forward another twenty yards and aimed at the underside of the machine when it happened.

From her elevated position on the dunes, Kim saw it first. "Rich! Take cover!"

He looked up to see an AGM-65 Maverick air-to-ground missile racing from one of the Super Hornets toward the fleeing chopper. He turned on his heel and sprinted away from the doomed helicopter as fast as he could, but in his heart he knew no one outruns a missile travelling at over a thousand kilometres per hour.

The chopper spun around and pulled up in a vain attempt to dodge the Maverick but it was like a dairy cow trying to outrun a hyena.

The gigantic explosion blasted the chopper into a fireball and propelled Eden through the air in the terrific heat and flames of its shockwave. Kim gasped as she watched the ECHO leader spinning through the burning chaos and crash down hard on the rocks dividing the berm from the backshore.

In the sky, the three Super Hornets turned in perfect unison to the north, their afterburners roaring as they accelerated and gained altitude for the ride back to the strike group. Far below, Kim Taylor ran through the smoke pouring from the Black Hawk's wreckage to reach Eden as fast as she could.

When she got to him she thought the worst. He was unconscious and his head was smashed into the rocks. Blood was dripping down over his face from the terrible gash on his temple as she dropped to her knees beside him and cradled his head in her hand.

"What happened?"

She looked over her shoulder and saw Alex pushing her wheelchair as far as it would go.

"It's Rich," Kim said. "I'm not sure... he got blasted pretty bad when they blew up the chopper."

"Oh Jesus..." Alex ran her hands over her face. How much more of this could they endure, she thought.

"We need help, Alex."

"It's on the way," Alex said. "The Captain of the Harry Truman just radioed and said he's sending a Sea Hawk from the ship to get us."

"How long?"

"Any minute," she replied, straining to see Eden's condition. "It left the same time he dispatched the fighters."

Kim Taylor stared down at the blood on the rocks and then up through the smoke and heat to see Alex Reeve's anxious face looking back at her. She hastily rubbed sand from her eyes and shook her head in disbelief at the horror that had unfolded around her. She wasn't sure any minute was going to be fast enough to save Sir Richard Eden.

CHAPTER FORTY-FIVE

Joe Hawke and Scarlet Sloane fought their way inside the Seastead but then the resistance grew even greater. The Athanatoi keeping Lea and Camacho hostage burst into action, firing back at them and determined to keep them at bay.

"There she is!" Scarlet shouted. "They're trying to get her in the elevator."

"Not on my watch," Hawke called back, aiming his weapon and taking out one of the men holding Lea. The man dropped to the floor and the other man spun around to see what had happened.

It was the only chance Hawke needed and he seized it. "Get down Lea!" he called out. She dropped and he took out the second man, but a third leaped forward to grab her. This time Lea was ready and she kneed the man in the groin and darted for cover.

"Another one!" Hawke yelled.

Yet another Athanatoi jumped over a nearby couch firing constantly from a handgun as he flew through the air. The muzzle-flash pulsed as the rounds fired out and then he stopped firing just in time to pull his arm around to execute a perfect parkour shoulder roll and disappear into the shadows.

"Jesus, these guys make Han's Shaolin monks look like couch potatoes," Scarlet said.

"That's what worries me," said Hawke.

Across the room Camacho was fighting his way to freedom via a savage knockout punch to his guard's face. He dusted himself down and pulled the pistol from the unconscious man's hands before running over and joining Hawke and Scarlet.

"Where did they take Lea?" the Englishman asked as they fired on some men defending the higher levels from a mezzanine.

"To the top level," he said, wiping the sweat from his eyes. "That's where they said their boss was."

"Then let's get after her."

Hawke pounded up the steel steps beside the elevator, gun in hand and ready to fight but starting to feel his energy levels drop. He'd been going full-on since Munich and he wasn't getting any younger. Much more of this and these bastards would get the better of him and Lea would be lost.

At the top of the stairs he saw another wave of Athanatoi rushing into position, and at his feet were the corpses of the fallen enemy they had taken out a moment ago on the mezzanine. He grabbed a machine pistol from a dead man and emptied the magazine at the enemy, blasting chunks off the walls and puncturing holes in the brushed chrome elevator doors.

Out of rounds, he moved forward to the next dead body and snatched another of the guns, raising it into the aim and loosing another angry flash of bullets into the enemy. He would tear a hole through every last one of them if that's what it took to get Lea back.

But the response was equally as devastating, and whoever these men were they were shockingly well-trained in their tactics and gun control. They operated almost as if they had a hive mind, but the reality was they were coordinating their movements over a comms system... taking orders from strategic command over ear pieces and reporting back on concealed palm mics.

Scarlet winced as another burst of gunfire blasted the ceiling tiles above her head and the pieces rained down on her. "They look like they're out of the bloody Matrix!"

"And they act like it too," Hawke said, emptying the second mag and angrily tossing the gun behind him. He looked ahead and saw Lea just for a flash – the men who were holding her had dragged her to the front line.

"Drop your weapons or she's dead."

Hawke, Scarlet and Camacho exchanged a glance. The former SAS woman looked at Hawke for the next move, but she already knew what he was going to do. One look at the carbine jammed into Lea's neck was enough.

Hawke got to his feet and raised his hands. He knew there was no way he could fight through this army. He was experienced enough as a soldier to know there were other ways to get what you wanted. The fact they had now decided to use Lea as leverage to force his hand sealed the deal.

"All right... I'm unarmed."

"And the other two!"

Scarlet and Camacho followed his lead and stood up with their hands above their heads. "Easy darlings, don't shoot what you can't afford to replace."

Two of the men padded over to them and raised their submachine guns into their faces. "The Oracle desires your company."

"He wants to meet us before he kill us," Lea said.

The man looked at her. "You're already dead."

*

Reaper's mind was racing as he thundered along the top of the steel pipeline on his way back to the main platform. He was struggling to maintain his balance on the oily surface as he ducked and dodged incoming enemy fire, this time fired not by Korać or Kruger but by the men in black, the self-styled crazy cult who called themselves the Immortals.

He fired back, but thanks to his precarious position on the pipe his shots were all over the place. At least it would force them into cover, he thought. He reached the area where they had broken into two groups and made his way along the western perimeter. His plan was to catch up with Maria, help her finish Luk and Kamchatka if they hadn't already done the job, and then regroup with Lexi and go topside to find Hawke and the others.

There were fewer Athanatoi on this stretch of the Seastead, and he was able to slow for a moment to reload and get his breath back. He watched his breath cloud out in front of him. Beyond was the startling dichotomy of two grays – paler in the sky and darker in the sea. He had almost forgotten they were in the middle of the ocean since the fighting started, and he had no idea how to win a battle like this.

His mind moved to Ryan, the youngest of the team and the least violent among them, who had leaped from the substructure's scaffolding to stop that bastard Dirk Kruger from getting away and given his life in the process. It wasn't right but he'd died a hero. How he would break the news to Maria, he didn't know.

And then up ahead he heard a gunshot.

And then another.

He took a deep breath and began pounding toward the action as fast as he could.

CHAPTER FORTY-SIX

The penthouse at the top of the Seastead was unlike anything they had seen before, with a level of opulence that would have embarrassed a Saudi prince. Lea could hardly believe what she was seeing. She had no idea that such wealth existed. The entire Seastead plus its lavish furnishings must have cost indescribable billions.

The men who had escorted them stepped back and exited the room, closing the doors behind them, and then a new, dark silence fell.

Her eyes lowered from the chandelier on the ceiling to an enormous mahogany desk at the far end of the room. Safely behind it, a man was sitting in a leather swivel chair. He was facing away from them, and all she could see was the top of his head. Above him was an antique Georgian mirror angled slightly downwards, but his face was still obscured. On the desk, set deliberately in view, was the idol the men had snatched from Kruger on the helipad.

"What's the matter – can't you face me?" Lea said.

Hawke, Scarlet and Camacho said nothing.

The man made no reply.

"I said, haven't you got the *bollocks* to face me, you bastard?"

Outside they heard the chatter of submachine guns and random grenade explosions as Reaper and the rest of the team fought with the Athanatoi foot soldiers.

"I see you were appreciating my chandelier a moment ago. It's the Givenchy Royal Hanover from Germany.

Beautifully crafted from solid silver in 1736. I bought it a few weeks ago for seven million dollars."

"Who are you?" Hawke said flatly.

"I am many men." The voice was calm and the accent mildly foreign. Lea couldn't quite place it but she thought she'd heard it before.

"You have no idea how much I want to shoot you through the back of that chair," Lea said.

"I understand your anger, but fortunately you do not have a gun."

"You understand nothing, you bastard. Why did you murder my father?"

The Oracle laughed, but it was a low, humorless chuckle. Lea felt the evil as it almost pulsed from his side of the room, flowing like poisoned wine spilled on a clean tablecloth. She had never felt a rage like this before. It was so great it had started to tarnish at the edges, and turn to fear and sadness.

She was standing with the man she loved and some of her closest friends, but inside her head her mind forced her to watch a never-ending motion picture of her childhood memories: her mother making a cake in the kitchen as the Irish sun pierced the mist outside; her brothers playing in the garden; her father showing her how to fit a lens to a camera.

Her father.

Simple childhood memories more important to her than all the gold and treasure in the world, and now the last remnants of a previous happiness were nothing more than dusty relics, destroyed by the monstrous animal on the other side of this room. A wave of revulsion crept over her like a cloth soaking up that poisoned wine.

"Give me what I want, you son of a bitch! Why won't you just tell us what we want to know?" She took a step closer. "What happened to my father?"

"You want answers, I understand that... and you're not alone. Your father was the same. He was digging too deep."

Hawke saw the anger on Lea's face and took a step forward. "You can start with who are the Athanatoi?"

"That cannot be answered. It's like asking – who are humans?"

"I don't understand."

A long sigh from the man in the swivel chair. "You have caused me much trouble. I respect your courage, but you understand why I brought you here."

"You're full of shit," the Irishwoman said, almost spitting out the words.

But the Oracle merely laughed.

And then he turned around.

Hawke, Lea, Scarlet and Camacho took a step back in shock. None of them could believe what they were seeing.

Lea spoke first. "I can't believe it."

"Better believe it," Scarlet said in disgust. "We've been played like violins."

"Otmar Wolff," Hawke said coldly. "If that's your real name."

"It's my real name... at least *one* of my real names."

"You're the Oracle?" Lea said.

He nodded once. "I'd shake your hands but we already did that back in Liechtenstein, plus you're filthy and covered in blood."

Hawke fixed his eyes on Wolff. "Bond got Hugo Drax and I get you – at least you're wearing the Nehru jacket – nice touch, by the way!"

Wolff rose from behind his desk and walked to the window. It stretched three hundred and sixty degrees around his penthouse suite, with views over the Atlantic in every direction. Slipped his hands in his pockets casually. Sighed with irritation. "I brought you here to take the idol and kill you, and instead you destroy half my home."

He picked up the idol and weighed it contemplatively for a few moments. "But I have her now, at least."

Lea bristled with anger. "Why ask us to get it, you son of a bitch?"

The reply was cool and measured. "Set a thief to catch a thief, and all that. After the desecration at Mictlan and the Mexican's thieving of the idol, I decided you must all die, but I knew I needed that idol first. I have resources, but they are mostly political. On the other hand your team has proved itself to be rather, shall we say *adept* at locating ancient relics."

"True story. We found you, after all," Scarlet said.

Wolff ignored her. "My plan was simple – invite you to Liechtenstein, find out what you learned in Mictlan before the Mexican Government sealed it off again, and have you retrieve the idol for me. I must say it worked like a dream. The consummate wild goose chase."

Hawke took a step closer. "It's not over yet, Wolff."

He laughed. "It was the ultimate revenge – turn you into puppets to do my bidding and then when you have served me by furnishing me with this idol, execute you – oh, and you might like to know I had your little Caribbean island annihilated today." As he spoke he caressed the idol in his hands. "She's mine now. That is all that matters."

"Using us was a pretty cheap trick, Wolff," Camacho said.

"Not at all. In fact it makes perfect strategic sense. I realized that setting a team of my own men against you in a race to find the idol was inefficient and would waste my time and resources. I asked myself: why not simply use the ECHO team as my puppets and have them find the idol for me?"

"Such a nice man," Scarlet said.

Wolff ignored her. "You had already proved yourself extremely capable, and it would only cost me five million dollars as well. I made more than that playing on the commodities market before breakfast today so you were very cheap to buy. All I had to do was sit back and wait for you to bring the idol to me, but when you stumbled across Atlantis I knew I had to intervene. Sadly, I doubt there can be much left there now for future surveys."

"How kind of you," Lea said.

Wolff smiled and tipped his head to one side. He reminded Lea of a chameleon looking at a fly a second before firing its tongue out and catching it. "In many respects it's lucky you didn't die when I destroyed the Tomb of Eternity in Ethiopia or I wouldn't have been able to use you now."

Lea could hardly believe the words she was hearing. So he had also been responsible for the destruction of that mountain. Now she knew she was closer than ever to learning the truth about this man and his powers. "What's the significance of Atlantis in all this?" she asked. "Why did you destroy it?"

"Atlantis is nothing," he snarled. "A burned-out husk of a colony that was annihilated during the wars. My destruction of it today was nothing compared with what put it under the waves in the first place."

"A colony?" Lea asked. "What does that mean? And what wars?"

Wolff laughed. "If you thought Atlantis was the greatest civilization of all time, just waiting to be discovered and plundered then surely you were sadly mistaken. Atlantis was nothing more than a failed religious order of traitors, and not even unique – just one of many, all created by *them*." He let a sour, bitter laugh escape from his clay-colored lips. "Created by them just as if they were playing a game…"

"I don't understand," Lea said. "Who created Atlantis?"

Wolff stared at the young Irishwoman for several awkward seconds while drumming his fingers on the desk. The relentless tapping filled the tense silence as the old man clearly wrestled with his own thoughts. "The story of human civilization is not at all as you have been taught. Everything you think you know about humans and the world we live in is a lie, and worse than that, your rulers know it."

"Liar."

"What you see in your world today has all happened before, and I will destroy mankind before I let you shine a light on the truth."

"Now I know who you are, you *bastard*," Lea said, spitting the last word out, "I'm going to bring an end to all this shit."

He laughed, mocking her. "This isn't the end, Donovan – only the beginning."

Far below a tremendous explosion ignited the refinery and rocked the entire Seastead. Wolff grabbed hold of the side of the desk to stop himself falling over, and for the first time Lea thought she sensed something other than cool control on his face.

"Looks like the tide is turning," Hawke said.

"You cannot destroy me," Wolff said, a malevolent smirk spreading on his face.

Before any of them had a chance to reply, a second tremendous blast knocked them off their feet and flung them through the air like confetti. Lea felt the full force as the shockwave struck her. It felt like a horse had kicked her in the stomach and she hit the deck like a rock, rolling over several times before she hit the wall and stopped dead. When she looked up the room was filling with smoke.

"Is everyone okay?" Hawke yelled.

"Fucking fantastic," Scarlet said, coughing. "Thanks for asking."

"He's gone!" Lea said. The desperation in her voice was clear for all to hear.

Hawke looked through the smoke to the Oracle's desk and saw she was right. He was gone.

He leaped to his feet and ran to the desk, smashing his fist down on top of it with frustration. "Damn it to hell!"

"Where did he go?" Scarlet asked, scanning the room.

Hawke sighed. "There's an escape hatch."

"Are you freaking *kidding* me?" Lea said.

"And he remembered to pack the idol before he went on vacation as well," Scarlet said.

*

Maria Kurikova felt confident as she moved deeper into the fight. She knew that somewhere behind her Reaper and Ryan were advancing to the north in pursuit of Dirk Kruger, but her sights were set firmly on Luk and Kamchatka.

She struck out on the pipe, her boots slipping here and there on small streams of leaking oil, but it was the fastest way to get to the other side of the substructure. If she went all the way around the safety scaffolding she knew she would lose them.

Below her the raging black sea pounded and roared like a trapped bear and sprayed her with freezing saltwater as she made her way across to the other side.

And then she saw him.

Luk.

He was standing in the shadows of the scaffolding on the far western side of the substructure and he looked scared, which surprised her. All around them the battle raged and now somewhere above her from the main platform she heard a loud explosion and felt the vibration from the shockwave as it emanated into the substructure. *Lexi got the refinery*, she thought.

And then Luk pulled a knife from his belt and tossed it in the air so he was holding it by the blade… *ready to throw it at me*.

She flicked her eyes down at the violent sea and knew there was nothing down there but a terrible, lonely death.

She looked back up.

The next seconds went like lightning.

Luk pulled his arm back to throw the knife.

Maria fired her gun and dodged to the left to miss the knife.

She slipped on the pipe and tumbled over it.

Luk staggered backwards, his hands clutching the savage bullet wound in his stomach.

Maria grabbed hold of the pipe as she fell down, and just managed to grab hold of a riveted plate holding two segments of the pipe together. She was safe, for now, and had stopped herself plummeting into the sea, but it was only now that her hands were grasping the pipe's metal that she realized it was hot – too hot to handle.

She cursed in pain as she hauled herself back up the pipe and then staggered to her feet. Not taking any more chances she made the last few yards of the pipe and stepped off onto the substructure's platform a foot away from Luk.

"Please…" Luk murmured. "Make it fast."

"You want it fast?" she said, her heavy Russian accent concealing only part of the utter contempt she felt for the man kneeling in front of her.

She raised her boot and placed it on his chest. "Нет…*No*."

And with that she booted him off the platform.

He screamed as he tumbled over the edge of the Seastead and crashed down into the Kort nozzle of the moored container ship below. Sucked down by the force of the enormous ducted propellers he was drawn helplessly toward the savage, whirring blades. The last thing she heard were Luk's blood-curdling screams as his body was sucked inside the industrial cowling and minced by the vessel's azimuth thruster. This was followed by a terrible noise that sounded like an industrial meat grinder. Seconds later the heaving Atlantic was bright red with blood and then it was all gone, washed away with the tide forever.

"Death by a thousand cuts, you bastard," she said coolly, and slipped her gun back inside her holster.

And then saw the muzzle flash.

And heard the crack.

And felt the shot.

It felt like someone had run a hot poker through her heart.

She gasped, but felt no air fill her lungs, and then she dropped to her knees as the hot blood poured from her mouth.

She knew what had happened… or thought she knew, because now she was losing consciousness. Her blood pressure was dropping because of the nine mil hole in her heart and there was nothing she could do to save herself.

The battle seemed to move in slow-motion as she turned her head and saw Vincent Reno racing toward her with his gun raised. He was screaming *Non!* and then he fired three successive shots above her head to kill the assassin. She never knew if he got him because instead she chose to close her eyes and go to sleep.

CHAPTER FORTY-SEVEN

"Who the hell has an escape hatch under his frigging desk?" Lea asked, sighing angrily.

"The President of the United States, for one thing," Hawke said. "I know because Alex told me she saw it when her Dad introduced her to President Grant. It's right under the Resolute Desk and leads down on a slide to the Secret Service's Horsepower Command post in the White House basement."

"Well, this arschole has one too," Lea said. "And he's just used it to get away. Damn it all!"

A man rushed into the room with a gun raised. He was wearing black and Hawke immediately saw the Athanatoi mark on his wrist. He burst into action ready to fight him when he saw it was the man they had called Lazarus.

"Where is the bastard?" Lazarus said.

Scarlet pointed down the escape chute. "He left the party early."

Lazarus ran to the chute and cursed in a foreign language none of them recognized. He stared down into the gloom of the escape route, his face crossed with frustration, anger and fear.

"Where does this lead?" Hawke asked.

"He has an aircraft."

"Shit," Hawke said.

"Double shit," Lea said.

Scarlet sighed and rubbed her eyes. "Make that a triple."

"No, this is definitely a four turd situation," Camacho added.

"Let's get after him," Hawke yelled. "This is what we've been waiting for. If we want kill him it's now or never."

Lazarus shook his head. "Many have wanted to kill him, but all have failed. Today I will succeed where they all failed."

Then man from the helipad burst into the room with a gun. "Lazarus, you traitor!"

They exchanged gunfire, both striking each other. Lazarus's aim was better, hitting the other man in the head and killing him instantly, but his own wound was in the stomach. Death would be slow and agonizing.

"Jesus!" Lea said, running to the wounded man. "Oh God…"

"Get after him!" Lazarus said, his voice barely a whisper. "He *must* die. Take this." He handed Hawke his M4 complete with grenade launcher attachment. "You'll need it."

"Scarlet – with me," Hawke said. "We're going after Wolff. Lea and Jack – stay with Lazarus. He could help us."

Hawke slid down the escape chute at speed, folding his arms over his chest as if he were using an aircraft's evacuation slide. Seconds later his journey was over and he found himself on a sheet steel platform beside a narrow-gauge railroad leading off into a tunnel.

"What the fuck is this?" Scarlet said, now standing beside him. "Disneyland?"

"He's gone, Cairo – and whatever he used to get away was the only one because there's nothing else here."

"Then we have to run along the tracks," she said. "Now's your chance to get back from Pork to Hawke."

He gave her a look and readied the grenade launcher. "Let's see who gets there first then shall we?"

*

Lea stared down at the dying man. "Why did they call you a traitor, Lazarus?"

He tried to smile. "Because I wanted to tell the world about what we really are."

She took a deep breath. "Are you... *gods?*"

He shook his head. "We have lots of names – the Athanatoi is a very old word we use but there are others – the Shadowmen, the 10ᵗʰ Floor Group, the Priesthood – it depends on the country. In China we're called Bāxiān, a group of eight *xian*, or transcendental saints."

"How many groups are there?"

"There are many sects, or factions. Some refer to these as churches, or creeds, others even use the word denominations, but it all comes to same thing. There are lots of us, more than you know. We are immortal, but not divine. We are human, just like you. We were given the secret of immortality and we guard it with our lives, as you have seen. You can think of us as priests serving a higher power."

"What higher power – the Oracle?" Camacho asked.

The man laughed, coughing out more blood. He shook his head and gasped in pain as he clutched his stomach. "The Oracle serves the higher power just like the rest of us but now he's locked in endless skirmishes in the search for..." he doubled over in pain and made an agonized wheezing sound. His blood pressure was falling too low. "I'm dying... I'm finally dying."

"No you're not!" Lea said, leaning forward and tightening the tourniquet, but it was useless work and they both knew it. She gripped the man's head in her hands. "Searching for what, Lazarus?"

He looked up into her eyes as he released his dying breath. "Knock, and the door will be opened to you."

And then he was gone.

Lea closed her eyes and sighed, and then laid the man's head gently down in the rubble.

*

Jack Brooke picked up the phone and dialled through to the CIA headquarters in Langley, Virginia. A few seconds later Davis Faulkner picked up the call.

"What the hell is going on in the Caribbean, Davis?"

"I don't know, Jack."

"A lot of people are talking to me about some kind of military strike on an island down there." Brooke knew the island, but Faulkner didn't need to know that.

"I'm the same – just getting crap flying in all over me, six ways from Sunday."

"Find out what the hell is going on and get back to me."

"Yes, sir."

"Oh, and Davis…" Brooke rubbed his hand over his face and took a breath. "I'd kinda hoped I could bring this up when we were face to face, but you heard about Harper, right?" His shook his head with sadness as he thought about Harper Cavazo, one of the senators for Florida.

"Sure did – no wonder they call those damned things Doctor Killers."

Brooke clenched his jaw. He had known Harper for twenty years. Her death in a light aircraft accident a few days ago still felt raw. The NTSB was still investigating.

"Listen, Davis... we've known each other a long time so I guess you know what's coming."

"Oh no..."

"You don't think you're up to it?"

"I wouldn't say that, exactly..." his voice trailed off and Brooke heard a long inhalation on the famous cigar.

"So what do you say?"

"I was thinking about retiring somewhere tropical with a cool drink in each hand."

"But instead you're going to join me on the ticket and be my Vice President, right?"

A long pause. "I'd be honoured to share a ticket with you, Jack."

Brooke smiled. He liked Davis Faulkner – to a limit, but more than that he was a Florida man, and that was a major battleground state in the up-coming election. Brooke was going to have to carry the Sunshine State if he wanted the keys to 1600 Pennsylvania Avenue.

"Thanks, Davis. Now – find out just who's been blowing the hell out of the Caribbean. It's in our sphere of influence and no one plays down there without us knowing about it."

"You got it, Jack."

Brooke cut the call. He'd done the right thing. Not that he was going to tell Davis Faulkner about it, but his daughter had been on that island when it was attacked and he wanted to know who to pay back for the favor. At least the old Floridian had agreed to join him on the ticket and run as his Vice President. If Davis could deliver Florida's Electoral College votes he was sure he could win the Oval Office and if something ever happened to Brooke, Davis Faulkner would be a safe pair of hands in the White House.

At least not everything today had been a disaster.

CHAPTER FORTY-EIGHT

Hawke and Scarlet emerged from the monorail and found themselves exactly where Lazarus had described. They were standing on a rain-lashed section of the Seastead's upper level on the northeast of the platform by a runway. A sky slick and greasy with rain loomed above them and dead ahead was the hangar. Trundling out of it was a small Eclipse 500 business jet.

With the grenade launcher the dying man had give him gripped firmly in his hands, and only three rounds for it in his pocket, Hawke knew they only had one chance to stop Otmar Wolff, and that chance was now.

"We have to get closer!" he said. "This thing has a two hundred meter range so we couldn't hit a barn door from this range."

They ran across the platform in the rain and wind as fast as they could, never taking their eyes off the jet. Its two Pratt & Whitney turbofans were already fired up and the Oracle was trundling it out of the tiny hangar and lining it up on the runway.

"He's on his way, Joe!"

"We'll see about that."

He aimed the grenade launcher and fired on the small jet. A puff of smoke and then two seconds later the small hangar exploded in a fireball.

"Strike one," Scarlet said, looking anxiously at the jet as it began to speed up.

Hawke fired the second grenade. Two seconds later another large fireball exploded into the air, this time on the runway twenty yards behind the accelerating jet.

Scarlet sighed and turned to look at Hawke. "Strike two... only one grenade left."

Ahead on the runway, Wolff had pushed the throttles forward and the afterburners lit up at the back of the small jet. It speeded up rapidly and began to race away down the runway.

"Now or never, Joe."

Yes, thanks, Hawke thought. *I got that.*

*

Reaper turned the corner one second too late to save her. He'd just watched Ryan Bale and Dirk Kruger die in a boat explosion caused by Dragan Korać , and then wasted Korać for it. Now, he was thundering toward the sound of gunshots and arrived just in time to see Maria take Luk out. She'd booted him off the platform after he'd tried to kill her with a knife. It was a job well done, but then things had gone badly wrong.

He tried to stop it but was a second too late.

Another fatal shot, this time from above.

And Maria fell down. She swayed back and forth and then it was over.

Reaper immediately scanned the rigging above her and saw the assassin. He was already trying to get away.

Ekel Kvashnin.

Kamchatka had claimed another victim, but this time, Reaper swore, it would be his last.

The Frenchman jammed the gun into his belt and started to climb up into the support scaffolding in pursuit of the Russian hitman. The weasel had now reached the top of the scaffolding and was on a small mezzanine level, taking cover behind one of the Seastead's enormous electrical turbo generators.

He watched with hatred as Kamchatka reloaded his rifle and took up a defensive position. Seconds later they were engaged in a high-intensity fire fight. A fire fight Vincent Reno was determined he had to win.

High above on the next platform he heard the chaotic noise of battle and what sounded like the whining of an aircraft's jets, but dismissed it, not believing an aircraft could take off from a platform of this size.

Kamchatka fired on him. He was high in the substructure's support scaffold, like a pirate in a galleon's rigging. By the looks of it, he was loading a Russian-made VSSK Vykhlop sniper rifle, and he was doing it with impressive calmness and efficiency considering the circumstances.

Reaper knew this was his moment. He slowed his breathing and took the shot.

And Kamchatka took the bullet in his heart, just as he had done to Maria.

"Goodnight, you bastard," Reaper said.

As Kamchatka fell from the rigging into the sea, Reaper closed his eyes and gave Ryan and Maria a silent prayer.

*

Hawke aimed the grenade launcher for the final time and fired it at the jet. They watched as the grenade round tore through the air, their hearts full of hope. The former Commando had judged the speed of the aircraft and the crosswind, aiming the projectile ahead of the moving jet and to its left to compensate for the three seconds it was in the air.

Time seemed to slow down.

Lea and Camacho emerged from the monorail and ran to them.

And all four watched as the jet lifted into the air, flying right over the top of the end of the runway as the grenade exploded into a third and final fireball. The aim was good enough to knock the jet to starboard for a few seconds, but they watched with grim disappointment as Wolff pulled it level and banked hard to port. Seconds later he vanished into the low cloud ceiling and all that remained was a stormy sky.

"You missed him!" Lea said.

Hawke threw the grenade launcher to the ground and cursed.

"What about Lazarus?" Scarlet said.

"He's gone."

"What did he say?"

"It's from the Bible," Lea said. "Ask and it will be given to you. Seek and you will find. Knock and the door will be opened to you. Matthew. " She looked at Scarlet who was staring at her. "Oh – I'm a recovering Catholic schoolgirl."

Lexi arrived next, panting hard with the effort of the sprint. "I got the refinery."

"Good work," Hawke said. "But he got away."

And then Reaper turned the corner, hands on his hips and doubling over to get his breath back.

"Where are Ryan and Maria?" Hawke asked, unsettled by the bleak look on the former legionnaire's face.

The Frenchman took a deep breath, straightened himself up to his full height and looked at them. He said nothing, but gently shook his head.

They all knew what it meant.

CHAPTER FORTY-NINE

Davis Faulkner relaxed his posture and tried to remember everything he had been told about the basic golf swing. Sometimes in life it was just too easy to forget the fundamentals, and this was one of those times. He was a busy man, and he had too much on his mind to remember the little things.

He gently corrected his balance, shifting his weight to the middle of his feet and gently angling his spine down towards the Bridgestone B330 ball awaiting its fate down on the tee. He flexed his knees and lowered his right side to ensure the ball was in perfect alignment with the left side of his head.

Faulkner remembered what his instructor had told him about the swing – bring the club head back first, then the hands, shoulders and hips should all move in one gentle, fluid motion. As he raised the club higher he shifted the weight to his right side. The momentum of the swing gained pace, and his shoulders were now a good way into their full rotation in preparation for the attack.

He began the downswing with a lateral shift, dropped his arms, pulled his right elbow into his hip and rotated his body towards the ball, making sure to keep his head up and away from the ball as he went. Then, with an accuracy and power than surprised him, he made contact with the ball, kicking his right knee inward and keeping his left leg straight. The club head smacked the ball high and fast into the bright, crisp Virginia air.

He straightened up as he watched it fly through the sky. Not bad for a beginner.

It was then he was aware of someone talking to him. It was Aaron Carlson his personal assistant, and he sounded even more anxious than usual.

"What's up, Aaron?"

"It's about the, er... *mission*, sir."

"What about it? I don't want any bad news right now, Aaron – not if it's going to mess up my handicap."

"It's Colonel Geary, sir. He says they failed to take the island."

Faulkner turned to face Aaron, and raised his club up to rest on his shoulder. This was not good news, and he had been expecting better from Geary. "What?"

"He says they had a greater defensive capacity than he had anticipated for such a small, private island."

"And isn't just how he would put it, too?"

"And there were jets... *our* jets, sir."

"I see." His mind began to whir.

"What should I tell him?"

Faulkner sighed and turned back around to face the driving range. He swung the club off his shoulder, nearly hitting Carlson in the face as he did so, and tried all over again to relax his posture and regain his composure. The Oracle wasn't going to like this one little bit.

"So what do I say, sir?"

"Tell him to keep his goddam mouth shut."

"Yes, sir."

Davis Faulkner watched Aaron walk off the course and his mind began to race with this new development. The Oracle rarely accepted failure but there was a good chance his notorious bad temper might be soothed by his good news about almost certainly being elevated to the Vice Presidency in a few weeks. Davis Faulkner clung to that hope and took another swing into the great blue beyond.

CHAPTER FIFTY

Lea Donovan turned to the window so the others didn't see the tears and stared at the smouldering wreckage of the Seastead. It reminded her of the pictures she had seen of burning oil rigs. Great clouds of filthy black smoke bloomed into the cold Atlantic air, rising a few hundred feet before getting caught by a strong wind and whipped west over the ocean. In a few days it would reach the African coast, but they were going in the opposite direction. They were sailing into the setting sun in a boat taken from beneath the burning wreckage of the Seastead.

They had destroyed the Oracle's oceanic inner sanctum, but it brought no pleasure because the cost was too high. Maria Kurikova was lying in a body-bag in the cargo compartment and Ryan Bale was missing, presumed dead and buried at sea. When she thought about it she felt like someone had hollowed her out.

Two of her best friends were gone and for what? A strange golden idol that meant nothing to anyone – and which was now in the Oracle's grotesque grip. All they had was the Valhalla idol, exactly what they had started out with. A weird avatar forged from gold and offering nothing to them except the inscrutable expression of an elderly mandarin… She hated those idols. It was because of them that her father was dead, and now Maria and Ryan were added to that grim list, as well as so many other innocents.

Ahead of her Joe Hawke was idling past the marina's no-wake zone and taking the boat out into open water.

As he pushed the throttle forward the bow rose ten degrees into the air before getting on plane and then it dipped again, allowing a better view of the stormy horizon ahead of them. With the extra fuel on board he was happy that they would reach Elysium in a little over one day's sailing. At least then they would have the safety of their sanctuary to recover and regroup before deciding how to deal with so much new information. It was bewildering, but he never let his enemies get the better of him. There was no choice but to fight to the end.

Lea dried her eyes and looked behind her into the cabin. Jack Camacho and Scarlet Sloane were asleep, the English SAS officer's head resting on the American CIA man's broad shoulder. Lexi Zhang was staring out the opposite window, no doubt her usual worries scattered to the wind by the thoughts of this terrible day. Reaper was smoking on the stern, collars up and wordless.

Hawke now gripped the wheel and trimmed the boat at five degrees, instantly smoothing the ride and allowing the vessel to increase in speed. He checked the compass and nodded with inward satisfaction that he hadn't forgotten how to drive a boat. A small consolation after the terrible disaster of the Seastead battle, she guessed.

She knew he was thinking about Ryan and Maria, and adding their deaths to the list of all the others who had died since this all began – Sophie Durand, Olivia Hart, Bradley Karlsson, Ben, Alfie, Sasha... the roll-call of the innocent dead went on and on and made her want to scream with rage. She knew he felt the same.

At least Mendoza, Soto, Luk, Kamchatka and the bastard Kruger were all dead. It brought some small comfort to her that her friends hadn't died for nothing. Dispatching Luk and Kamchatka to the ocean floor for eternity was a particularly comforting thought.

Hawke put his arm around her and kissed her check. He hadn't shaved for days and he looked tired and yet there was still a kind of energy around him and that was comforting too, but the truth they had learned from the Oracle felt like it was crushing her and making it hard to breathe. It changed everything. There really were cults of immortal beings who worked in the shadows to control governments and the Oracle was some kind of leader who possessed the power to destroy mountains on the other side of the world.

None of it made any sense, but it was the new reality and they all had to rise to meet it with a show of force. The Oracle's vow to annihilate mankind had not fallen on deaf ears and the ECHO team had to stop him. But where to start... she knew it had something to do with those damned idols.

The former Commando checked the compass and put the boat to sea, his heart heavy with the knowledge he was leaving two fallen comrades behind. It wasn't the first time. As a commando and an SBS canoeist and even now as an ECHO team member he had lost colleagues and friends before, but this time felt different. This time felt extra raw.

Reaper felt the same way, and he knew he had to step up and be there for his new friends. It was time to put his reluctance to join things behind him and request a formal place on the ECHO team. He picked up his tobacco tin and cigarette papers and moved forward to the wheelhouse. Lexi was trying to hide her tears, but not doing a very good job of it, and when he saw Camacho and Scarlet sharing a hug and a few quiet words of consolation, he knew he had to be with these people.

"I want in," he said.

Hawke looked at Lea, and she shrugged her shoulders. "As soon as we get back to the island we'll speak to Rich."

"You think he'll accept me?"

Hawke nodded. "He'd be crazy not to, Vincent."

Reaper gave a solemn nod and began the intricate process of rolling a cigarette at sea. Not his first time, the slim cigarette was made in seconds and hanging off his lower lip as he searched through his pockets for a lighter. Before he found his own, a flash of light in front of his face startled him. He followed the arm back to the inscrutable face of Scarlet Sloane, who was now also smoking.

"Ah – tu as du feu," he mumbled. "I lost mine in the battle, je crois."

Scarlet sighed. "I'd lose my soul before I lost my lighter."

"I can believe that," Hawke said under his breath.

Reaper took the light and moments later he was puffing out a cloud of fresh tobacco smoke as he wandered back to the stern.

Scarlet went back to Camacho and Lexi went below decks to be alone.

Hawke settled on taking the boat back to Elysium.

Beside him, Lea Donovan looked back out to sea. The smoking Seastead was now nothing more than a smudge on the distant horizon.

She wasn't going to let any of this stand, and she knew none of the others would either. She clenched her jaw as she fought the rage back once again, her mind spinning with thoughts of justice and revenge as she heard those terrible words echo in her mind once again... *this isn't the end, Donovan – only the beginning.*

You can bet on it, she thought.

You can bet on it.

THE END

AUTHOR'S NOTE

Here is a great place for me to thank you for reading my book, and also give a special thanks to everyone who has followed Hawke's journey from the beginning. Regular readers will know how I feel that writing/reading a novel is a shared experience and I hope you enjoy reading these tales as much as I enjoy writing them. I have some really exciting and new ideas about the future of the Joe Hawke Series and I can't wait to share them with you. I'm also hoping to be able to bring you some good news about a release date on the standalone thriller I've been working on, which is called *The Armageddon Protocol* as well as some other projects.

Let me add that all reviews at Amazon are gratefully received as they are essential to the series, so please allow me to give a big thanks to everyone who has taken the time to leave me a review in the past. I also want to say thanks to everyone who has left me a review on Goodreads as well. It means a lot to a writer and I value your opinion

Rob

The Joe Hawke Series

The Vault of Poseidon (Joe Hawke #1)
Thunder God (Joe Hawke #2)
The Tomb of Eternity (Joe Hawke #3)
The Curse of Medusa (Joe Hawke #4)
Valhalla Gold (Joe Hawke #5)
The Aztec Prophecy (Joe Hawke #6)
The Secret of Atlantis (Joe Hawke #7)
The Lost City (Joe Hawke #8)

The Sword of Fire (Joe Hawke #9) is scheduled
for release in the spring of 2017

**For free stories, regular news and updates,
please join my Facebook page**

https://www.facebook.com/RobJonesNovels/

Or Twitter

@AuthorRobJones

Printed in Great Britain
by Amazon